CURSED BOYS *and* BROKEN HEARTS

ALSO BY ADAM SASS

Surrender Your Sons

The 99 Boyfriends of Micah Summers

Your Lonely Nights Are Over

CURSED BOYS and BROKEN HEARTS

ADAM SASS

VIKING

VIKING
An imprint of Penguin Random House LLC, New York

First published in the United States of America by Viking,
an imprint of Penguin Random House LLC, 2024

Created by Dovetail Fiction,
a division of Working Partners Limited, 9 Kingsway,
4th Floor, London WC2B 6XF, England

Visit us online at PenguinRandomHouse.com.

Library of Congress Cataloging-in-Publication Data is available.

ISBN 9780593464816 (hardcover)

ISBN 9780593692912 (international edition)

1st Printing

Printed in the United States of America

LSCH

Edited by Kelsey Murphy

Design by Lucia Baez

Text set in Dante

For the grandparents no longer with us:
For Angelo, who always raised his glass to me
For Cynthia, who lives on through her recipes
For Joe, who opened his home to me
For Bill, who loved telling stories
For Herbie, who built the home in this book
And for Shirley, who created the family in this book

AUTHOR'S NOTE

Have you ever felt cursed? That no matter what you do, no matter how charming you are, no matter how good your work or art is, that it's all simply . . . not enough? Is something controlling your fate, stopping you from reaching your dreams? Or is the curse, in fact, you? Are you getting in your own way?

This book doesn't have all the answers, but it will guide you through the forest of uncertainty, which is thick with brambles and sharp thorns. In *Cursed Boys and Broken Hearts*, Grant Rossi believes his entire eighteen-year-old life has been ruined by a single red rose.

Is he wrong? You be the judge.

Who here hasn't had something so small in their lives become so big that it blocks out everything else? In fact, this story tackles the realities of such a thing—depression. Be forewarned, this story takes a look at characters in the throes of depression and self-hatred, but there are also depictions of pathways forward, like therapy, SSRI medications, and—shockingly—self-forgiveness.

Of all my characters, Grant Rossi is the one I'd most like to meet because he is me at my angriest, my most inconvenient, and my most in-need-of-a-hug. Writing Grant, by allowing him his anger, I could allow myself the anger I hadn't let myself comfortably feel my entire life. Please, from the bottom of my heart, give my angry boy a chance—a chance at being himself, a chance to find his own way, a chance to win you over, and a second chance at love.

With these caveats out of the way, I am proud to present the grand romantic destiny of Grant Rossi.

INVIDIOSO E GRATO

Envy and gratitude. The two sides of romance.
Each exists in the other's shadow,
yet neither can live without the other.

How will you know the value of what you have
until you have tasted the pain of being without?

Taste the difference at Vero Roseto Garden Inn & Vineyard!

After more than a decade, Mama Bianchi is once again
touring her famous vineyard, home of the Wishing Rose label,
where she asks you to choose between her
Grato reds and Invidioso whites.

Invidioso or Grato? Envy or gratitude?
Where does your heart truly lie?

Only Mama Bianchi and her Wishing Rose know the truth!

Vero Roseto, now accepting reservations.
(Two nights for the price of one through
the end of the summer!)

VALLE, ILLINOIS, JUST OFF US HIGHWAY 20

CHAPTER 1

INVIDIOSO

I design fashion. I design art. I do not design chintzy two-for-one flyers for my aunt's failing B&B. Yet Mom still sent over the mockup of my aunt's upcoming ad so she could make use of my "design eye." But all I could see was a once-great destination spot offering massive discounts throughout their busiest season. That's all anyone else will see, too. Two-for-ones through the whole summer? Even during the Rose Festival in August? That festival is our crown jewel. Yet here my family is, admitting we can't even give these reservations away.

On the off seasons, Vero Roseto's rose garden and vineyard are crushed by unforgiving Illinois winters—totally deserted except for the most desperate tourist. And thanks to climate change, spring doesn't exist anymore (vanished along with the visitors who used to seasonally escape to the vineyard). Summer is all Vero Roseto has—and summer is not enough to break even.

"Ma, there's three exclamation points in this," I say, looking over the abysmal ad. "Aunt Ro's gotta cut it down to one or none."

Over speakerphone, my mother grunts impatiently. "We just thought it was so drab without them! She wants people to know they're excited."

"Every time she adds an exclamation point, her desperation goes up a font size."

Mom snorts. "You got judgmental in the city."

I don't blink. I just stare up at my nonmoving ceiling fan. My studio apartment is stifling in the early summer heat, but I don't have the willpower to switch on the fan. My clothes lie on my body as heavily as an X-ray vest. My ratty gray T-shirt is due for a wash, but at least I can't smell myself anymore. My nose has acclimated to the wretched sad boy fragrance that's currently strangling this airless room.

Look at me. Two weeks out of graduating high school, and I'm already thriving.

The city has done wonders for me. Truly, so grato about it.

"Yep," I say tonelessly. "I got judgmental in the city. Judgmental and sad."

Over the phone, Mom clicks her tongue—*my poor, pathetic son*—and says nothing. For long seconds, we stew in silence. I've done the thing I'm not supposed to do: mention my depression. She lets me talk about whatever I want, but the truth makes her quiet. It reminds her of the meds I used to take—and should get back to taking, once I make an appointment. It's nothing I'm embarrassed about, but she doesn't like thinking of me needing them, like I have a terrible infection she's doing her best to ignore, and I'm rudely reminding her of it.

"Grant," she says, lowering her voice, "it's almost been a year. There's more than one boy in the world—"

"I thought you called to talk about this crummy ad." Anger whips through my chest like a cobra. Guilt immediately follows, but I don't take it back. If I can't mention my sadness, she can't mention my ex.

My heroic, romantic, sweetheart ex everyone fell in love with—his thousands of Instagram fans, my design program friends, and my family (who didn't even meet him before I was dumped). They adored him—that sweet bunny *and* his new bunny boyfriend (the best friend he fell in love with) who couldn't hurt a fly.

Except they hurt *me*.

But I don't count. I'm a beast, not a bunny. A beast with baggage and a curse on my head where no relationship lasts longer than a month. When my ex and I were dating, he and I were the golden couple. Then he fell in love with someone else, and I had to go. But where was the sweet, simple fairy tale his followers demanded? From their point of view, our broken fairy tale wasn't nuanced reality, it was just . . . my fault. But in reality, I'm a cursed boy, so where was this honestly gonna go anyway?

So, the bunnies get to keep their little dewdrop love story while the beast remains shut away in his dungeon. Just like in those fairy tales my ex tricked me into believing in.

"Back to the ad!" Mom says, fiddling with loud pots and pans. "Instead of exclamation points, what if we put some words in all caps?"

"No," I moan.

"Why not?"

"Writing in caps is for millennials who are too online. Vetoed."

"Well, we've gotta show enthusiasm somehow!"

"We don't. Enthusiasm is desperate, and Ro's discount looks desperate enough. People come to Vero Roseto to feel classy, exclusive, like it's a club they can't get into. If Ro plays it cool in the ad, nobody will notice the place is in trouble."

"Speaking from experience?"

My heart screams, but I don't judge her too harshly. It's an Italian thing, gagging your kids like this, and I'm the youngest of eight, so she had lots of practice before she got to me. "Ouch, Ma."

"Well, ouch, yourself. You just said our family's business is in trouble."

"It *is* in trouble."

"And so are you," she says firmly, but with extreme care.

She's right, but I'm too empty to respond. Mosquito bites roar across my ankles, but I can't even find the energy to reach down and scratch them.

Mom sighs. "Why don't you get away to the B&B? I can tell you aren't taking care of yourself, and Ro would *die* to have you over. Spend a few weeks. Get out of that city. She'll cook. She'll clean. And she gets a cool, artistic teen who'll tell her everything she's doing wrong with the business." Knowing she hasn't closed her hard sell yet, Mom laughs. "I'm giving you an open invitation for free food that doesn't come out of a microwave AND to criticize your family without back talk! How else can I sweeten this deal?"

I clear my desert-dry throat. "I'm just busy. I can't get away."

"Busy sleeping in past noon?" Mom's exhale blows out my phone speaker. "Okay, so you moved to the city, and some rich boy was careless with your heart. So *what*? It's a tale as old as time. You're creative. Take all that crap he gave you and feed it into your work—"

"I've done that—"

"You're handsome! And tall—gays love that."

I retch. "Okay, but how do *you* know that?"

"There's other boys—"

"I've *tried*."

"Enough! Grant, he wasn't that great—"

Like I've been jabbed with adrenaline, I sit up in bed for the first time in hours. I can almost hear my body peeling off the mattress. "Ma!" I practically wail. "He wasn't a bad guy. He just didn't love me." Phlegm collects in my throat as my fourth cry of the day approaches. "What was he supposed to do? Stay with me forever just because I'm cursed?"

"Piglet, no . . ." Mom's voice fills with fear.

Hot tears build behind my eyes. I set my phone on my nightstand cluttered with empty pop cans and cartons of Easy Mac. After wiping my eyes dry, I hurl my top sheet onto the floor. "It's so *hot* in here!"

"Well," Mom clears her throat, "the AC over at the B&B is freezing."

"I'm not going to Vero Roseto, Ma." My head collides with my pillow as I pick up the phone again. "Sorry, but I don't think it would help me to be around something that's dying."

There—that comment ought to scare Mom enough to leave me alone.

We mutter goodbyes to each other, and I let my phone slip down my chest, where it settles somewhere beneath my ribs. With my last ounce of energy, I search around the carpet for The Bad Magazine, the one I hurt my feelings with when I get in these moods. It's a complimentary promotion for the Art Institute of Chicago's student design program— the show I worked on with my ex last year. The last thing we did together.

We were the stars of the show, so a publicity photo from the event's red carpet entrance made the cover: me and him, the fairy-tale couple that was going to conquer the industry. When he left, he took my love for my work with him. That has to be why I'm still like this after a year. I'm just not me anymore. I'm something else now—*a beast*.

Or maybe this is the real me. Maybe the person I was with my ex was the fake.

Months ago, during a spiral, I scratched out my face with a black pen. Traces of my smile—a silly, ignorant smile—appear around the edges of the scratch marks. I couldn't stand looking at myself that happy. It was a lie.

Looking at this photo, it helps me remember—I'm cursed.

My ex is just the latest of many who realized they were dating The Training Boyfriend before coming to their senses.

My ex got his fairy-tale ending, but there's none of that for me. A low, scalding flame simmers beneath my heart knowing that even if I do find someone who wants me, it will be too late to get my pure, wholesome fairy tale. That chance is gone. Whoever this new boy will be, he'll have to deal with neediness, repressed anger, and—yes, Mom—desperation.

He'll have to deal with the curse, something no boy has ever survived.

Who would even have the patience? The time? The strength?

Who could ever learn to love a beast?

CHAPTER 2

EVERYONE WANTS TO BE US

In my studio apartment, a half-body mannequin taunts me as I measure a sleeve's length of fabric. Mint-green satin. Very tricky material to work with, even if there wasn't a storm in my head blotting out any trace of sunshine. My clothes are four days old. My curly hair is matted flat with oil. I have a faraway stare in my eyes, but oh yes, I'm still going to create A Look.

No more half-finished sketches. No more endless doodling on my tablet.

I'm going to get my hands dirty, put an actual needle and thread to actual fabric, and work. Get my body feeling it again. Touch something other than metal, glass, and pixels. The old Grant Rossi is somewhere inside this snarling, sunken-eyed beast, and I'm going to wake him up.

It's not just about my exes or my curse. It's about getting back to my future. Becoming the most famous designer of all time—even if that means also becoming the loneliest.

To hell with boys. The curse can have them. Right now, I

have one job: cut this sleeve and sew it. If I can do this, make the satin look crisp, I can do anything.

Twenty minutes later, clutching a ball of utterly ruined satin, I know I'm screwed.

I glance at my phone, like maybe *this* is the time to reach out to someone, poke my head up from the sand. And this time, my brain doesn't stop me.

I text my friend Eshana: **Hi, I'm alive. Sorry I ghosted your texts. Nothing bad happened, just the usual.**

As if she'd been waiting by the phone, Eshana texts back instantly: **How're you holding up, kitten? Your mom texted me to see if you were alright. I lied and said I just saw you. But that felt jinxy.**

I let out a pained moan. **Very jinxy,** I text. **Sorry you had to do that. I'm reachable if my mom texts you again, btw. I just need some time to think about my next move. I still don't have college lined up.**

Fuck college, she replies. I laugh into my palm, and miraculously, a bit of blue sky pierces the clouds in my head. Eshana texts: **And are you doing this thinking alone? I'm happy to chill if you're free.**

Maybe I'm not up for the challenges of needlework just yet, but some company wouldn't be a bad idea, though I'm not quite ready to hang out with my friends. Their faces would reflect how lost I look. So, strangers are best. Like clockwork, when my brain chemicals turn upward again, I plan a date.

After so much "down," I feel my brain turning, getting back up and running. When my energy returns, it's like that day in January when you finally decide to get rid of your Christmas tree. The tree used to be so important. It was the centerpiece of the room, but now it looks wrong. What is a *tree* doing in my home? Why haven't I gotten rid of this thing?

Depression acts the same way.

And now I can suddenly smell how foul my room has become—how foul I've become. Why did I let my clothes pile up like this? I have a hamper! What is this layer of grime on me, when a scalding shower feels blissful? Here I'm awake and shedding this old skin. After two conditionings, my dark curls get back their bounce and shimmer. After toning and moisturizing, my light olive skin gets back its golden sparkle.

I'm so cute! Not a troll at all. The mirror exposes my brain as a liar.

I pull on a hunter-green Henley, which fits snugly around my still-muscular arms and chest. My body hasn't softened! Once again, the mirror reminds me how my brain lies.

I'll always trust you, mirror!

The mirror winks and says if I stick with him, I'll be just fine.

When I text my other friends that I'm doing better, they return with joyful messages. Like nothing ever happened. I appreciate that.

Whenever I go to ground, I can't talk to anyone because

they always ask how I'm doing, and me being the emotional hoochie that I am, I can't resist spilling the truth. An hour later, I've scared them with my spiraling—and I end up feeling worse than ever. So, instead, I just warn people I'm going into my hobbit hole, and I'll see them when the weather changes.

Text me your location, my tall drink of limoncello! Eshana texts. **Boys are BEASTS!**

I'm counting on it, I text back. **Rawr.**

Who better to love a beast than another beast? Belles are out this year.

Before leaving, I need a jacket. My hand wraps around my closet handle . . . but stays there.

This is where I hid it.

The forbidden jacket is shoved to the back, but it's there, in a garment bag, waiting. I made the jacket myself: black vegan leather with a hand-stitched design across the back of a pumpkin swarmed by vines. That jacket got me into my design program. It's mine—it's me. I made it months before I even met my ex! So, when I look at the jacket, why do I see him and not me?

I was wearing it when I met him. It got him to notice me. It's part of our story.

Our love story is over—but then what am I writing now? A tragedy? Some queasy mix of both?

A cold hand grips my heart, and I smile wickedly. *Hell with him. I'm reclaiming this.* I throw open the closet, shove my other jackets to the left, and snatch the forbidden garment bag. Its weight feels powerful in my hands. I've missed this.

I am more than just an obstacle on the way to someone else's happy ending.

I pack my tablet (in case the boy stands me up; I can work while I eat) and take the long route toward Old Town. This journey will be a great banishing, strolling past all the places that remind me of my ex. Everywhere I've been avoiding this past year.

The train where we met—I cast him out.

The sandwich shop on our first date—I cast him out.

The fountain in the park where I sang to him, where I would later sit and realize it was really over—I cast him out.

God, this is a lot. Why did I take him to so many places? Why wasn't I more careful? I should've kept parts of the city cordoned off just for me in case it fell apart, but I didn't. I allowed every corner of Chicago to become tainted. Even as I walk up the redbrick Old Town street to meet this new boy, I realize my error too late: it's L'Antica Magia, the Italian restaurant where my family met me after my show—after I was dumped. Saddest shrimp scampi I've ever forced down.

With the sun setting beneath the tree-lined streets of this charming brick village, intense rays catch my reflection in L'Antica Magia's mirrored door. The reflection is harsh. Chiaroscuro, the art masters call it. Light and dark. The sun cleaves my face in two, which isn't flattering to my heavy eyelids and round cheeks. The light creates steep, drooping shadows that make me look . . . old. Ghoulish. A heartbroken ghost haunting the city.

This mirror says maybe my depressed brain made some points.

I don't walk inside. Shuffling around the patio's iron chairs, I peek through the window into the golden-lit restaurant. It's bustling. Servers deliver platters of calamari and freshly baked bread to laughing families. My heart slumps. That should've been me and my family, but I ruined it with drama. We couldn't even celebrate my successful show because my mind was stuck on what I'd lost. I couldn't just lie for one night, just to laugh and eat with them again.

Sitting alone next to one family is a very cute boy with light brown skin, a bleached crew cut, and round glasses. My date, Luca. Our pre-date chat was promising when I learned he's starting prelaw in the fall. A chance to break my cycle of free-spirited, artistic bunnies. After Luca politely waves away the server, he smiles nervously until he's alone again . . . then he chugs his goblet of ice water and checks his phone.

I'm late. He's worrying I stood him up.

I hop out of sight before he sees me. My feet take me down the street, but they don't stop. I keep walking until the restaurant is far behind me. Opening the app where we found each other, I message Luca: **I'm sorry. I'm not ready to do this again. Sorry.**

I'm running. To where? I don't know, but I can't do this.

This behavior is *sick*, Grant. Everyone else has gotten over these relationships but you.

"Yo!" I cry, leaping into the road to stop a cab with its light on. Brakes scream as the cab stops. It's not even close to hitting me, but that doesn't stop the dark-bearded driver from leaning out his window to cuss me out. After jabbering my apologies, I climb into his back seat and ask him to take me to the LaSalle Street Station.

"Hey, Joe Jacket, don't do stuff like that, jumping into the road," he says. "This isn't a movie."

My chin trembling, I open my phone, scrolling past several disappointed but understanding messages from Luca. "Yeah, well," I say, "this is the scene in the movie where you take me to the train station so I can get out of this city and get a life." I pull up Aunt Rosalie's number.

With an amused chuckle, the driver takes off south. Moments later, when my aunt answers, she doesn't get out a syllable before I whimper, "Aunt Ro?" My chin shakes so much, it feels like it's gonna fall off. "I'm getting on a train to Valle. Is that okay? Mom says you've maybe got room for me?"

Instead of a coherent response, I'm met with a gale of excited whooping.

A smile wants to rise, but I'm not ready for that yet.

The Beast of Chicago is leaving. Maybe it's for the best that I spend some time around a dying old B&B.

It's one place I know my exes have never touched.

CHAPTER 3

VERO ROSETO

The train arrives in Valle after midnight. After stepping off the train into the quaint gas-lamp-filled station, I briefly forget I'm still in the Midwest, let alone a suburb of Chicago. Valle looks like an alpine ski village—just with giant, vaulting trees instead of slopes as it sits in the lap between two enormous forests. The buildings are humble, small, and brick. The only lights around for miles are the station's lamps, a few home windows, and the lightning bugs. Deep in the distance, a low chatter of insects swarming over Lake Valle clears my brain of five years' worth of clutter.

Suddenly, I'm thirteen again, here to spend the summer with my siblings and cousins. No other plans but swimming, Nintendo, and roasted vegetables from my grandfather's garden.

The summer I turned thirteen, June was glorious. I laughed every day.

That July, I made a wish on my family's famous Wishing Rose. I'd never wanted anything so badly.

By August, my grandmother died, my wish became a

curse, and I never saw Vero Roseto again—until now.

I hug my arms across my chest as the Uber driver delivers me to Vero Roseto, that great big memory place. Ten miles outside the cottages and shops of Valle, Vero Roseto Garden Inn & Vineyard awaits, untouched since I left it five years ago. The cream-colored sixteen-room estate is set back deep from the main road. An archway, covered in hand-carved roses and vines, marks where the road ends and the B&B's gravelly path begins. The vines—fashioned, like all of Vero Roseto, by my great-grandmother—are so distinctive. They must've snuck into my subconscious, somewhere inside my brain where I tuck away happy things, because they're nearly identical to the pumpkin vines I sewed onto my jacket.

"You can drop me here," I tell the driver.

"It's no problem to take you to the door," he says.

But my hand is already eagerly gripping the handle. "I want to walk."

Truthfully, I just don't want an audience in case the memories become too much. With no luggage but my tablet satchel, the long path to the front door will be easy. I pass under the arch, reaching an elegantly painted sign advertising the Rose Festival. In August, the festival is a walking tour encompassing most of the home gardens in Valle, ending with a grand finale at Vero Roseto. In our prime, we were stunning, but in the last few years, my Instagram snooping has revealed Vero Roseto's Rose Festival contribution has become less "showstopper" and more "show's over." Aunt Ro needs pizzazz lessons, and

I don't mean littering an ad with so many exclamation points that citizens of Mars wouldn't miss her enthusiasm.

The main house comes closer, and I pick up speed.

This was always the part of the road where we'd run to the door. Mom would drop off me, my brother, and my sisters at the arch and then drive back to town while the rest of us ran inside to get sandwiches from our grandmother. My siblings were all bigger than me, but I pushed myself the hardest, so getting ahead of my sisters was easy. Beating my brother, A. C., who is ten years older, was the real challenge.

In the dark, I run. This time, there's no one to race, but it is tradition, so I let myself become a hyper-driven thirteen-year-old again.

The gravelly path forks. Continuing straight is the guest entrance that leads to a parking lot. Curving left—the path I take—the road becomes a paved, semicircular driveway leading to the main home. I can't see it in the dark, but behind the estate is where the magic happens: the vineyard, pie stand, and gardens that stretch until you reach the dense Valle forests. Somewhere in those gardens, I realize with a sickening lurch, is the Wishing Rose—an actual rose bush that's become our family wine label.

It's also where my curse began.

The entire grounds appear in my mind, right where I left it. But it isn't exactly the same. My grandparents are gone, the economy tanked our business, and the little boy Grant is now a cursed beast, but . . . there's still pie!

My full sprint stops the moment I reach the veranda, and I slap my hand against the wide column, the finish line where A. C. would usually boast how he'd always be faster, no matter how hard I pouted.

Well, big brother, I'm not a kid anymore, and you're a tired old dad now, so I'd like to test that theory.

As I catch my breath, a porch lantern switches on, and Aunt Ro rushes out in a fluffy, canary-yellow bathrobe. A small, plump woman in her fifties with swirls of long, dyed-black hair, Ro thrusts her arms around me before I can even say hello.

"Grant!" she shouts in a whisper, burying her cheek in my chest. Her hug is as tight as a boa constrictor, but so, so comforting. Oh my God, how long has it been since I've hugged someone?

"I was gonna text you I was downstairs," I whisper. "You stayed up for me?"

"I've been cooking! Can't sleep at all. Not with you coming in!" She merrily swats my chest and scans me up and down. "Where are your bags? I'll wake up Paul—"

"No need, no bags!"

Standing on the veranda with nothing but my phone, tablet, and forbidden jacket, my thoughts return to Chicago and the mess I abandoned there. Yet, as usual, Aunt Ro chops through awkwardness with her machete of knowing: "You just jumped on a train without a plan, didn't you?" She chuckles, waving me inside. "You're impulsive, like me."

The entrance hall is dark, but the smells are the same: fresh flowers, fireplace embers, and that special tang that only occurs when tomatoes meet wine. My heart grows three sizes at the memory. The two-story hall is bisected by winding staircases. On the left is the West Wing for guests; on the right, the East Wing for family. Connecting the top of both stairs is a landing, separated by a communicating door so we can easily help guests, but they can easily leave us alone. Finally, hanging on the landing is an old portrait of Great-Grandmother Anne-Marie Bianchi.

Mama Bianchi.

She was a commanding presence, but still approachable. She died when I was six, so I don't remember her much, but as far as looks go? She's me in old lady drag. Broad shoulders, round cheeks, deep-set eyes, and a head full of curls. Oh, and what my exes have always referred to as "big kissy lips."

So I owe my looks and artistic style to Mama Bianchi, but not my romantic luck. She was happily married for sixty-seven years. Two out of three ain't bad.

As Aunt Ro leads me toward the family's kitchen in the East Wing, she chatters excitedly. "I was so mad I couldn't make it to your show. This place can't be left alone for a second. How long has it been since I've seen you in person and not on FaceTime? *Five* years? God, life is just passing me by. You were a sweet little butterbean, now you're this tall? My sister only knows how to grow big galoots. You angelic little boys are all *men* now, I can't stand it. I'm surprised you're not bigger in the tummy. Don't worry, it gets all of us. Your parents, me, your brother. Not that there's anything wrong with it, it's genetics and *beautiful*." She elbows me. "And from what I hear, in Chicago, if you got bigger and slapped on a beard, you'd need rainbow repellent to keep 'em off you."

Lot of information at once, Ro!

With a small laugh, I stop her under the stairs. "Aunt Ro, as much as I love you discussing what may or may not happen with my body, I'd rather we didn't right now?" I want to add, *At least not until I've been more than a few days out of my depressed self-image hell.* "And wait—did my mom tell you I needed dating help?"

Ro doesn't blink. "She didn't need to say anything. You're the busiest person in this family other than me, but suddenly you jump on a train, no bags, and come out here to watch your aunt peel apples?" She shakes her head. "Something's up. And you don't get career troubles, you get boy troubles. So I don't know exactly what you want out of being here . . ." A smile broadens her face. "I just know that you're here, and Mama Bianchi is gonna look over you."

Ro clutches my cheeks with both hands like she's gripping a steering wheel, but still, golden, shimmering relief spills down my body. She's always known me on a deeper level than Mom. I could spill my guts to her right here—sobbing, screaming, tantrumming about the injustices of the universe and its cold, uncaring inhabitants—and she'd let me. Because she knows sometimes that's what you've got to do to get over something.

In the kitchen, everything is the same: black-and-white checkerboard floor, immaculately maintained mid-century appliances, and a breakfast island with a wood top. I climb onto a stool and let my jaws close around the heaping plate of fried green tomato sandwiches and—my favorite, favorite, FAVORITE—bread patties. These are fried pancakes made from egg yolks, parmesan, and the seasoned breadcrumb batter left over from making chicken cutlets. It's like biting into a heavenly hockey puck of salt and burned cheese.

I close my eyes as the flavor strikes my memory like a mallet.

I'm ten. Grandma is frying cutlets while ten kids (me, my seven siblings, and two cousins) swarm around her, begging her to start the bread patties early. Her cast-iron pan spits oil in every direction, so she shoos us away with a rag. I—the smallest—don't leave. Like a stubborn alley cat, I remain by Grandma, staring patiently. Then Aunt Ro's hands close around my tiny shoulders, and she guides me away, telling me to get my swim trunks on if I want Uncle Paul to teach me cannonballs before dinner. Before I leave, she slips a warm, still-sizzling bread patty into my hand.

When I open my eyes, Aunt Ro is smiling expectantly across the island like I'm unwrapping a present she's bought me.

With a mouthful of bread, I clutch my chest and say, "They're exactly the same."

She grins triumphantly. "I finally perfected your grandma's recipe—which was really Mama Bianchi's recipe. I'm convinced Ma left ingredients out of the recipe card, so after she was gone, anytime I'd make them people would say, 'These are good, but there's just *something* missing.' But I trial-and-errored it until I found it." Aunt Ro leans across the island, her voice low and conspiratorial. "Locatelli cheese on top of the parm."

"You cracked her code," I say before shoving a full patty in my mouth.

Ro knocks happily on the table. "She's up in Heaven right now going, 'Damn you.'" My aunt makes a sign of the cross, as if to ward off the aforementioned damnation. "Love you, Ma, but Grant needed the real deal."

"From the bottom of my heart, I did." As I wipe off my greasy fingers, my body relaxes. "You're the only one in this family who can make an actually delicious vegetarian meal. Dad would be like, 'Here's your bag of lettuce,' and Mom would be like, 'It *is* vegetarian. It's just a little chicken. Also, there's eight of you. I'm supposed to make two separate dinners?'"

Being the last kid of eight means "be glad for whatever you get" in all matters practical and emotional. I'm lucky my parents and siblings stop to consider me at all.

Chuckling, Aunt Ro retreats to her big metal coffin of a fridge and shuffles back with a small plate of chicken cutlets and a chilled, half-drunk bottle of Wishing Rose–brand chardonnay.

Invidioso—our envy label.

"So, I saw your ad," I say. Halfway through a gulp of chardonnay, Ro is about to respond when I hold up my hand. "More thoughts coming in the morning when I'm not a zombie, but are *you* doing the Mama Bianchi tours now? What's going on, what's happening, who's Mama Bianchi? Are you raising people from the dead?"

"Please, no evil magic required!" Ro nibbles on a cutlet. "Your great-grandmother is already everywhere. She's in the walls, more powerful dead than alive."

"Mmm, like Obi-Wan."

"What? No, I'm Mama Bianchi now. I wear the shawl, I do the tour, I ask them where their hearts truly lie, the whole show. People love it. Well—*person* loves it. Reservations have been slow." She eyes me before taking another sip of Invidioso. "The rate we're going, I'll be the one stomping the grapes, too."

My joy, always so temporary, deflates seeing Ro worry. "It's that bad?"

She throws on a smile again. "Don't worry. I scared up some money to bring on a new gardener for the Rose Festival. Didn't have many options with my budget, so . . ." For some reason, Ro can't look me in the eyes. She shrugs. "But he's a pro, he loves Vero Roseto, and I think it'll be an . . . interesting summer."

"Interesting?"

But Ro is already scooping up plates. "I said 'interesting'? My head. Sleep-deprived. You know, uh, I just mean . . . it'll be fun. Rose Festival, yay!"

I pivot on the stool, my eyes narrowed. "Ro, what's going on?"

"Nothing!" She lands the plates clumsily in the sink with a loud crash. She heads for the open doorway leading upstairs to her bedroom. As she turns back to me once again, I get the uneasy feeling of being scanned. Ro smiles, softer, and with enormous love. "Your old room is ready for you. We'll have to figure out clothes in the morning, but . . . it's good you're here. We need you. And Mama Bianchi is looking out for you."

I smirk. "You or the ghost?"

"Both."

Once she's gone, I toss back one more bread patty, drop off my dishes, and climb the East Wing stairs to "my room"—a tiny suite I used to share with half my siblings, the youngest ones. The East Wing stairs are pitch-dark, but in my mind's eye, my memory takes over and I anticipate every pivot without missing a step.

I can't shake the feeling that I'm home again. But this place has never been my home. It's hosted more bad memories than good, and as soon as I figure out where the hell I'm applying for design school, I'm gone.

Still . . . for the first time in months, my insides aren't a tornado of chaos.

24

As I reach the landing at the top of the stairs, a large window lets in a shaft of deep indigo light. Not enough to see my way around, but enough to make out hints of the rose garden across the back lawn. As the high green hedge walls appear, I hold my breath.

The Wishing Rose is there.

The rose is a tourist trap and the symbol of our wine label that's kept my family clothed and fed since World War II. It has brought together four generations of Bianchis and Rossis. It's a family myth I believed in so hard, I cursed myself. From the moment I laid my hands on that rose five years ago, no boy has ever loved me for longer than a few weeks.

Welcome home, Grant, the rose whispers from the dark. *Do you have another wish to make?*

CHAPTER 4

THE GARDENER

If it wasn't for the grandfather clock gonging outside my room, I would've slept past lunchtime. It's noon. Can't believe I slept past the other hour chimes. Thank God I did, because the sound is triggering. With each noon clang comes a bitter taste in the back of my throat. The last time I slept in this room, it was filled with kids. My three oldest siblings were out of high school, so they stayed in their own rooms. The younger kids all bunked here—me, the youngest, plus my older cousin and four older sisters. Sometimes, my best friend Ben would stay over.

Best friend.

It's weird, saying that now.

Unlike me, Ben lived in Valle year-round. His dad knew our family, and he was my age, so I was desperate to have him over. The rest of the time, all the older kids filling the house snapped up every inch of attention. But when Ben was here . . . we carved out our own world.

Each time he slept over, Ben stayed in a sleeping bag next to mine on the floor. Weirdly, last night when I collapsed into bed, I had to fight the urge to curl up in our sleeping bag spot instead.

On the floor, Ben and I would stay up later than the others, whispering . . .

Gong . . .

The grandfather clock chimes again outside the door, and I nearly choke on my tongue.

I had forgotten about the clock. That last summer five years ago, after Ben fell into snores, I lay awake, eyes staring at the ceiling, my stomach rotting from anxiety. The grandfather clock outside rang twelve for midnight, and I made a bet with God, or the universe, or whoever the hell was in charge of my life, because I knew it wasn't me. I bet that if I could count to one hundred before the twelfth gong, I would wake up the next morning and be someone else.

Someone who didn't like Ben.

I made this bet every night for a month—but every morning I'd wake up and see Ben lying there asleep with his dimpled chin, the ceiling fan tossing around his shiny red hair. I'd know that neither God, the universe, nor anyone else was going to help me.

I was secretly dating another boy, Hutch, who lived in town. Only Ben knew—but he didn't know I wished I could be with him instead. The choices were making me sick, and because I wasn't out, there wasn't anyone to talk it through with . . .

So I asked the Wishing Rose for help.

But as soon as I made my wish, Ben swooped in and stole Hutch. In a way, I got what I wanted: my life became much simpler. I was alone.

I never saw Ben, Hutch, or Vero Roseto again, and my curse began.

Gong . . .

Finally, the clock finishes, and my uncle's scratchy baritone voice shakes me from my traumatic memory. I crawl out of bed, barefoot, still in my good date jeans, and stagger toward the window that looks out across the vineyard and gardens. It's a magnificent view.

At least, it used to be.

Not to kick my aunt when she's down, but this B&B looks effed. Full disaster. Junkyard. The sprawling lawn leading to Valle Forest is shaggy, brown, and patchy. Grandpa's vegetable garden is choked with the corpses of rotting food. The swimming pool is bone-dry, and a brownish-yellow ring hints that it hasn't been cleaned since the last presidential election. In the distance, a sculpture garden stands as another sullen cemetery of gardening. Topiary arrangements are overgrown, long past losing their shape. The pretty white trellis lies in pieces, collected in neat piles as if it's about to be used for firewood. And the rose garden—home of the Wishing Rose, our B&B's centerpiece—is lost in mounds of overgrowth.

The only thing that's been maintained is the vineyard and

winery barn to the west of the gardens. It must be the only thing still dependably turning a profit.

But worst of all, directly beneath my window, the expansive deck connecting the pool with the winery has an actual hole in the middle of it. The surrounding planks are splintered or otherwise compromised, and the whole thing seems to be slouching. Jesus, it must've collapsed from a heavy snowfall or rainstorm. The deck used to be the hot spot where guests took their wine or brunch plates to enjoy the sun while their kids swam. Now it's a death trap.

Why would anyone stay here while the place is in this condition? Aunt Ro's going to need a whole team to get this thing running again.

But she doesn't have a team, she just has Uncle Paul.

Paul—a beefy, round man in slacks, suspenders, and a paint-splotched tee—clomps through the remains of Grandpa's vegetable garden to reach the foot of the deck. His face is simultaneously pale white and lobster-red sunburned as he squints against the sun at the job ahead of him. Aunt Ro, dressed in a raspberry-colored frock and floppy sun hat, joins him to survey the hopelessness.

"This is all gonna have to go," Paul sighs, his voice floating up to my window perch. "I can get the lumber. I just can't afford the extra guys. Maybe we see what me and Gardener Boy can do with it."

"Oh, Paul," Ro groans. "He's already got so much to do

getting the gardens show-ready. What about our contractors?"

"Those guys only have so many hours in a day, Ro. Either they renovate the West Wing rooms, or they fix the deck. Can't do both."

Ro lets out another long moan. Quietly, she adds, "I could ask Grant . . ."

Paul chuckles. "When *is* our nephew getting up? Tomorrow?"

Eep.

I retreat from the window lest I be spotted, snatched in a butterfly net, and dragged down to . . . rebuild an entire deck? I don't know how to do any of that! I'll end up making something so rickety it'll get somebody killed. I came here for one reason only—to be a depressed gay artist hurtling down one painful memory lane after another.

Please respect that!

But Uncle Paul would just roll his eyes and say, "That's not a real job," and "That's no way to live," and "Please help us."

I plan on returning to bed when I spot something else outside the window, the last thing I ever expected to find in my family's backyard: a 100 percent smokeshow of a man. Halfway down the lawn, a tall, muscular young man in a navy-gray tank top pulls a hoe and a bag of fertilizer over to the vegetable garden.

It's *Gardener Boy.*

After he drops the fertilizer, the young man mops his face with the back of his gloved hand. He's drenched in sweat.

Dark freckles cover his deeply tanned shoulders. When he lifts his arm again, he reveals a dark, furry pit. At this point, I realize I've been clutching the drapes with both hands like I'm trying to stop myself from falling.

"Hullo," I mutter.

I can't see his face clearly, but . . . this is someone to investigate. I'm sure Aunt Ro will understand my talents are much better suited to critiquing her designs and making sure her gardener has everything he needs than to working on any sort of deck-building nonsense.

The increasing heaviness in my pants tells me it's time to go. After putting on the tee I pulled off in the middle of the night, I sneak into the hallway. When I pass the cursed grandfather clock, I'm greeted by another memory I hadn't noticed last night in the dark: the laundry flap. A metallic window, painted the same calming green as the wall, leads down a chute into the basement next to the laundry machines. When we were little, Ben and I used to line up our Avengers figures along the chute's ledge and fire Nerf darts to make them plummet to their doom.

I played Thanos. He was Loki.

And hoo boy, was Ben a Loki.

I graze my finger along the laundry flap's edge. With a squeeze in my chest, I can almost feel the action figures still standing there. I stick my head into the laundry chute and gaze down the shaft—three stories deep—into the basement. The basket is still there at the bottom. Literally nothing has changed about Vero Roseto; it all just stayed and rotted.

Downstairs, the team of contractors Ro mentioned trudge into the West Wing, which is draped floor-to-ceiling with plastic tarps. There's no way anybody could stay here with this amount of construction going on. Ro *really* needs that two-fer sale. As soon as I'm finished introducing myself to Gardener Boy, I'll fire up my tablet and get that ad shined up.

I travel through the East Wing parlor to get outside. A galley hallway is lined with black-and-white photographs of my great-grandmother and my great-grandfather as a young couple, standing outside the construction site of Vero Roseto and holding their newborn baby—my grandma—in the rose garden.

The parlor's sliding door spits me out onto the patio surrounding the abandoned swimming pool. My aunt and uncle aren't here anymore. They must be in the winery. Good—a little privacy with the gardener won't hurt. Speaking of our new mystery man—just beyond the pool, his muscular back ripples like machine pistons as he hacks away at the vegetable garden. Unlike the massive, showplace rose and sculpture gardens, the vegetable garden is a humbler open-air box, about the size of a small garage. Grandpa used to grow tomatoes, carrots, squash, and zucchini; maybe even more than that. He'd been doing it for decades.

The gardener will need to dig deep to clean it all up.

He grunts as he hacks at the dead stalks and weeds. His work noises sound like Link attacks in *Zelda*. Very cute.

The grass—dying as it is—feels nice as it slides between my bare toes. I don't mind being a bit unkempt approaching this hot, soil-driving man. I'll show him I can look rough, too. I'm not afraid of getting a bit country. I run my fingers through my curls, which have become matted and tangled in the almost twenty-four hours since I conditioned them for my failed date.

As I come closer to the grunting young man, courage drains out of me, but I stay focused on creating a casual intro line:

"Need a hand?"

"You look like you could use some iced tea."

"Who am I? Just some sad creep who was staring at you. Don't let my handsomeness fool you. The damage runs deep. You'll have to hoe pretty hard to fix my garden."

"Hey there," I say brightly. Eh, that was my best choice.

Without turning around, the gardener stops working. With an exasperated grunt, he drops the hoe onto the soil. His shoulders pulsate as he catches his breath and mops his brow.

Why won't he turn around? Okay, rude.

My plan is crumbling, so I start biting my nails. "Sorry to bother you. I'm Grant. I live here, sort of. I'll be around in the house if you need water or lunch or . . . whatever."

Sweat beads down the gardener's speckled shoulders. Why does he have to look so sexy while he's ignoring me?

"I was wondering when you were gonna come down," the

33

gardener says, unlatching a water bottle from his belt and guzzling deeply. His voice, so deep, has the slightest trace of a Scottish accent. The sunlight catches his stubbled Adam's apple as he throws his head back and chugs.

Oh God, I'm in trouble. He caught me watching. I don't know how, but he saw me creeping and knew I was going to come strolling up, half-chubbed, like, *"Hey, I just woke up at noon. I'm gonna go do some very hard graphic design and eat some bread patties. Want to have sex in the laundry room?"*

"I, uh, I didn't, uh—" is all I can stammer.

"Oh boy," the gardener laughs to himself. My cheeks couldn't feel any hotter. Maybe I can jump into the hole in the deck before he laughs at me again. "Grant, Grant, Grant . . ."

I blink, stung. That soft way he said my name. There's something familiar to it.

Like he knows me.

Then the gardener turns. He peels off his backward cap and drags a forearm across his glossy red hair. The handsome young man—with vibrant hazel eyes, long lashes, and a dimpled chin—smiles.

Now all I want is to cannonball into that empty pool.

"Ben?"

CHAPTER 5

BEN

Ben McKittrick.

My ex–best friend and the originator of my curse—the gardener my aunt was so mysterious about. Now I know why. When Ben and I had our falling-out the summer before eighth grade, we weren't quiet about it. Everyone in my family knew our friendship was over, but no one knew the truth.

I loved him, then he stole my boyfriend. And when they both left me, there wasn't anyone I could tell. Ben had been the keeper of my secrets. That was the real ass-kicker of it all.

Now here he is, chumming around with my aunt and getting *paid* to do it.

Ro said it helped that the gardener loved Vero Roseto. I should've known what that meant. Ben adored this place—and me, at one point. We ran around these grounds for years, two little Nerf-gun-playing twerps.

But we're not twerps anymore. I'm tall, he's tall. I've got big arms, he's got big arms. I smell like I haven't changed my clothes since yesterday, and he smells like a hardworking gardener. Everything about him is different—defined. Bigger.

Hairier. Jawline-ier. He's so beautiful, I instantly recall everything about my body and face I don't like: my soft waistline, my round, shiny cheeks that are in a constant skincare battle against acne. Things I like or don't mind in other boys but despise in myself.

We're the same age, but Ben McKittrick has become a man, while I'm still a boy. But young Ben—the boy I wrongly trusted—is in there somewhere, beneath the surface.

This hot guy in front of me I can deal with, but the boy and I have baggage.

"You're back," I say, more breathless than I meant to.

"You're back, too," he says, chugging more water (probably to show off his beautiful, stubbled throat again). He laughs as he wipes his lips with his forearm. "Is this gonna be awkward?"

A smile stiffens on my face. "Why would it be? I'm happy you're here to help. The place really needs it." Ben stares in silence as he circles his finger around the nozzle of his water bottle. Those feline eyes of his that never blink. I laugh, but it comes out agitated. "What?"

"I just think it would be better if we got shit out in the open," Ben says.

"There's nothing to get out! It was all a million years ago. It's fine."

"You're not angry?"

"I'm not—what? No, I'm—" Ben tilts his head quizzically, and my body goes into lockdown. Short, quick breaths. That flushed, squeezed feeling, like being crushed by a garbage compactor. He's doing this on purpose to get a rise out of me. "Whatever. What does it matter? I said I'm happy you're here."

He smirks. "Which is bullshit."

"I'm being polite. That's what adult human beings do, Benjamin!" With each second I speak to this boy, a new joint in my body freezes up.

Ben shrugs. "It's all right to be angry."

"No, it isn't!" I blurt, but then my voice deflates. "It's a bummer and no one likes it." Ben sends me a look, like he can see right through me. "But I can't hide it either, apparently, so . . ."

I'm a homosexual. Of course I have no idea what to do with my anger.

Even worse, now that I'm looking at him, the feeling shoots through me. I missed his face so much. That playful, almost mean look he has, like I never know what he's going to say next. He's as sharp as an axe, and sadly, I like it. I've spent the last five years dating boys who never surprised me, even when they were dumping me. But Ben always feels new.

What the hell am I supposed to do with any of this?

"Look," I say, exhaling myself back to normal. "I'm glad you brought it up, but I really—"

Ben turns away, picking the hoe back up. "You're not glad."

There goes my normal.

"What do you want from me?" I ask, curling my hands into

fists. "Want me to cuss you out? I've done that already, and it didn't help. Are you trying to get me to kick your ass?"

Ben's eyebrows lift pleasantly, like *Hey, that's an idea.* "You probably could," he says, surveying my body. "You got big, bro."

An exasperated laugh slides out of me. "Well, *bro*, I design dresses now, so I don't really do the kicking-someone's-ass thing a whole lot, even if I wanted to."

Ben crosses his arms over the hoe to lean against it. "You don't want to kick my ass?"

"No."

"Liar."

"I'm not lying."

"So, what do you want?"

"I *want*"—I take a giant step toward him, so we're inches apart—"to offer you a cool beverage because you look like you need a break. Now can I get you a fucking iced tea or not?"

Ben smiles. "Sure."

Minutes later, I return from the kitchen to the yard with two freezing cans of Brisk iced tea. Ro is the luckiest person in the world that she was nowhere to be found when I went back inside. Every room in the house transformed with my triggered memories of that last summer with Ben. The kitchen absorbed most of my anger. Every door got a hearty slam: the patio, the parlor, the fridge, the patio again.

Ben, no longer antagonizing, accepts the can and holds my

eyes as he taps the lip of the can before opening it.

After a long gulp of tea, I snort, "Why do you always do that? That *tap-tap-tap* on the can."

Shrugging, Ben sips. "Stops it from exploding in case the can got shook up."

"It's tea. It's flat. There's no carbonation."

"It can still explode."

"And your little tapping stops it? You're living in a fantasy world."

Ben blank-faces me as we descend into a thick silence. He doesn't need to say anything, because he's already in my head: *Grant, this is what I'm talking about. You're clearly angry. I'd rather you just slap me now than spend the whole summer snipping me to death.*

Well, Ben-in-My-Head, you have a point, but this is how I choose to punish you.

"Want a tour of what I've got to fix around here?" he asks, breaking through the tension.

"Yeah." *Finally*, a topic other than us.

Since I've seen the disaster that is Grandpa's vegetable garden, Ben walks me farther down the lawn (making his hips extra swaggery *on purpose*) toward another graveyard: the sculpture garden. I'd already seen the chopped-up remains of the white trellis, stacked neatly in piles, but I wasn't prepared for what a junkheap the rest of it would be.

The sculpture garden grounds used to have a chessboard-like tiling of light- and dark-shaded grass. In its prime, it was kept so neatly trimmed you could play golf on it. Now it's so overgrown, you wouldn't know there were different shades unless you were looking for it. Six large shrubs rise from the overgrowth like terrifying monoliths. They used to be trimmed into different animal shapes: a swan, a wolf, a hummingbird, etc. But those well-defined shapes are long gone.

"Bunch of shite, right?" Ben asks, disappointed.

"Awful," I agree. "How long has it been nasty like this?"

Ben absentmindedly kicks a divot in the lawn. "Since everything got nasty between us, I think." He nods. "After your grandparents died."

We made it forty whole seconds without referencing our baggage. A record. Five years ago, not only did Ben and I fall out, my grandmother died, followed a few months later by my grandfather, and the joy of coming to Vero Roseto as a family sort of went away. Ro took over the business but just couldn't hold it together alone.

"Ro wants me to dig up all the sculptures," Ben says, rustling his hand over the bush that used to be a wolf.

"Why?" I ask, looking at the overgrown topiaries. "They're historic."

Ben nods and crushes his empty can. "Yeah, but she can only afford me, and I can't make the animal shapes. You're the artist, not me."

Sweet as that observation is, I glance up at what used to be a swan with a heavy sigh. I can sew and sketch, but these sculptures need an actual topiary artist. Grandma was ours.

Her mother, Mama Bianchi, taught her, but they didn't pass that knowledge down any further.

"So they've all gotta go," Ben says. "Gotta make this place spiffy in time for the Rose Festival. Two months isn't a lot of time with just me working. Ro says this year's festival could make or break Vero Roseto."

"Make or break?" I ask, turning from the swan. "Like . . . we're really in trouble?"

"Dunno. Don't think she'd say it if it weren't true."

I laugh bitterly. Ro is very much at home exaggerating, so it can't really be that bad . . .

Nursing my warming tea, I say, "I can't believe Ro didn't tell me you were here. She just said she got some cheap gardener."

Ben snorts. "You know me, cheap and tawdry."

Inside my head, I cackle so violently it calls down lightning. But I resist taking his bait. "I didn't even know you gardened."

"Oh yeah." He slaps his empty can against his palm. "Picked it up from my stepdad in Scotland. Freshman year, I moved back with my mam."

"Ah, I was going to say: welcome back, accent."

So many lifetimes have passed in five years, I didn't even realize Ben had been living in Scotland. Yet the soft rumble of his newly invigorated accent doesn't lie. What else have I missed about him?

My insides roil as I hold back the questions I really want to ask, like *"What about your boyfriend—aka my boyfriend—that you were so in love with? Did you ditch him, too, when you left?"*

I'm glad Ben went to Scotland. When we were friends, his parents fought nonstop. Hanging out at Vero Roseto brought him some much-needed peace. I thought it would help when they finally divorced, but it ripped him up even more. Ben stayed with his dad while his mother left for Scotland. He missed her, and middle school—the era when you're figuring out what a big homo you are—is no time to be left alone with a dad who isn't good with feelings.

As I hold back my own feelings, I ask, "So, are you going back to Scotland for college, or . . ."

"That's the plan." Ben bites his lip. "I've been back over a year. My dad had a kinda serious health thing . . ."

"Oh." My posture straightens. "I'm sorry—"

"He's fine. It's fine." Ben exhales on a pained grunt. "All better. And it's been nice, being around this old place again, but once it's fixed up by the end of the summer, I'll head back. There's nothing really keeping me here." He smiles, almost angrily. "So don't worry, you'll only have to deal with me for a little bit."

I snort defensively. "I'm only here for a little bit, too."

"Right, right. You've got more important things to do than deal with us. Very good of you to spare some time."

We fall silent.

I had no idea Ben was as angry with me as I am with him. His resentment gets my blood riled, like, what does *he* have to resent? I'm the one who got screwed over, not him.

But when Ben talks like this, he sounds so weighed down, it almost makes me want to forgive him. It sounds like we both got our asses kicked last year. Five years doesn't feel like a long time, but here we are, two *radically* different people from the last time we stood in this garden.

The tour continues back up the lawn, as Ben knows to skip the Wishing Rose garden altogether. Besides fixing that and demolishing the sculpture and veggie gardens, he'll have to resod this entire sprawling lawn of God-knows-how-many acres. "And that's just the gardening," he says as we circle around the filthy, empty pool. "Deck's gotta be rebuilt, the pool's a mess, and they're redoing the West Wing guest rooms."

"Is that the most necessary thing right now?" I ask. "I mean, the deck's in pieces. This place is a hazard. Seems weird to put remodeling first."

Ben just snickers as he throws open the patio door. "You'll see."

Upstairs in the West Wing, past the curtains of contractor plastic, I do finally see. Room after room of the ugliest moth-eaten rooms I've ever laid eyes on. Every pipe is rusted through and has stained the wall a yellowish black. Speaking of stains, large brown ponds of filth cover the low-pile rose-patterned carpets. The sofas and comforters on the bed are littered with dozens of feather-spewing moth bites.

"What's that smell?" I say, pinching the dust respirator mask Ben made me wear.

"Sewage backup," he says through his own mask. "Over the winter, the old pipes corroded. It all let loose at once. Ro couldn't pay to fix everything, so she just stopped the leaks. That had a domino effect. The stains. Mildew set in. Moths." He shakes his head in amazement. "I've seen shithouses in Edinburgh that are more sanitary."

"Ro . . ." I whisper. She really is on her last leg.

Construction equipment and ladders sit abandoned while the workers have lunch downstairs, but I don't even know where you'd begin on something like this.

"Do you think it can get fixed?" I ask Ben.

With masks covering everything but our eyes, his gaze seems kinder. "We've been working on it, don't worry."

Down in the entrance hall, underneath Mama Bianchi's portrait, I snap off my mask and finally breathe fresh air again. Ben returns from the kitchen with two more ice-cold Brisks.

"So that's Vero Roseto today," he says, winking as he knowingly tap-tap-taps his can again, which gets a small laugh out of me. "And allegedly, it all needs to get fixed before the Rose Festival—or we close for good."

"We have to get all that done in two months, huh?" I ask, drowning the West Wing's foul stench from my nostrils as I drink.

Ben smirks. "We? I know what me and the contractors are up to. What are you here to do?"

This boy was born to push my buttons.

I don't take his bait, and I certainly don't say "To copyedit a social media ad."

What I do instead is go for the throat.

"How's Hutch?" I ask pointedly, sounding angrier than I meant to.

His brow furrows. He didn't miss my tone. "Hutch?"

I could crush my can of iced tea in a single squeeze! I know he's not going to look me in the eyes, Mama Bianchi as our witness, and *lie* that he does not remember Hutch, the boy he stole from me. But I just smile and ask, "Your boyfriend?"

Ben's lips curl into a mean grin, the way they always would when he was about to rag me. "My . . . eighth-grade boy-friend?" He snorts. "Yeah, that didn't work out."

Heat boils under my cheeks. *Why* did I have to go bringing up Hutch? I was trying to play it cool, but now I just brought up his thirteen-year-old boyfriend like I was inquiring about the missus. Of course they're over. Of course all that carnage was for nothing.

Ben shrugs those huge, freckled shoulders, and I'm annoyed all over again at how hot he's become after all this time. No way I'm winning the "who got hotter?" contest.

"I don't really do 'boyfriends' anymore," he says. "I mean, I'd like to be romantic. Had a few in Scotland, but none that lasted more than a few weeks."

"Sounds familiar."

Has Ben really had as impossible of a time finding love as I have? Getting dumped again and again? Mad as I am, it's nice to not be the lone loser in the house.

After downing his drink, Ben adds, "Yeah, when it starts getting hard, I just lose interest and cut 'em loose."

Aaaaaaaand never mind—I'm still the loser here.

"Ever feel that way?" he asks, so innocently, as if he were wondering if I ever thought about murder. "Ever feel like no matter what you do, a new guy's just gonna end the same way?"

"Like you're cursed," I say through gritted teeth. "Sometimes."

Two boys, two curses. Mine, to be always dumped. Ben's, to always do the dumping. I guess we cursed each other.

CHAPTER 6

BASEMENT GAMES

Our tour ends in the basement, which I've been looking forward to since the moment I arrived. The basement was the true kid paradise of Vero Roseto. Adults ran—or at least heavily supervised—every other part of the B&B, but the basement was where we roamed free. Whole worlds were invented down here. Somehow it's where we became our true selves.

Not that my straight siblings and cousins had any other selves to be. They were the same kids upstairs and downstairs. But me and Ben were the D word: different. For seven summers in a row—age six to twelve—he and I had no idea our differences were the same. By that eighth summer—age thirteen—we knew. But we found out too late. After my grandparents died, after my siblings got too old to hang around, and after Hutch, there would be no ninth summer.

I guess *now* is our long-delayed ninth summer.

The basement door opens, and I almost start bawling at the top of the stairs. It's all the same. The steep, vinyl steps, patterned with florals that haven't been updated since Mama

Bianchi built this house. The staircase ends at a T-boned wall that cuts the basement into two sections. To the left is the game room—a well-lit, adult-approved kid play area. To the right is the cellar—a poorly lit, adult-*not*-approved area that was irresistible to us. If adults caught us over there, we'd be shooed away to the game room, even though we always crept back. The basement was like a personality test to see if you were "good" or "bad."

A beast or a bunny.

Ben and I were—and are—beasts. We turn right into darkness.

Part of me is more afraid to look in the game room now. Everything is so well-preserved, it feels like I've time traveled, and Ben and I are about to bump into our child selves, still hanging out as if nothing is about to disrupt their lives.

In the dark, I grab the hanging light cord, which used to be hard to reach on my tiptoes but is now dangling near my neck. I tug on the light, and the cellar says, "Welcome back!" and reveals a long corridor of cracked cement, rusted piping, and wooden doors with heavy iron handles. The cellar is objectively off-putting, aesthetically. Yet it fills me with warmth to look at it. While the rest of Vero Roseto used to be postcard-gorgeous but has now fallen into junk, the cellar is like, "What's up? Been ugly. Still ugly."

That's comforting.

Down here, there's the furnace, breaker boxes, and two rows of laundry machines to manage the guest linens. Like the kitchen appliances, these laundry machines are older than most of my relatives, but it's part of the charm. I'm sure I'll still think it's charming when they combust in the middle of the night, and all this rotting wood becomes my fiery tomb.

As Ben wanders beside me, he gazes at the labyrinth of pipes covering the ceiling, his long, muscular throat exposed to me. I eye it like a vampire, with all the lust and violence that particular monster intends for his victims.

"When I first started gardening here, I came down to the basement," he says, eyes glued to the ceiling. "It wasn't right being here without you, so I left."

How *dare* he sweet-talk me! It's like he spanked my heart—immediate pain, with an almost pleasant bouncing sensation afterward.

I smile awkwardly but don't respond. If I speak, I worry I'll sound all warm and friendly, and I intend to remain icy at him for the duration of my stay.

Behind us are my grandfather's tool benches—with walls of medieval-looking devices still hanging where he left them the day he went upstairs, shut his eyes, and never reopened them. Next to the benches is the spare bedroom where my Uncle Dom stayed until my grandparents passed. We don't hear from him much these days, but he would always be a star on the Fourth of July. Dom kept loads of illegal fireworks down here. God only knows how the Valle Forest avoided being "accidentally" burned down every summer—but Dom had plenty of cop buddies, and they're all crooked as a box of snakes, so his antics were just ignored.

"Let's open the Big Four," Ben says, his voice lighter and brighter than it's been all afternoon. Once again, being in the basement allows Ben to loosen up. Will it have the same effect on me? I'm standing next to a boy who has become two hundred degrees hotter since I swore to never speak to him again, so I'm going to say . . . no.

The Big Four are the cellar's four wooden doors, lined side by side next to the laundry machines. Each one leads to a room of treasures and memories. Also, each one is filled with a highly distinctive scent. My fingertips crackle with anticipation at the mere *idea* that I'm about to smell these heavenly rooms again.

"Well, I was just thinking about Dom, so this one's first." I charge ahead. The door sticks. Clearly, it hasn't opened in years. The wood whines stubbornly against its cement frame. Ben and I both grip the iron handle, our biceps flexed and kissing, and pull until it gives way. The scent is instantaneous, conjured perfectly from memory: soot and aging paper. The shallow pantry is filled with shelves of the largest fireworks collection I've ever seen. Bottle rockets the size of tiki torches. Trays of tennis-ball-sized smoke bombs. Black Cat firecrackers wrapped in red paper. A box of multicolored batons I recognize as Roman candles (my favorite—the color, the sparks, the drama!). And then there's a shelf of pure weapons-grade explosives: M-80s and mortar shells.

Illegal with a capital *I*.

My mouth is on the floor. Ben's eyes are almost out of their sockets.

"911, I'd like to report a *terrorist operation*," I say, aghast. "What is this? I've been sleeping with this down here? These look like landmines!"

"Ro said she had some stuff she'd need me to get rid of," Ben says, shaking his head. "But . . . I don't know where to take this. It's safer getting rid of toxic waste."

"Doors closing, bye!" I shut away the death trap and add it to my list of things—starting with Ben—to demand an explanation about from Aunt Ro.

The next door opens more easily. A strong scent of brine smacks us in the face as we see the pickling room. It's identical to the fireworks room, only these shelves are filled with less dangerous items: massive jars of pickled vegetables. Grandpa Angelo kept this room immaculate. It was his baby—the second phase of his garden. When he'd grill burgers or cook a roast in the open pit outside, the side dish would always be fresh, salted-to-death pickles. In middle school, when I stopped eating meat, I'd still get excited for the barbecues because it meant pickle time.

"Paul does the pickling now, but he brings veggies from town," Ben says, shrugging. "You saw how nasty the garden got."

"I'm sure you'll get it growing again," I say. Inside my head, I roll my eyes at myself for being so polite. Guess this basement is loosening me up after all.

The third and fourth doors are bigger than the others, and above them is an overarching plaque reading IL DIAVOLO TI ASCOLTA.

"'The Devil's listening to you,'" I say, waving at the plaque.

Ben rolls his eyes. "You told me like a million times."

A steel cage clamps tightly over my chest as I narrow my eyes. That smug smirk! Smacking my arm, he asks, "You still trying to impress guys with your big Italiano act?"

"*No,*" I huff, lying, my blood hotter than ever. "You still try to impress guys with your Scottish . . . pain-in-the-ass asshole act?"

"It's not an act." He grins. "And it's a jock dropper."

Damn him. I grunt, "Okay, well, I don't need to hear about all the jocks you've dropped."

Ben sighs and dabs his dripping cheeks with a hanky. "That's funny coming from you."

"Why?"

Ben leans boyishly, carelessly, against the last wooden door and laughs. "I had to hear about every speck of your last relationship totally against my will."

My brow darkens. "What did Ro tell you?"

"Nothing. I follow you on Instagram."

Suddenly, I want nothing more than to shut myself in the fireworks room and start pounding on mortars with my fists. I clear my throat angrily. "You follow me? When? I would've seen."

And blocked your ass, I want to add.

Ben shrugs again. If he shrugs one more time, I'll have those shoulders surgically removed! "I don't know," he says. "A while? I don't have any posts, or a profile pic. Anyway, sorry it didn't work out. But your Art Institute designs looked cool—"

"Thank you." Cutting him off, I hurl open the third door to find a deeper pantry. The pleasing scent of oak and whiskey arrives exactly when I need something to stop me from strangling him. Grandpa's casks are still here. Five large barrels of rye from different years. I don't know what the dates are exactly, but I remember the one on the end is at least five-year aged. He barreled it after Grandma's wake in August. He died that October.

Mama Bianchi and my great-grandfather also died a few months apart.

Aunt Ro says that's the mark of true love, when you really can't live without your partner. And both couples found each other because of the Wishing Rose. The jerkoff family legend attached to that rose has pumped more toxic ideas of romance into my brain than all the movies in the world combined.

So, if someone outlives their spouse by years, they're what, not really in love?

It's an awful thing to attach magic to grief.

I slam the door shut. This basement is annoying me.

Ben's eyes flare at my loud racket. "Problem?" he asks.

"No, why?" Now it's my turn to shrug as I haul open the final door—"*Il diavolo ti ascolta.*"

The deepest, longest-winding pantry of them all. Mama Bianchi's wine cellar. A dark, electric-lamplit corridor greets us. Countless dusty bottles of richly hued Wishing Rose labels await us. Some of these bottles are from back in the forties when my great-grandmother built the whole place to impress my great-grandfather.

Everything smells darkly sweet and spiced with cedar.

Ben playfully knocks his hip into mine, sending shock waves of disgust through me. "Aren't you gonna tell me the story again?" he asks in a goofy voice.

I roll my eyes. "I thought you didn't want me repeating stories?"

"Such a sensitive little scrotum. Just tell me again. I want to hear it."

My breaths are getting shorter. That trash compactor tightness is returning.

But still, I don't think I can handle being made fun of for one more second, and I already feel like enough of a loser baby, so I oblige him: "*Il diavolo ti ascolta*. My great-grandmother carved 'The Devil is listening to you' above the wine cellar to keep out her nosy kids. Blah, blah, blah, that's the story."

Clicking his tongue with disappointment, Ben smacks my chest. I jump again. "You used to tell the story so juicily. How your mom got scared that she thought she saw the Devil—"

His giggling gets interrupted by my quiet hyperventilation.

The lamps overhead are growing dimmer.

The corridor is closing in.

Ben. Me. Here. Again.

This is where it happened. This exact spot is where I knew my wish became a curse.

It was during my grandma's funeral. Weighted by guilt, Ben took me down here to confess he was hooking up with Hutch and that they were gonna try dating each other. I thought he was going to say he was in love with *me*, the way I was in love with him. But no.

Everything broke. My family. Our friendship.

"You okay?" Ben asks, concerned and reaching for me, but stopping just shy of touching. I step back, my ass clattering against the bottles in the cubbies behind me.

"Just claustrophobic. Can we go?"

I spin around, halfway toward the stairs, when Ben's deep, throaty voice commands, "Hey."

I turn. He hasn't followed me. He's still waiting by the laundry basket.

"What?" I ask.

"I have something to show you. Found it here last time."

Ben drops to his soil-stained knees and crawls toward one of the washing machines. He sweeps a furry forearm under the basin and pulls out something. Whatever it is, it's small enough to fit in his fist. As he walks to me, I have to control my breathing, or it'll get erratic again.

He's close enough to smell. Dirt and ocean-scented body spray.

His scent turns my boiling blood into a cool, placid lake.

What is it about these smells—soot, brine, rye, and Ben—that on paper should be repulsive, but in reality excite me?

Grinning sheepishly, Ben opens his fist. In his chapped, ruddy palm is a Nerf dart. A shockingly orange foam finger with a rubber tip. It's been lost under there since we were kids shooting action figures down the laundry chute. He remembered and went looking for it the very first chance he got.

"Been a long time," I say, forced into a whisper by how powerfully my heart is pounding.

"Not that long," Ben says, smiling. "Just been a busy five years."

When he smiles, the boy appears beneath the man. And that boy and I have unfinished business, so the brief softness in my heart hardens. Swallowing, I lay down my boundary: "Ben, we can't hang out like before."

"I wasn't asking to." Again, he laughs, and again, anger tightens my jaw.

"I don't know how long I'm gonna be here. I'm figuring stuff out."

Ben nods, his lips curled angrily, and he pulls his cap backward. "In other words: shut up and garden." Before I can defend myself, he drops the Nerf dart into my palm and closes my fist over it. "Still bugging over some shit that happened back when we still played with toys." He stomps up the stairs. "I thought you were a man."

"A MAN?" I shout, laughing. "Didn't realize I was suddenly talking to your dad!"

He's gone. I thrust my bare foot, hard, into the cement wall next to the dryers. Pain enters my big toe and rockets up the back of my leg. I hop in place until the pain subsides—but nothing dulls my dread. How am I supposed to spend the summer with him?

Aunt Ro rushes downstairs. "What's all the noise about?" she asks.

Hissing at my scraped toe, I smile nastily. "Hey, Ro, you just missed the *gardener*."

Her face floods with fear. Busted.

THE FAIL FESTIVAL

Two grilled paninis arrive on the kitchen island in front of me so quickly, they might have been conjured by magic. Arugula, banana peppers, pepperoncini, sliced olives, veggie gravy, oil and vinegar, and tons of cheese smashed between two halved baguettes. Aunt Ro wrings tension out on her dishrag as she watches me take my first kingly bite, which is salty and divine.

I then set the panini down, clean my fingers of oil, and say, "Thank you. Now . . . What. Is. That. Awful. Boy. Doing. Here?"

Her crimes finally laid bare, Ro slumps onto an island stool and chomps into her own panini. "Ben was cheap," she says, thinking through her bites. "And more importantly, he loves Vero Roseto. We need this place to be like it was again, or we're not gonna make it. The tax bills are doubling. And I can't take on any more debt. Paul and I don't have kids. I can't spend the rest of our savings just to hang on to a place you all barely even visit. I have to get serious about Vero Roseto as a business, or it's time to move on."

"Move on?" A chunk of panini goes down hard. "Like sell it?"

"There's already been offers." She shudders. "Vultures are circling. The Wishing Rose brand is strong, so we're looking like very tasty roadkill. Pretty soon, I won't have a choice."

I'm speechless. For eighty years, this place has been our family's beating heart, and overnight, it could all just . . . stop?

"But I have a plan," Ro says, steeling herself as she chews. "Ma always said during lean years, the Rose Festival kept us in the black. We're the crown jewel, the last stop on the tour. If we do the festival big, and I mean *big*, it could keep us in fighting shape. The festival's in August. That gives us two months. You, me, Paul"—she mutters her next words into her panini—"and Ben."

My sandwich drops to the plate with a dramatic thud. "I knew staying here was a trap."

Aunt Ro grabs my wrist to stop me from leaving. "It's perfect for all of us! You're a designer, and I need something designed! You won't have to build anything! Ben will do whatever you want."

My gaze bores flaming holes into my aunt. "Designing is one thing. Working with Ben is . . . something else. Did you and Mom plan it this way?"

I don't have the stomach to remind her my last ex and I fell in love designing a show together. It ruined me in six million different ways. Go through all of that again, but this time with someone I *already* have baggage with? A HOMICIDAL IDEA, RO.

"If it's too much, I get it. It's just . . . I'm not good at these festivals." Ro dabs her eye, careful not to dampen her eyeliner. "Losing the home my mother was born in, and it'll be all my fault . . ."

Italian opera at its finest.

Quietly, I reach across the island and stroke Ro's hand with my thumb. "Aunt Ro, that's not a tear, that's vinegar. Stop fake crying because I caught you lying about Ben."

Huffing, she hurls a balled-up paper towel at me. "You!" She waves her panini like a weapon. "I'm gonna slip meat into the next thing I cook you."

"Answer the question, criminal! Are you plotting to smoosh me and Ben together again?"

"The last thing on my mind! We're in big trouble, buddy. We've got more things that need fixing than people to fix them. Ben McKittrick is a gift from God—"

I sputter into my sandwich. "Did Ben tell you that?"

As Ro chews, her narrowed eyes study me. "This is why I said nothing."

The oodles of cheese in this panini are soothing my beast into a more patient creature. After a long moan, I say, "By not telling me, you really made sure I found out in the most hilarious way."

"How'd you find out?"

"I looked out the window, saw a hot gardener outside, and strolled outside to chat him up."

Uncontrollable giggles take over my aunt. "Oh no, I really

set you up. I told you all my angel boys grew into men when I wasn't looking!" Her laughter dies as her brow darkens. "Wait, what were you gonna do if the gardener ended up being some regular guy? Were you gonna romance some *grown man* in my house? You're still a baby! That's not why I invited you here."

I jab my finger in her direction. Ro and I can duel better than anyone. "You're up to something besides this festival."

Ro grows quiet. Coyness creeps into her smile. "Fine. It's not *just* about the house." With a new seriousness, she slips her cool, painted fingers inside mine. "I know you think you've got a curse. That Ben—and the Wishing Rose—started the curse."

I wasn't expecting that much accuracy.

"We're a superstitious family," Ro says in a mea culpa. "Sorry, but it's in your blood. And I believe healing things with Ben will break your curse and heal you, too."

I try to pull my hand back, but Ro holds firm. "I don't know how you know all that," I whisper dangerously, "but Ben doesn't seem like he wants to *heal* things. And neither do I."

"Leave that to the Wishing Rose! Make a new wish and set things right. The rose has brought together four generations of this family. Your great-grandmother, your grandmother, me—"

"Then that's how it works for straights!" Now I pry my

hand back for real. "For little gay boys, we make a wish on it and"—I flick my hand under my chin—"cursed. It happened instantly."

I collect my plate to leave, but Aunt Ro follows me from the island to the sink to the fridge and back again. "Grant, that last summer, I saw you sneak out to the garden at night . . . I heard you make that wish." A tear breaks down her cheek. "Sweetie, that wish was bad. That's not how it works. The rose reveals your true love, not—"

"Ben *was* my true love, but he blew up my life instead. And the rose can't fix that."

Ro wipes another tear from her cheek. "Believe what you want, but what I believe—and remember, I'm Mama Bianchi now—is that Ben's going to fix the rose garden, you're going to fix the Rose Festival, the Rose Festival will fix Vero Roseto, and the Wishing Rose is gonna fix *you*."

As Ro pulls me into a desperate hug, I let it happen, even though I'm as rigid as a statue.

That wish was the most private moment of my life, and she was snooping?

Better her than my brother, but *Jesus*, Ro.

After finishing the hug, I pull open the fridge for something cold and sweet. I pop open the bottle cap on a Mexican Pepsi with the real sugar, and try to pivot. I don't want to talk about my curse or my wish anymore. "So, we need to design a five-star festival *plus* fill the renovated B&B rooms. How am I supposed to do that? Copyediting your ad?"

Grinning slyly, Ro unfastens the oil-stained apron from her raspberry-colored frock and returns it to the hook on the side of the fridge. "Yes. I need a social media teen to help me fill these beds through the summer into the festival. You're not getting paninis for free around here."

I roll my eyes. "You olds think we're all just sitting on the nuclear codes about how to make a viral post. It's luck. It's about trends you don't even know are happening. It's like saying, 'Teach me how to get struck by lightning.' You just get struck by it."

"True," Ro says, sliding back on the rings that she took off while she was cooking. "But you can teach me how to wrap myself in metal and hold up a golf club in a rainstorm."

As I sigh, an invisible weight settles on my shoulders.

"I'll take a look at your social stuff," I say, "But . . . I'm off my game. I don't even have school lined up for the fall yet." Each word exits as stubbornly and painfully as an extracted tooth. "My portfolio was *way* stronger a year ago. I stopped sewing. Stopped planning. My spark just went away."

Ro watches from across the kitchen. Her face is soft and sympathetic. "It happens."

I laugh bitterly. "Happened at the worst time. It's hard to explain to colleges you took a gap year for a mental spiral."

Silence fills the kitchen as I, apparently, got too real. And so it goes with this family. I miss talking to Dr. Patty, my therapist. She had this way of taking the roller coaster in my head and making it all make sense. She didn't try to tell me I wasn't on a roller coaster. She didn't ask why I didn't just get off the roller coaster mid-loop. She just . . . let me ride it and talked me through it.

I'd love to see her again, but it's been so long, I doubt she'd have room in her schedule. Anyway, apparently I'm about to be a lot busier here than I thought, so maybe I won't have the time either.

Finally, my aunt nods, her eyelids growing heavier. "This house is important to so many people, and I'm failing them. Bad things happened out of my control, but I also made mistakes. I know what it's like to have one thing after another come down on you hard, throw you off your game, and you can't correct it no matter what you do."

She gives me a little smile, and I return it.

"But it's not over," Ro says. "I know we can fix things."

"Sounds like I came at the right time," I say.

Grinning more broadly, Ro extends her ring-laden hands. "That's what I've been saying."

I sigh. "The thing with Ben . . ." I wince. "I would love it if things could be better—if Ben could magically be a different person, and I could magically not be messed up about it—but that true love shit is out of the question. It's off the table. It's in the trash can. In the garbage truck, heading for the dump. I'll be nice. We'll work nicely together. But anything more than that, forget it."

Ro starts to protest again when—*creaaaaaaak*—the floor

outside the kitchen doorway whines noisily. Aunt Ro—closer to the sound—leans through the arch. "Hello?"

Sheepishly, Ben emerges from around the corner. He wrings his ball cap in his hands, his wavy red hair sticking wildly in every direction. When he actively avoids eye contact, I know the truth: he's been creeping on our conversation.

A sour sneer comes over me as I turn into a gargoyle by the fridge.

"I need the wheelbarrow for the compost," he says. "Can't find it where I left it yesterday."

"Paul's got it!" Ro says with a nervous laugh. "He should be done by now—let's find him."

Aunt Ro floats outside merrily, repressing that she just tricked me into confessing my jagged feelings for Ben while the dickhead himself was eavesdropping. Of course she doesn't care. She's another eavesdropper, listening in on my lowest, most desperate moment at the Wishing Rose!

That's Vero Roseto. Ears everywhere. Privacy nowhere.

Ben doesn't follow her out. He lingers in the doorway, half looking in my direction as if he has something to say. But he doesn't. He heard me admit I'm a flop, still wounded by his carelessness, and all he has is pity.

"She runs fast," I say. "Better catch her."

He shuffles outside. And I'm left alone.

Before heading upstairs, I open a rear kitchen cupboard to see how little this place has changed. On the floor of the cupboard, surrounded by loose pantry items, is Grandma's Singer suitcase—the first machine I ever learned to sew on. She taught me, but at first she just let me watch her work, whether it was hemming our clothes or mending the drapes.

I am the amalgamation of the skills of everyone in my family.

Lugging the suitcase in one hand, with its ancient iron weight, I open a kitchen drawer full of a dozen dishrags, each patterned with different fruit. I choose two towels with strawberries and take everything to my East Wing bedroom.

The silence is nice, especially after such a noisy day.

I open the suitcase, plug the 1960s monstrosity behind my room's writing desk, and get my fingers feeling needle and thread again. Hours pass. The sun sets. I trace an outline of my hand on the strawberry dishrags, slice out the patterns, feed the cloth into the machine, and proceed to sew myself a matching set of strawberry fingerless gloves.

As I flex the gloves open and closed, my power returns. My skills are all still there. I just need the intent and to focus on what I'm *doing*. Yesterday's fog—dissipating slowly since arriving at Vero Roseto—now clears entirely.

I'm me again.

I raise my eyes to the ceiling and ask Mama Bianchi— not Ro, the real one inside the walls of Vero Roseto—what I should do. Stay, save the house, and deal with Ben? Or leave and rebuild my life—and my portfolio—some other way?

I don't hear a voice, but the answer still emerges.

Stay. Save the festival, the house, and the family, and use your new designs to get into a great school.

Then I'll start a new life somewhere else with zero baggage.

And for God's sake, I won't ever let a boy get in my head again.

CHAPTER 8

THE WISHING ROSE

That night, I return to the scene of the crime. I know what I have to do.

Nobody in Vero Roseto is awake except me and the spirit of Mama Bianchi. Ro and Paul are in bed, and Ben went back to his dad's house in Valle. I pull on the gray sweats my uncle lent me and creep downstairs with a flashlight. Pausing in the hall beneath my great-grandmother's portrait, I whisper, "Sorry to bother you so late." Her oil-on-canvas face—warm yet stern—seems to brighten as she stares downward. I draw an angry breath. "You only knew me as a baby, and you probably don't like who I fall in love with—which is why you had your rose backfire on me—but tough shit. Because I'm gonna save your house. And without me, your portrait is gonna get sold online to some wine snob, and your magic rose garden will get bulldozed into condos." I flash my dimples. "Which would be fine by me, but a lot of people care about that ugly weed, so I'll save that, too!"

My respects now paid, I cross the hall toward the under-construction West Wing. Curtains of protective plastic still drape from the upstairs landing where the workers left it. As quietly as I can, I grip the plastic curtain and pull it free of the painter's tape fixing it to the railing. It plummets softly to the ground, collecting in a massive pile. The plastic crinkles noisily as I fold it into a shape I can more easily carry.

I can't be any quieter, so I at least try to be quick about it.

When I'm finished, I listen to the silence in the hall. No voices. No doors opening.

Everyone's still asleep.

Exiting outside to the backyard is easy, but making it over the lawn to the rose garden is far more treacherous. Knowing what I know about the yard, there's a million ways to get killed or maimed in the dark. I could fall into the drained pool or into the collapsed deck—and I need a shattered leg like a hole in the head, so I keep my flashlight on and take the journey slowly.

The night is pleasantly warm. A symphony of crickets and frog song keeps me company as I retrace my steps from the night I cursed myself—the night Ro apparently followed me. The closer I get, the more the moonlit sky disappears behind the massive shadow that is Valle Forest. With the sculpture garden trellis still lying in pieces, there's fewer obstacles to maneuver around on my way inside the rose garden. The entire garden is housed within shrubbery walls. It's like something from *Alice in Wonderland*.

Or the hedge maze in *The Shining*.

Next to the archway is a switchboard buried in the shrubs.

When I made this nighttime trek at thirteen, I was so short I needed a stick to throw the light switch. Now, as a fully grown beast, it's a cinch. The lights still work—the interior garden illuminates with cool footlights and overhanging stadium lamps. It's not oppressively bright, just enough to pretty up the space.

If Ro looks out her bedroom window, she'll be able to see the lights, but I won't be long.

Gathering a courageous breath, I cross under the arch . . . and find a mess. The rose garden used to be the grand centerpiece of Vero Roseto—an open-air topiary masterpiece with fountains and rose-covered walls of green. Walking inside used to feel like you had shrunk down to the size of a bee and were walking inside a rose itself. Today, the fountains are as dry as that swimming pool—and they've become toilets for forest animals. The rose vines covering the walls are still there, but they've withered. Blackened corpses of rose bulbs droop pathetically off their stems.

However, one piece of the rose garden remains untouched.

When I see it at the end of a long stretch of horticultural death, my heart stops.

The Wishing Rose.

It's actually several roses filling a large, spherical bush. The bush is brightened by its own ring of overhead lights, dimmed softly so as not to overheat the flowers. The dim lights lend the Wishing Rose bush a romantic aura of magic. I can almost see tiny pixies encircling the bountiful, cherry-red hybrids, which (unlike the rest of this garden) continue to be meticulously cared for. Looking at the Wishing Rose, it's easy to believe in its myth, its magic, its power.

The hairs on my arm frizz and stand at attention.

I'm a child again.

Five years wasn't that long ago, but it feels like a century. I was so little. Not a drop of anger in me. The beast wasn't awakened yet, but it was there, just under the surface—a hurt child, begging for help but given claws instead.

"Hello there," I say to the Wishing Rose. Particles dance through the light surrounding it. "Don't worry. I'm not here to wish. Not making that mistake again."

In under five minutes, I've dressed the scene. I toss three plastic curtains over the garden—the fountains, the rotting walls—everywhere but the Wishing Rose. No one needs to know how dreadful it looks under the curtains; we're just undergoing some remodeling.

Rule number one in social promo is conceal everything that would distract from your narrative. My narrative for Vero Roseto is mythmaking—we remain as powerful as ever. Everything can rot except the Wishing Rose, our family label. People used to come from other countries just for the chance to trust their heart's desire to Mama Bianchi's roses. That's what matters. The rest is window dressing. So, if the rest looks like garbage, cover it.

Pardon our fairy dust. Vero Roseto is getting some work done to make it shinier than ever.

Rule number two for promo is get personal.

We do so much to hide our scars, but you can't look shiny and plastic. There must be something organic, something imperfect, something raw and maybe even wounded. Show them one scar so they won't go looking for the others.

That's where I come in.

In my phone's front-facing camera, I check my hair—bouncy but careless. I can't look camera-ready. After some consideration, I pull down my hoodie's zipper another two inches. This communicates that I'm in sweats, so I don't care how I look, but here's a flash of pec cleavage.

I'm depressed but still a cutie, America!

I position myself in front of the Wishing Rose, its magical, healthy light shimmering behind me in the dark. When you're getting real, it's best not to over-rehearse these things, so three, two, one, action—

"This is the Wishing Rose," I say, recording. "These hybrids have been in my family since World War II. During the war, my great-grandmother—Mama Bianchi—grew these roses, started a winery, and built an entire *mansion* around it. Why? To win back my great-grandfather, who was fighting in France. Before the war, they were engaged, but he broke it off. She was rich, and it made him feel small. Not cool behavior, but it was the forties, and she loved him anyway, so she doubled down. When he came back, he saw this place—Vero Roseto!" I gesture grandly behind me, but never move the camera off the Wishing Rose. "The roses won him over, and eighty years later, here I am. There's a myth that any bloom on the Wishing Rose bush knows true love. It's brought together four generations of my family. My great-grandmother, my grandmother, my aunt, my parents, and my sisters."

I pause to swallow painfully. Here it comes. Tell them, Grant.

"How it works is, um . . ." My voice cracks, but I don't stop. "You hold one of the roses, think of the person you'd like to be with, and then you wish for a sign that they're The One. It doesn't work just for my family. People come from all over to stay at Vero Roseto and buy a rose to wish for the person they want to marry. We get dozens of messages from people saying it worked for them. Within a week of making their wish, they're engaged."

I brush back a tear, and on a wounded breath, I tell the truth:

"I wondered if the magic would work for me, too, because I'm gay. When I was a kid, I came out here when everyone was asleep. I had a crush on a boy—but I was with someone else. I felt so chaotic, I worried my problem wasn't choosing between two boys, but the fact that they were boys at all. My family wasn't homophobic, but you see stuff on the news, you hear people talk, and it gets you thinking maybe you're the problem. I just didn't want to be alone. I loved my family. I loved coming to Vero Roseto every summer for the Rose Festival. I never wanted to be the sad, alone person in the family."

I take a deep breath and go on. "All I heard growing up

was how the rose brought my family together and made it grow, but . . . I was a kid and didn't think I'd be able to. I wanted to be part of the magic and the myth. So, five years ago, little me put my hand on the rose"—I walk backward and reach for a petal—"and I asked the rose to reveal my true love. But because I'd been society-poisoned into believing that my love couldn't be a boy, I lost my courage. When I wished, I thought of the boy I wanted to be with, but for a split second, I thought about wanting to change. I said, 'Or just take all these boys away. Show me my *real* love. A girl.'"

A quiet tear drops down my cheek, but I don't let my phone drop.

I breathe out a loud moan and keep recording.

"Shocker, the rose didn't change me," I say. "That can't happen. I was wrong to wish that, and my wish backfired. The next week, those boys I cared so much about got together with each other, and I *did* end up alone. But the curse didn't stop there. Because I asked the rose to take *all* boys away, that's what it did. Ever since then, no one's stayed with me longer than a few weeks." On a deep, cleansing breath, I deliver the closer: "I'm cursed, but I'm also proof the magic is real. We've got another Rose Festival coming up this August. Vero Roseto is a dream place, and there's still reservations for rooms in our newly renovated West Wing." I spin the camera around to show the tarps slung over the garden walls, and then pivot back to me. "We're almost done with our renovation, and the Wishing Rose *will* be accessible to paying guests of the

B&B, so snatch up those reservations quickly. But a word of warning . . ." I bring the camera closer, so they can see my tears are real. "Phrase your wish carefully."

I flash a peace sign and stop recording. In the cricketing silence of the rose garden, relief floods my nervous system. I did it. My ugliest secret is now free. Hopefully, my confession should be enough mythmaking to draw in superstitious visitors.

Rule number three of promo: sometimes, a warning works better than a welcome.

Before leaving, I turn back to the Wishing Rose. Its petals stare blankly, unconcerned about the wreckage they've made of an innocent kid. I want to scream, *How could you do this to me?!*

But I'd just be yelling at a plant when I'm really yelling at myself.

CHAPTER 9

JACKPOT

Thanks to the feelings dredged up by my public late-night therapy, sleeping upstairs is impossible. One gong from the grandfather clock outside my room, and my thoughts instantly spiral toward Ben. Ben—back in my life again. I'm still into him, but that's only because my dick can't understand the danger I'm in if I fall for this boy again. The damage I absorbed from my exes is a scratch compared to the gutting when I lost Ben.

Each day I spend here will be a challenge.

Since the upstairs bedroom is too haunted by bad memories, I opt to smother myself in good memories instead and sleep in the basement's game room. Uncle Dom's old camping cot is still there from the seventies. It was made for a large child, but I curl into enough of a ball to fit. Its earthy, stale-cracker scent and the texture of the hunter-green canvas activates a happy memory from when I was young, safe, and still loved Ben.

Well, back when I only knew the simple side of Ben. And of myself.

Finally, my brain lets me sleep.

In the morning, I have no idea what time it is. The storm-shielded basement has no windows, and I didn't bring a charger for my dead phone. Upstairs, the workers' bandsaws rumble faintly as they continue renovating the West Wing. In the dark, I grasp for a light switch near the stairs. Like the rest of Vero Roseto, the game room is as preserved as a museum. Behind my cot, an ancient dollhouse sits open, its flooring—made of contact paper patterned with sunflowers—now curled and peeling. Dolls and toys of every size (and era) lie scattered throughout the house like the morning after a raging party.

Next to the dollhouse, a library of children's books wraps the entire back wall. Little Golden Books with shimmering foil spines, stacks of baby-blue titles I recognize as a Nancy Drew collection, and two full rows of Goosebumps. During those frequent summer storms, my sisters would read them out loud by flashlight. There was one that freaked Ben out about a mask that turned a boy into an old man. If it hadn't been pitch-black, I wouldn't have had the courage to reach over and rub his back to calm him. It's something a straight boy wouldn't think twice about doing for a friend, but when you're confused—and touching a boy's back *means* something—a million internal negotiations happen all at once.

When Ben didn't flinch at my touch, I knew what I did was okay.

When he took my hand in the dark, I knew I was *not* okay.

A few years later, I'd wish him out of my life forever. And the rose cursed me instead.

Don't ever wish straightness on yourself.

The rest of the game room is taken up by a full-size pool table. The older kids played pool on it, but the rest of us used it as a stage. Ben, my sisters, and I put on an impromptu production of *Tangled*, with each of us taking turns being Rapunzel. My brother, A. C.—ten years older than me and annoyed he couldn't use the pool table—would always interrupt. As the youngest of eight highly vocal and opinionated Italians, it was impossible to do what I wanted in peace. A. C. was infuriating until he started calling Rapunzel "Ra-Pinball," which cracked us up so much it set the tone right again.

Don't ask why! When you're that young, anything silly and random is top-shelf humor.

Beyond the Ra-Pinball table, at the farthest wall, is the slot machine my great-grandfather allegedly inherited from a friend of a friend of Al Capone. Nearly a century old and made of heavy iron and brass, the slot machine rests on a table mounted to the wall. It was the coolest thing any kid—young or old—could play with down here, even though we mostly just lost hundreds of nickels to it.

Next to the slot machine is an old, plastic McDonald's cup. A drawing of Catwoman wraps the cup, its vibrant colors faded, but it's still filled to the brim with nickels. A smile rises as my twiddling fingers reach for the slot machine's lever. I take a nickel from the cup, plunk it inside the dirty slot, and pull. Maybe *something* with my luck will change.

Shuddderrrrrrrrrr.

The mechanical beast trembles loudly as three wheels spin. Familiar painted icons—lemons, a bushel of grapes, green apples—whirl past my unblinking eyes.

The wheels spin to a stop—one at a time landing with a tinny *clunk*—until I see exactly what I hoped for. Three in a row. Rose. Rose. Rose.

Jackpot.

On another, happier whirl, the machine belches a decade's worth of nickels (all failed jackpot attempts) into the basin below.

"Helloooooooooo!" I shout, thrusting my arms in the air.

If I close my eyes right now, I'd be able to see A. C., Ben, Kimmy, Traci—everyone—all of us children again, cheering me enviously as I achieve the unachievable rose jackpot! Young Ben wraps his arms around me, and . . .

"You got a jackpot?" asks grown-up—real life—Ben behind me.

My heart in my shoes, I spin quickly, biceps tightened and fists raised to fight whoever just spoke (even though I know it's Ben; my fists aren't communicating well with my brain). He stands at the bottom step, a new tank top—this one teal blue—already sweated through from a morning in the garden. Here I am in nothing but gray sweat bottoms, praying my morning wood has already deflated.

Ben snorts. "I've been playing that thing for weeks and keep getting green apples."

I laugh. "It knows you're a sour asshole."

"Yeah, 'cause you've been such a rose," he sputters. After a brief wince, Ben's tone softens. "I caught your video from last night."

Tension stiffens my spine. "And?"

"Thank you for not bringing my name into it."

"That's it?" My eyes narrow. I poured my guts out, and this is all he has to say?

"Well, you're a popular guy, and I don't want to be the new villain in your life, so I appreciate you keeping me out of it."

"A new *villain*?"

"Your exes must be flattered you can't get their names out of your mouth, and you keep pointing to them—sorry, this *curse*—for why you're so miserable."

"God," I groan, my joy at winning the jackpot already dead. "I don't blame *them*. I blame—"

"A rose, yeah."

I almost said *"I blame you,"* but that might start our festival plans on a bad note.

Clearly agitated, Ben blows out sharp breaths and adjusts his backward cap. "You and your family—all these jinxes and curses and hex talk." He shakes his head. "Look, I'm sorry you were going through all that back then, and I *am* sorry about what happened with us, but . . . you think Hutch and I got together because of a wish you made?"

Ben's sneer exposes my self-centered viewpoint. Standing here, half-naked, all my curse talk suddenly seems as childish as the games in this basement. Some mildewy idea I should have put away years ago. But brains don't behave rationally like that.

I shrug, rake my fingers through my curls, and lie: "I was just trying to make the video sound witchy enough so people would want to come here. I promised Ro I'd promote the festival. This might be our last year if we can't make it work."

Rather than soften him, my words toughen Ben's expression into a cold grin.

I hate it.

"*What?*" I say. "I'm trying to help!"

"You don't know?" he asks.

"Know what?"

Ben scrunches his face in disbelief. "We're already booked through next month."

"Booked? Like . . . the rooms? People made reservations?"

Ben nods. "Your video kind of blew up. Ro's losing it. Her website crashed, and she's enlisted your uncle to help renovate the rooms now because people are coming *today*. She might have to put guests in the East Wing family rooms until the West Wing is ready, so get used to that cot."

For a long moment, I sputter nonsense, overflowing with confusion that in the time between posting my video and waking up, my family's fortunes have turned around. "But . . . *when* are people coming? We're not ready. The West Wing looks condemned. There's a frigging sinkhole in the deck. There's not even a rose garden to have a *rose* festival!"

"*Yep,*" Ben barks, looking irritated. "Could've used more time to prep, but guess I'll just work around the clock to make a pretty party for all your fans."

"Okay, *wait.*" I close the gap between me and Ben. He already smells like sweat and soil. *Do not look at his chest, Grant! Eyes up!* For a moment, Ben's gaze flicks up and down at me (I haven't been feeling like my chest is anything to stare at lately, so thanks for looking, Ben). "What do you mean 'my fans'?"

Ben smirks—his bear face already in place if he ever gets a bear body. "Your video, Grant. Our middle school bullshit, dragged up for everyone to see."

I take Ben firmly—but gently—by the wrist and meet his eyes. His jaw hardens. I've only seen him this angry once before. "I didn't make that video to rag on you. I did it to make people believe the Wishing Rose brings people together, so they'd come to make it happen for themselves."

Scoffing, Ben messes with the flecks of red hair peeking out from his cap. "Well, it worked or whatever. Just if anyone starts prying about our drama, I'm gonna take it out on you."

He jabs my bare chest, hard at first, but then he pulls back, looking unusually self-conscious.

Weren't expecting my boob to feel that nice, were you, Benji?

"Yeah, I grew up, too," I laugh, but he rolls his eyes. "I'm sorry I didn't warn you I was making that video. I didn't realize it would go that far that fast."

He casts his eyes to the pool table. "Your ex reposted it. The one with all the followers."

My *popular* ex. He saw everything and shared it. To embarrass me? Out of pity?

I pace around the pool table and mutter, "What are we gonna do? People are gonna see this place is a dump and know *I'm* still a dump . . . I should've blocked him."

"You'd block him?"

His soft, wounded tone halts my spiraling thoughts in their tracks. "Yeah?"

Ben clutches the green felt ledge of the pool table and lowers his head. "If you'd known I was following you last year," he whispers, "would you have blocked me?"

Neither a yes nor a lie comes to me in time.

"That would've really, really sucked if you'd done that, but I wouldn't have been surprised." Ben's chest rises on a sharp, furious breath. His jaw is so tense, just like when . . . Well, I haven't seen him this angry since our friend breakup. He snorts. "I hope you didn't get the story wrong about your ex, too." Ben flicks an eight ball across the table and clomps upstairs.

"'Get the story wrong'? What does that mean?"

If he's talking about himself, how else was I to interpret Ben running off with Hutch? I'm the wronged party, and I

83

have every right to be mad at everyone and everything!

"Saddle up, city boy," Ben calls from the top of the stairs. "We got lots of work to do. That fancy new chest of yours better not be just for show!"

Oh, it's not, sweetie. I'll show you—and everyone—what I can do.

CHAPTER 10

THE OLD GRANT

One shower, oatmeal breakfast, and phone charge later, I gather Ben, Aunt Ro, and Uncle Paul outside on the back lawn to discuss my strategy for dealing with Vero Roseto's sudden popularity. As usual, my strategy involves a lot of improvisation and faking like I know what the hell I'm doing. But fortunately, my instincts usually end up being spot-on, and my fake confidence becomes real. While my aunt and uncle are tense, and Ben leans casually against a fence post, I stand confidently astride the collapsing deck's stairs in my borrowed denim shorts and oversize tee.

The bottom step whines under my weight. Clearly, we can't keep a scrap of the existing deck, which stretches almost the entire width of the manor. It has to go now.

"Ro," I say. My aunt, lost in thought, startles at the sound of her name. "When are the first guests arriving?"

"Ten of them *today*!" she says, tugging on her self-manicured nails.

"When's check-in?"

"Four o'clock, but I've already had a few ask for an early

check-in . . ." Spiraling, she throws up her hands. "I wanted guests, but I didn't think we'd book all the rooms, or I would've noted they can't all be filled yet." Her brow darkens. "And your video said everyone who books a room can see the Wishing Rose, but I wasn't planning on having it open until August for the festival! What's gonna happen when they want to see it today?"

Ben's eyes drift bitchily to me, as if to say, *Well? Answer her.*

I step down from the deck toward Ro, and all three of them flinch. My move looked impressive and confident, but I was actually just scared I'd break through the stairs. I shake it off and shrug casually. "If the guests see everything like this, they'll go online and talk about how nasty it is."

Ro and Paul stare, the color draining from their faces. Smiling, I raise my finger to the sky. "*But* they're not going to see it like this."

Ben rolls his eyes. "If I worked nonstop, no meals, no water, no sleep, I still couldn't get the rose garden ready for at least a week. We don't have the materials or the bulbs or . . ."

I raise my hand calmly. "I understand. This is actually going to be simple. I want to introduce all of you to the art of addition through subtraction." The three of them lean closer. "We have seven hours before check-in. All we have to do *today* is provide guests with a room, a glass of wine, and the Wishing Rose. Vero Roseto and Valle Forest are beautiful enough to do the rest."

"But what about the deck?" Uncle Paul argues, his eyes disappearing into a squint.

Nodding, I point to my aunt. "Ro, those reservations you got, did they put money down?"

"They all had to for the first night," she says, still fiddling with her nails.

"Great! So, we've got cash to work with." I spin toward my uncle. "Paul, could you get people up here right now to get rid of this deck? Not to rebuild it, just demo and clear."

Uncle Paul, his furry arms perpetually crossed in agitation, finally drops them. "Yeah, I can get my guys," he says, his voice suddenly brighter. He scans the deck, cautiously studying it, likely mentally going over the geometry of how he'd attack the problem. "We could chop it up by lunch and have it hauled out before check-in."

A rush of adrenaline surges through my chest. I can't fight my smile.

There it is. The old Grant, still in there, elbow-to-elbow next to the wounded child and the cursed beast. It's getting crowded inside me, but at least I know the artist and leader still exists.

"Ro, it's gonna be great," I say, taking her into a hug, but she wobbles queasily, as if she needs more convincing.

"I'm so glad you're energized," she says, "but we've known for weeks about everything we have to do. It's just been so busy. I don't think there's time—"

"People are coming. We have to try, right? You wouldn't let me be this negative."

Ro laughs, exhausted. "No, I wouldn't." She sighs. "The guests can stay in the East Wing. That means you've gotta stay in the basement again."

I nod. "Done."

She glances at Ben and Paul, who look wary but waiting to accept her approval. She's running this operation, not me. "Paul, I think you and the guys should focus solely on the deck. Specifically the middle section with the hole, but remove it all if you can. Like it was never there. That means, Ben, you're in the rose garden."

"Aye, aye." Ben salutes.

She winces at us both. "*With* Grant. It's a two-person job. You boys okay with that?"

Ben and I meet eyes only briefly. If I lingered any longer on his face, the enormity of what a *bad idea* this is would break my confidence. A day of laboring side by side with a boy I can't go five seconds without fighting with. What a treat for everybody!

After Ben nods grimly and I say "Sure!" fakely, I address all three of them again: "Don't get distracted making everything pretty. We can repair everything later. We just need to subtract everything that's broken or dying. The winery and the Wishing Rose itself are still pristine. We'll throw some extra construction tarps over the sculpture garden, and then all we have to do is clean those fountains and take down the rotting vines . . ." Stepping back from my aunt, I stomp over to the back lawn and point at various places like I'm appraising the land. "Ben already cleared Grandpa's vegetables, so we just need to seal up the pool and . . ."

As my pointing finger finally lands on the lawn, my shoulders slump. The vast majority of the grass is patchy, yellowing, and hideous. "The lawn sucks," I moan.

"That's all right!" Ben yelps, hurrying to meet me, his can-do spirit newly alive. His eyes sparkle as he scans the dying lawn. "Paul, if you've got a spare guy or two, we can pull up the lawn so it's just sod. People don't mind something unfinished if they see it's being worked on. Progress, right?"

It's such a wonderful fix, I almost forget to be mad at him.

"It's all perception," I agree. "And if anyone gets here early, Mama Bianchi will give them an extra-long tour of the winery."

Ben chuckles. "After a few glasses of wine, they won't care what the lawn looks like, eh?"

I laugh and smack his bare shoulder. He smacks me back.

For one plummeting moment, I forget everything I was ever mad about. In that moment, he's not Ben, the boy who shredded me to pieces, he's someone new. Someone . . . sweet.

He isn't sweet, I remind myself. *He cosplays as sweet until you drop your guard. So, don't drop it.*

Aunt Ro hasn't spoken in a minute. At least she's stopped picking at her nails.

"Well, Mama Bianchi," I say, "any last thoughts before we begin?"

Everyone turns to her. On a cleansing breath, she unfastens

the cream-colored sash under her chin and fans herself with her sun hat. She grins, a twinkle in her eye. "I think it's a good thing you're here, Grant. You and Ben." She sends Ben another warm smile, which he returns—not the usual catlike smirk he has for me, but something genuine and touched. This whole past year, with Ben's dad sick with something serious enough to bring his son back from Scotland . . . I'm glad he had Ro and Paul here for something familiar.

He really does love Vero Roseto.

"Hands in the middle," my aunt says, thrusting out her ringed, crimson-nailed hand. Paul slaps his furry-knuckled mitt over hers, and Ben places his hand—large, freckled, and veiny—over his. "So cheesy," I say, placing my hand over Ben's. The shock of touching his hand is instantaneous.

Don't think about how nice this is, don't think about how nice this is.

Luckily, Ro ends my misery with a "Vero Roseto!" rallying cry, and we all break.

Paul returns inside to call his demolition guys, and Ro follows him to grab her checkbook, leaving Ben and me alone. We stand awkwardly opposite each other on the lawn, a hideous site of wreckage and neglect that with any luck will soon be presentable to outside eyes.

There's a metaphor somewhere in there, but I'm going to need coffee first.

A flurry of birds soars overhead, uttering proud calls that echo across Vero Roseto, its vineyard, and the barnlike winery. It really is a beautiful place. Tearing it up will be easy; making it the gorgeous oasis it once was will be harder, but tomorrow's problems are for tomorrow.

"Come here a sec," Ben grunts. He takes my hand too fast for me to stop him.

I freeze into a statue, easily placed in the sculpture garden, while Ben examines my palm. My hand is also large, but with shorter fingers than Ben's. His rough touch slides along my palm's ridges and hillsides—the divot in my finger where I cut myself sewing my pumpkin jacket—until he clicks his tongue disapprovingly.

"Soft hands," he says.

I snort. "Yeah, I moisturize. Don't get all blue-collar warrior on me, Ben."

He sighs. "After you and I are done fixing this place up, they won't be so soft anymore." Thanks to the sun, golden flecks flash in his hazel eyes. "Just wanted to feel them one last time."

Breath leaves me like I landed hard on my back.

Grinning, Ben trots away toward the rose garden, a devilish swagger in his step.

That's Ben McKittrick.

Hot and cold, cold and hot. Never letting me know where I really stand.

Cosplaying as sweet until I drop my guard.

Well, my guard is still up, but I'm starting to think Ben has some not-so-innocent things in mind for us. Worst of all, I'm getting some not-so-innocent ideas, too.

CHAPTER II

A THOUSAND THORNS

For all my bravado about being able to handle yard work, Ben is immediately able to tell I can't handle it. When getting dressed this morning, I chose comfort over utility. Why did I think denim would be my friend during this much exertion? Not only that, but my rose-tinted safety goggles keep fogging. Ben's goggles, for whatever reason, do not. What a delightfully uncursed boy. In under an hour, he has stripped an entire rose wall of its decaying vines. At the next wall, he scurries up a ladder as nimble as a cat, snipping and dropping compost into a pile below. Meanwhile, at the opposite wall, my knee trembles at the top of my ladder, visions of hurtling to my death filling my brain.

"Ow!" I yelp, clawing my forearm against a vine as thick as rope.

"Got a boo-boo already?" Ben calls from his ladder.

I insist I'm fine, but a minute later, after snipping another vine, I cut myself again. "Faaaaaaahhhh," I hiss under my breath.

"I'm coming over."

"Don't! I've got this. Finish your side."

A snide chuckle emanates from below. "I am finished."

My sweat-drenched shirt already clings to my body like a licked envelope, and I've only cut down one branch? How is this *possible*? And even though Ben was finally acting sweet when I was giving out orders, as soon as I'm tasked with doing actual labor, I'm flailing and he's laughing.

At least he's being goofy, and not baiting me like yesterday. Is he relaxing from staying in constant Attack Mode? Maybe Ben was just as tense meeting me again as I was meeting him. We ended on terrible terms, but he did care about me.

Does.

Maybe.

Groaning, I focus all my hatred on this next vine, which hangs just out of reach, snapped almost cleanly in half. I extend my shears . . . The scissor tips graze the edge of the vine . . .

"Grant, just let me—" Ben mutters below.

Agitation boils up, and my sweaty grip almost makes me drop the shears. "It'll go faster if you don't interrupt—"

"It'll go *faster* if you let me handle the vines, and you drop down here to power wash the squirrel shit out of the fountains. Come on, you're gonna kill yourself up there. We've got a hard deadline to get this done, and it doesn't matter who does it. We're not giving out awards for Most Stubborn Bitch."

Okay, Attack Mode is still on a little.

What I despise most about Ben McKittrick is how he always

pounces on opportunities to prove how right he is. He's right it'll go faster his way, but he doesn't have to say it!

I glare at my horrible vine, silently blame it for all my problems, and descend.

At the bottom, Ben wears a smug smile. Like me, he has rose-tinted safety goggles—but unlike me, his sweat looks good. His tank top sticks proudly to all the right corners and curves of his torso. Dirt and yard shrapnel cling to his matted chest hair. If I could find a mirror, I know I'd see my clothes sticking to me awkwardly, widening some areas and sagging others. Confidence dribbles out of me just to see Ben standing there, handsome and victorious.

Ben flaps a "gimme" hand to my shears, and I turn them over, handle first.

"Don't worry," he says. "I was already not impressed. You impaling yourself with shears wasn't going to change that."

My hand on my hip, I laugh. "You never miss a chance to dunk on me."

That smacks the smile off his face. Ben appraises me soberly. "I was just taking the piss. Don't get all sensitive."

"Don't be sensitive? You sound like my brother defending his gay jokes."

He stares. I stare. A moment later, laughter explodes out of us. Ben pulls me into a hug and claps me on the back (thankfully with his non-scissors hand). "See, now we're getting the old back-and-forth going again."

As Ben climbs the ladder without any of my wobbling, I

call after him: "What if I don't want the old back-and-forth again?"

Ben doesn't look down. He just gets to work snipping. "What, your other Romeos never gave you shit like I did?"

"No, they were all sweet guys who were careful with my feelings."

"Until they weren't."

". . . Until they weren't."

A thousand poisonous memories ambush me at once, but I don't let them in. This is what wanting Ben McKittrick does to me, even if I try to want just his body. There is no casual with us. I want his fierceness, his lack of bullshit. I want his protection in life.

But I can't trust him to not be yet another thing I need protecting from.

Vigilance, Grant. The goal this summer isn't to heal things with Ben—no matter what Ro thinks. It's to design the hell out of the Rose Festival, use it to beef up my portfolio for design schools, and then escape to safety.

Sliiiiiice. Half of the long vine plummets to the grass. Ben looks down, his expression soft and open. Dangerously so. "Maybe *that's* your curse, Grant. You keep thinking nice guys are the thing. But you get so up in your head, you need someone who'll tell you to knock it off."

Ben always could read my mind. We nurtured that closeness for years, and a bond like that doesn't just dry up and blow away.

With a frozen smile, I say, "That's very interesting, Doctor. But what I need right now is to clean up squirrel shit. Where's that power washer?"

By the time I get the washer hooked into the rose garden's water supply, Ben is almost finished pulling down the last of the vines. The hose gun kicks back powerfully as I guide warm water streams across the two stone fountains. The fountains wipe clean in minutes, gray stone peeking out beneath the brown and white until suddenly the stone is all that's left.

My chest booms with mighty laughter. The power of Poseidon in the palm of my hand!

Finally, what was once a toilet for woodland creatures is once again a showpiece.

Finished trimming, Ben hops down the ladder and hugs the wall to avoid the spray of the power washer. For one wicked moment, I consider turning the hose on him, but until Vero Roseto is operational, he and I must rebuild our fragile truce. Then without warning, Ben tosses his hat to the ground, strips off his shoes, socks, and top, and runs bare-chested into the glistening stream of water.

"Do me next!" he crows.

I pummel Ben without thinking twice. The hydro-blast nearly lifts him off his feet. He howls with laughter as I wash him free of dirt, sweat, yard work—and hopefully his sins. In my mind, the power washer becomes a flamethrower. As Ben burns to a skeletal crisp, I cackle with only a tiny morsel of regret.

"Okay, time-out, enough!" He laughs, gripping the rim of a fountain as his feet slide sharply in the mud. He sinks to the ground, getting muddy all over again.

It was fun while it lasted. My finger leaves the trigger, and the water slows to a dribble.

I walk to Ben, hand outstretched to help him up . . .

But down I go. He yanks me down, and my ass strikes a shallow pool of fresh mud. Giggling, Ben climbs on top of me, pinning both of my wrists to the earth. His recently cleaned face drips onto my lips as he grins like a fool. "You enjoyed hosing me *way* too much," he says.

"Not as much as I'll enjoy this," I say. The word "this" doesn't finish leaving my mouth before I've hurled Ben off me, finally using my sizable weight and strength to land him on his back. I scoop a handful of sopping mud like it's a snowball and smear it across that handsome, stubbly jaw of his.

"*Fwahhhhhh*," he roars, wriggling helplessly under me as I laugh.

"Come on, Scotsman. Eat the peat!"

"You sick *faaaaaawwwwwghhh!*"

Ben spits—*pitouyyy!*—in a vain attempt to expel the dirt from his tongue. Soon, he doesn't fight at all. But that just gives him time to surprise attack with mud he snatched while I wasn't looking. Two fistfuls land—*plop*—in my hair. I gasp, unable to stop my worst fear from happening. *NOT MY HAIR.*

Ben giggles, weasellike, as he massages the mud into my hair like shampoo. "There you go!" he shouts with a newly brown beard. "Get it allllll in those pretty curls. Mud will really give it volume."

"I HAAAAAATE IIIIIIIT!"

I scurry backward from Ben until my back reaches the fountain. He lies on the ground, laughter bouncing his chest as I claw mud from my hair. *Ew, ew, ew!*

"There are grubs in there!" I bellow, clawing, clawing, forever clawing.

"Yeah, and you put them in my mouth," Ben moans, spitting again. "Thanks a bunch."

Ben sits up. Out of breath, we look at the filthy messes we've made of each other and laugh again—but a deeply tired one. Fun's over. These vines still need to be hauled out.

And we need a shower.

"Did you get everything out of your system yet?" he asks, beaming.

My anger? Never, honey.

I avoid answering by power-blasting my hair until I'm convinced I've gotten out every speck. When I'm done, I flip my neck back dramatically, and a curtain of water whips off my hair onto the newly bare garden wall.

"Okay, supermodel," Ben says, taking the hose to blast clean his face. We pass the hose back and forth until we're mostly mud-free.

When he's finished, an awkward silence finds us. I hate those. They're always when my happy memories of Ben flood the space between my angry ones. In need of a topic we can't make flirty, I reach for a question I've been meaning to ask since yesterday:

"Your dad's okay now?"

Ben nods, his jaw dripping and a new, faraway look in his eye. "Yeah. Thanks." He glances around at the garden, heaviness filling him. "Lymphocytic leukemia. One of the best ones to get if you're gonna get it. The treatment took. He's been all right since just after New Year's."

"I'm sorry."

"I said he's all right." He looks away. "Thank you, though."

"I meant I'm sorry it's been a shit year, and you had to take that on alone. I know you and him don't . . . mesh well."

Ben's expression goes blank as his jaw sets. He nods, his lips pursed, holding back a million hard things he wants to say about his dad but would never, not to me, not to anyone. "Appreciate that" is all he can manage.

Ben has absorbed so much shit—his dad's toxic male attitude, his parents' fighting, their divorce. Nothing ever passed through him, it all just went inside to some big invisible landfill no one can reach. He's tough—he always has been.

"Do you miss Scotland?" I ask. Birdsong and dripping fountains fill the silence that follows.

"Yeah," he admits, eyes on his toes. He glances up. "It'll be nice going back soon."

"Sure," I say, imagining him off in the homeland. Gone again. It . . . doesn't feel good.

"Or not." He shakes his head, then looks back up at me. "I don't know what I'm doing for school yet."

"Same here." I shrug—didn't I torch my future already? Leaving the country for design school was always my dream, but every day this summer has been so *loud*, figuring out how to get there seems impossible. Seeing my therapist again wouldn't hurt, but . . . let's get through today first. And why should I care what Ben does with his life after this summer? He *should* go back to Scotland. He always got along better with his mother, and why be here when you could be there?

And then there's all of my mess.

Ben and I need to think of this summer as an opportunity to put the past behind us, save the home we love, and end on a good note before splitting off to our separate futures.

"Should we fill the fountains?" I ask, spraying the hose in the air for a moment, trying to get us back on a merrier subject.

"Negative," Ben says. "Not until we can fix the mechanisms that make them run. Still water attracts mosquitoes, and then your guest reviews will be nothing but mosquito rage."

While I didn't get to be the gardening hero this morning, a twinge of satisfaction does arrive when I clamber toward the arched entrance to view the entire expanse of the rose garden. I was right—we added by subtracting. Yes, the greenery walls are more blank than before, but without the dying vines, everything looks much more . . . purposeful. Designed.

The garden is a shrine to the Wishing Rose. Nothing else should distract from it.

I flick the special lights for a moment, giving the bush its mystical halo.

Even in daylight, it sparkles.

The myth feels stronger with the single bush inside such a cavernous garden. The Wishing Rose calls to us. With one last bitter glance at the rose bush—then at Ben tromping out with his clothes in hand—my heart winces like a scared dog.

I had it all with Ben. But then I lost it. We lost it.

A confused boy made a careless wish, we acted on our worst impulses, and it all went away.

I'd give anything to make my wish over again, but too much has been said and done. And I know the truth now—if I ever find true love, it won't be a wholesome fairy tale.

It'll be a crimson bloom at the end of a path of a thousand thorns.

CHAPTER 12

MAMA BIANCHI

We make it happen with minutes to spare.

Uncle Paul's buddy drives away in a flatbed truck with the last remains of the deck before the new guests pull into Valle. And with Paul ready to collapse from heat exhaustion and Ro wanting to maintain her Mama Bianchi mystery, it falls on me to check in our visitors.

"They're here to see you anyway, superstar diva," Ben says with an evil grin. He towel-dries his hair. After everything we've done to keep up appearances at the B&B, Ro wasn't about to let either of our mud-stained bodies inside without being sparkling clean.

"Your public is waiting, so I hope you have your heartbreak stories ready to go," he says, winking as he jumps into his sneakers and flings his sopping wet tank over his clean, bare shoulder. A water droplet races down his torso—which I'm too busy looking at to respond quickly.

"... Shut up."

"Brilliant comeback, as usual." Ben snickers as he clomps away in wet shoes—*squish, squish*.

"How 'bout you make some more noise with those shoes!"

Ben spins on his heel to face me, grinning like the Joker as he continues backing away. "That's all you've got? Are you even *trying* to hate me?"

"YOUR FEET SOUND LIKE THEY'RE FARTING!" I holler, my throat so hot and tight it feels like I've zipped a jacket all the way up my neck.

But that jerkoff just rolls his eyes and continues over the lawn toward the rose garden. "Oh my God, pathetic. I take my tits out once, and your brain melts. Get dressed, goblin!"

Hatred seizes me so hard, all I can do is spit at him from the pile of dirt that used to be the deck. "Me get dressed? YOU get dressed! These guests are important, and my aunt isn't paying you to strut around with your ginger jugs swinging around!"

As Ben turns around again, laughing, the shutters on the second story window above me fly open. Ro—half-dressed, her hair still in curlers—lunges out of the small window balcony. Her eyes are furious. "GRANT ROSSI," she yells, "what the HELL is the matter with you? People are pulling up any second, and you're harassing my employee?!"

Ben can't stop laughing, which makes cooling down impossible as I crane my head up toward Ro. "He called them tits first!"

Just when I think Ro's eyes can't flare any wider, there they go. "Stop saying that word! Stop shouting! Keep your voice down, for the love of God!"

My entire face must be as red as a brick, as twin dragons of humiliation and rage do battle inside me. "Ben *told* me to—"

"Shh!" Ro snatches at the air, as if she's Ursula plucking my voice away. Obediently, I fall silent, and she slams the shutters closed.

Anger subsiding, my embarrassment dragon bloodily victorious, I turn back toward Ben, who is laughing so hard into his hand he might topple over. On a deep breath, I say, "I'm sorry. You should change out of those wet sneakers. Let me get you—"

This stops him laughing. Now deadly serious, he waves me away. "I've got a spare pair in the shed. And knock it off with the fake niceness. You were just starting to cook."

Finally, Ben runs off to the rose garden—*squish, squish*—to clear the remaining collapsed vines and finish laying the temporary sod Paul brought from town.

My body goes as rigid as a diamond. My hatred for this boy knows no interdimensional boundaries. Quietly to myself, dripping with poison, I hiss, "How is he *worse* than before?!"

With no time to process how I'm going to murder Ben McKittrick, I head upstairs, where Uncle Paul is waiting with a new set of clothes: his nicest (and oldest) outfit, a black button-down and matching slacks. "I used to wear them when I was a server at Il Crostini!" Paul chortles, pressing a freezing cold beer to his neck. "I was younger than you back then. Nicest thing I owned, so every time I took out Ro, I was wearing that same damn outfit."

I tighten Paul's belt another loop to keep the large pants high-waisted. "She didn't mind?"

Paul laughs again, moving the cold bottle from his neck to his forehead. "Maybe she did, but she never said. I think she was eager to lock me down. The *rose* said I was the one . . ."

As I face the bedroom's standing mirror, Paul and I catch each other in the reflection. He saw me flinch at the mention of the rose. For Ro and Paul (and nearly everyone in my family but me), the rose is a source of positive, healing, binding energy, not a lightning rod of curses.

Paul knows it's a sore spot. His eyes drop to the floor.

"Don't feel bad," I say, fussing with my top shirt buttons. "I'm happy the rose works for other people."

Paul groans, finally drinking from the bottle. "Don't tell Ro, but eh, who you love—who spend your life with—it's too important to be left up to a flower."

My eyebrow arches. I undo my third button, giving me my signature Grant Rossi chest peek. "You saying you have regrets, Paul?"

"No!" A bit of beer sputters off his lips. "I'm saying . . . that rose just seals the deal. People make happen what they want to make happen."

"You're saying I *wanted* to lose Ben?"

"What? No?" Paul fidgets on the edge of the bed. "I don't know the story there. I'm just telling you, your aunt wanted me, she picked me. If she made her rose wish and, like, the next day, I suddenly joined the army, she'd have hopped a plane to wherever I was going and said the rose told her to do it. See what I'm getting at?"

My hope draining by the minute, I finally face my uncle. "I do. I always thought you two had such a great relationship. Way better than my parents did. But whenever I get with somebody, it's clear I'm a Rossi, not a Bianchi. And Rossis are better off alone."

Paul stares, studying me, circling his thumb around the rim of his bottle. "Back then, I remember you and Ben being close. A lot of us could tell." He raises his hands in surrender. "We weren't making jokes or saying anything bad. Ro ordered us to stay out of it. She'd read somewhere that with gay kids that young, who aren't out, you don't say anything or pry. You just create a good atmosphere so they'll come out to you when they're ready." Shaking his head glumly, Paul gazes into his bottle. "Then you and Ben fell out, he was gone, and you were sitting there at breakfast every day like a ghost. I couldn't say anything." Paul shrugs his mighty shoulders, and his dark eyes begin to glisten. "When I was that age, a girl dumped me. I would've cut off one of my toes for her, even though she kicked the shit out of me. But I talked it all out with my dad, and eventually, it stopped hurting. I can't even remember her name anymore."

Suddenly, Paul looks up with hardened eyes and says, "I couldn't talk to you about Ben like you needed. I knew it would help you, but I didn't know how to talk in code. I only know how to say it like it is and name it. You had to be alone with all that, and then we lost you, too. I'm sorry."

The ice in my blood doesn't melt, it cracks. Paul is picking at a very old scab. It won't heal easily, but I'm happy he's trying. I'd hug him if I didn't have to keep my shirt clean.

"Ben's here, and you're here," Paul says. "You're talking. Work it out. If I had to hold on to my crap with that girl like you are with Ben, I would've missed *everything* cool in life."

Hug him, Grant.

He's better than Dad. He'll hear you out. Hug him and tell him the truth.

Yet as my jaw toughens, I know my pain has won again. "You don't understand," I say helplessly.

Paul leans forward. "I want to."

Twiiiiiiiiinggggggggggg!

As the doorbell shudders the house's brittle walls, I jump with surprise. "Yoo-hoo!" an older English voice calls from the veranda below. "Mama Bianchi? It's Mr. Pembroke Cartwright! I hope I'm not too early. You did say check-in was at four, or am I misremembering? The gate to the rear of the property is closed and no one answered when I knocked. Oh, God help me if I've got the date wrong. I have a receipt somewhere . . ."

Paul waves me away to deal with Mr. Cartwright before he monologues himself into a stroke. Dashing into the upstairs hallway of the East Wing, I catch Aunt Ro hanging halfway out of her bedroom door, irritation splashed all over her face.

She now wears the Mama Bianchi uniform: a dowdy Sicilian black gown with a crimson shawl draped diagonally across her chest.

"Cartwright is a travel critic!" Ro pleads. "Treat him nice!"

"Oh, *nice*?" I ask. "Because I was gonna slash his tires. Good thing you said something."

Ro rolls her eyes. "And he's *gay*!" She drops her voice five octaves on the word "gay."

"*Gay*?" I mouth, mocking her. "So, like, I should go down there, give him my number?" Ro's expression crumples into a scowl. "Give him Ben's number?" She stomps her foot, her chunky heel clattering against the hardwood. "Okay, okay!"

Giggling, I hurry downstairs, check my freshly washed curls one last time in the hallway mirror, and open the veranda door. Mr. Cartwright is a short, bald man around seventy. He's Black, with dark skin and creases around his large smile. He wears an ascot, a yachtsman suit, and violet-tinted sunglasses. It's a fussy but eccentrically friendly look.

Smiling, I step onto the veranda, stand as tall as possible, and greet him: "Mr. Cartwright, I'm Grant Rossi. Welcome to Vero Roseto." I make sure to hit the Italian words hard. "Your room is being prepared. While you wait, may I interest you in a fresh pour from our winery? Mama Bianchi would be delighted to serve you there."

Smiling, Mr. Cartwright removes his sunglasses with a flourish. "The delight would be mine!" He glances around the veranda theatrically. "My luggage?"

Behind him, four matching houndstooth bags wait to be handled.

With each passing second, I continue improvising my bizarre new life role as hotel manager. After a brief out-of-body *what am I doing here?* moment, I nod. "Leave your bags where they are. I'll have Ben bring them to your room."

"'Ben the Bellhop'!" Mr. Cartwright laughs. "Charming!"

"You have no idea."

I'm about to lead Mr. Cartwright across the veranda toward the winery when four more cars arrive via the family-side driveway. Ro must've closed off the main guest parking lane so Paul's workmen could freely haul out debris and compost. At once, the other guests park in careless, haphazard lines before leaping out and asking if this is where they leave their cars.

My smile freezes. Mr. Cartwright elbows my ribs. "You're gonna need a lot more Bens."

Sir, that's the last thing I need.

Including Mr. Cartwright, ten guests leave their cars, keys, and luggage with Ben, who rushes to meet us as soon as he gets my frantic texts. With each new set of keys he's handed, his pockets grow heavier, and his eyes grow wider. "You paying me extra for this?" he whispers as guests mill about on the veranda.

"Yes," I whisper, "your extra is this needs to go well or you won't have a house to garden."

"You're gonna make a great landlord someday."

I bare my teeth like a challenged dog. "Why are you doing this to me?"

"I like watching you squirm." He knocks me on my shoulder before waving to the crowd of new guests. "Say hello to Mama Bianchi for me!"

With an infuriating flash of eyebrows, Ben begins the luggage retrieval, starting with Mr. Cartwright. Our fanciest guest palms a few bills into Ben's hand as he moves to take the luggage, and the rest of us set off toward the stone path to Vero Roseto's winery.

The crew is an odd bunch: Mr. Cartwright; a middle-aged lesbian couple with their shy, ponytailed teenage daughter; a middle-aged straight couple with two teenage sons; a twenty-something French woman traveling alone; and a young, sullen, dark-haired girl (not much older than I am) who keeps tossing me anxious glances as if she knows who I am.

In fact, every young person present is eyeballing me like I'm a zoo animal.

They all know. Everyone is here for my drama.

Vero Roseto had close to zero guests before I made that video. It's extremely likely that each of these people followed every detail of my video and are wondering what else could've happened to bring me to this pitiful state, giving B&B tours in the country dressed as a waiter circa nineties-era Central Perk.

I, too, am wondering.

Shoving down those thoughts for now, I lead my tour past

the sprawling vineyard, which thankfully has not deteriorated like the rest of the gardens. These vines are vibrant, green, and thriving. Bushels of bountiful, healthy grapes lie in garlands across the wired fencing. It's the best first sight in Vero Roseto. Truly postcard-ian.

Finally, we reach the winery, a high-roofed red barn with a small gift shop in front and massive catacombs of wine presses around back. A hand-carved placard, spanning the width of the outer wall, reads:

BLUE APPLE ORCHARD, HOME OF THE WISHING ROSE LABEL

Blue apples. That's what Grandma called grapes.

We spent a lot of time around this winery growing up. The family was firm about children knowing our traditions from an early age. Like the Wishing Rose. At Vero Roseto, my family drilled into me that we owe our lives to that rose. That it's brought generation after generation together.

And, therefore, if it *didn't* bring you together with someone, it wasn't true love.

My heart twists as I sink back into that thirteen-year-old thinking that got me cursed: closeted thinking. Besides my brother's gay jokes—and my other six siblings laughing at them—my family was never outright homophobic. So why didn't I feel safe sharing my heartbreak over Ben to anyone? Why didn't I just let Ro or Paul help me? Because of my family's myth. Because of that damn rose, my family's entire relationship belief system centers around the idea that continuing the family line is fate-ordained rose magic . . . and anything else—which I naturally assumed included *non*-procreating homo love—was an irrelevant waste of time.

The tour wouldn't start on a good note if I led with that nugget.

"There she is!" Mr. Cartwright exclaims, quietly clapping. "Woman of the hour!"

Aunt Ro emerges—Mama Bianchi–styled—from the door leading into the barn. She waves gently, making herself seem decades older (and, I suppose, wiser). "Welcome to the Blue Apple Orchard," Ro says, sounding like an ethereal, benevolent spirit. "You have come to see the gemello maledetto"— she grins cheerfully—"the cursed twin. Invidioso e Grato. Envy and gratitude, the two sides of romance."

"If you mean we've come to drink wine, then hell yeah!" crows the lesbian with a gray butch cut. Laughter spills across the crowd, and even Aunt Ro joins them. The woman's daughter buries her head in humiliation before casting me another brief glance.

The young dark-haired girl thrusts her arm in the air. "When can we see the Wishing Rose?"

At this, every teen stands pertly at attention. This is what they're here to see, not watch their parents get tipsy.

"Eh . . . ?" Ro glances in my direction, terrified and thrown off her game.

Oh Lord. Guess we're gonna start in on this topic right away.

Okay, Grant, it's grab-your-ass-and-go time again.

I step up to join Ro at the barn door and smile with the charm that's gotten me so many first (but rarely second) dates. "Quick show of hands," I say, "who here booked your stay because you saw my video?"

All hands go up. My throat tightens, but I will it to loosen. "Amazing!" I say, lying.

Ro glances at me nervously, guiltily, but I don't blink.

Anger gives me strength.

"Awkward!" I laugh. A few scattered, nervous chuckles emanate from the teens. "But it's actually not awkward. You came because you believe in love. That's a cool thing. It's rarer than you think. Be proud of yourselves for that. The Wishing Rose and I have a complicated history, but the Wishing Rose and Mama Bianchi have a great history." I gesture to Aunt Ro. "The rose wish is all about what *you* want."

The dark-haired girl fidgets anxiously, her arm wiggling in the air, and I realize I never answered her question the first time around.

"The Wishing Rose will be available to view after sunset," I say. "That's when it's most magical. For now, it's your parents' turn for wine, so take it away, Mama Bianchi."

Beaming, Aunt Ro reaches for me, snags my whole cheek in her talons, and faces the crowd. "Look at this wise boy," she exclaims. "He used to be just a tiny thing running under your legs, and now"—she throws up her arms, a few happy tears spilling out—"the pride of this family!"

I can't believe anyone in my family except her and Paul

think that, but I take Ro into a tearful hug anyway. "It's all right."

"I just love you so much. I would *die* without you. I'm okay. This way to wine, huh?"

Grateful laughter floats among the guests—and me—as Ro jerks her arm toward the barn door, and we follow her inside the catacombs.

CHAPTER 13

ROT CREATES SWEETNESS

I never got to see my great-grandmother give her original wine tours, so I don't know how much Ro is nailing the impression of her grandmother, but she's giving a stellar performance. Wrapped in a delicate shawl and cloaked in her frock from the old country, the new Mama Bianchi leads guests like a crypt keeper through the lamplit catacombs. The winery barn's dark, cavernous hallways are earthy-looking structures made from stone and exposed beams of timber. Everything creaks ominously. If Ro wants to keep business booming beyond the Rose Festival, she should turn the wine tour into a Halloween haunt.

Just being here, I feel more creatively alive than I have all year in my city design courses.

As we round another corner in the cool, vaguely humid corridor, I mutter a silent prayer begging God/the universe/ Mama Bianchi's ghost not to turn me into one of those "the country is better than the city" assholes. There are simply fewer natural predators here, so my ideas are consistently met with unchallenged enthusiasm. Anyone with half a creative light bulb in their head would thrive under these conditions.

Still, a spooky wine tour haunt would be cute.

A shriek rings out, and half the tour ahead of me jumps.

As the tour crowds into the next room, I realize Mr. Cartwright simply screamed with glee at the sight of four large basket presses—wooden-slatted tubs that have been smashing grapes since my great-grandmother built the place. Heavy iron arms, operated by massive clockwork machinery, fill the pressing room with more ghoulish, rhythmic creaking as they plunge wooden platters into the vats of grapes.

Two winery operators—a man and a woman—stand on a raised platform to the side while operating the presses. They're draped in heavy rubber aprons slathered with dark grape residue, and they're too intently focused on their job to interact with us.

"Basket presses!" Mr. Cartwright gasps, impressed, into his phone. He's been recording voice memos the entire tour. Each new detail of this old-fashioned winery has exploded his brain with joy. "Not a single piece of machinery here is younger than forty. I would've come years ago if I'd known."

While the other guests glance at each other, slightly irritated, Aunt Ro describes the use of the basket press, how it's more fragile than modern presses, and how the machines require round-the-clock maintenance.

"Guess that's where all her money goes, not to landscaping," a coarse voice whispers in my ear. The hairs on my neck prickle. I know it's Ben before he reveals himself. He must've spiffed himself up after parking everyone's cars and hauling their luggage. No more backward cap. He's finally run a comb through his tangled hair and put on a fresh shirt.

I smirk. "You're looking spit-shined."

"I do look foxy most of the time."

"I'll have to take your word for it. Usually, you look like a wet dog that got loose."

Chuckling, Ben flicks his tongue discreetly over his upper lip. "Boys in town don't mind."

"I bet they don't."

"Don't think you mind, either, the way your eyes have been falling out of your head at me since you got here."

"*Please.* Somebody get you a straitjacket." We're in the back of the tour, but the dark-haired girl and one of the two brothers keep turning around to hear what we're saying. "Sorry," I mouth to them.

"Don't get your undies twisted," Ben whispers, "I'm just here for free wine."

"My aunt's not gonna serve you," I say, baffled.

Ben shrugs. "I helped save her business today, I'm getting a sip."

"Don't celebrate just yet. We only slapped a Band-Aid on the problem. We've got two months to put on the Rose Festival. That's gonna be a whole new nightmare."

"That's a you problem. I'm just the muscle." Ben tosses me a wink and grazes his fingertips across my back. I stiffen like a snake has coiled around me. The problem is, I'm stiffening everywhere.

He's literally a human curse!

Each signal from Ben is radically different from the last. I have to think he just likes my attention, likes making me all mixed-up and paranoid. The boy who I used to love, who used to get under my skin, has now grown a foot taller and acquired chest hair and wide arms. He has weaponized messing with me, and if I don't keep up my guard twenty-four seven, Ben McKittrick is going to gut me all over again.

And I don't think I could survive it a second time. Not after this year.

Thank God Aunt Ro has arrived at her grand finale moment to force Ben and me to shut the hell up. It's the moment everyone has been waiting for—the Invidioso e Grato moment of choice. Uncle Paul, cleanly dressed in a white button-down and slacks, presents Aunt Ro with a tray of evenly dispersed tasting glasses of whites and reds. She runs through her spiel again that envy and gratitude are the two sides of romance, each one serving a purpose.

"Envy allows you to savor defeat enough to recognize your gratitude," she says, grandly gesturing at Uncle Paul's tray. "You all seek the Wishing Rose to reveal your heart's truth. But as some of us here have already warned you, that can be tricky."

Ro gestures toward me, and the teens on the tour briefly

pitch their necks backward to get a look at me, the heartbroken sideshow (their parents have their sights firmly set on Paul's wine tray).

If being a cautionary tale is good for business, so be it. It should do somebody good.

I smile to let everyone know Ro's comment was in good fun, but Ben isn't happy about it. His heavy brow scowls at the gawkers, and he spins his finger in a circle. *Get your eyeballs off him!* his gesture seems to say, and everyone takes the hint.

When everyone turns back to Mama Bianchi, Ben's strong, chapped hand finds mine. He squeezes, and my heart squeezes with it.

He stood up for me.

Even when I tried to laugh it off, he refused to join in.

My heart rises like a geyser, but my brain slaps a lid on it.

Stay strong, Grant. Ben is sweet until you drop your guard.

"Making a wish on the rose—finding your love—is a serious commitment," Ro says with gravity as she clutches her shawl. "You must know your own heart before making your wish. Invidioso or Grato? Where does your heart truly lie? Are you lovesick? Do you want to make your wish because you want to possess someone you can't have? Are your intentions pure? Or are you prepared to humble yourself and accept rejection if that's what destiny has in mind?"

Ben doesn't let go of my hand. With each passing second he holds me, the stitching around my heart—the sewing I had to do myself as a thirteen-year-old boy—comes undone. I can feel it bleed. The pain is sharp and quick, but the yawning ache that follows is worse.

Mesmerized, the crowd watches Ro. Even Mr. Cartwright has stopped talking. He holds out his phone to capture the show as Ro tosses the crowd a wicked, knowing grin. "True love isn't nice," she says coolly. "Is everyone ready?"

An anxious, tentative mass agreement erupts, and Ro sweeps through the tour. Uncle Paul follows with his tray. She studies each person, their panicked faces. She arrives at Mr. Cartwright, his creased smile struggling to stay up as his phone continues recording. Ro's many-ringed fingers twiddle over the glasses of red and white, and then a selection is made.

Invidioso.

Mr. Cartwright exhales a pained gasp as Ro closes his hand lovingly around a glass of chilled chardonnay. He gazes at it like he's been handed my curse on a platter. She warmly rubs his arm, reassuring him, "You have gratitude for beautiful things in life, like this winery. But you seek a traveling partner. Someone who will understand your particular ways. That hasn't been easy, has it?" Struck silent, Mr. Cartwright stares at Ro, who gazes back with love. Love, openness, and intuitive understanding she's shown me countless times in my life and on this trip. "Invidioso isn't anything to be scared of. It just means you should approach the Wishing Rose carefully, with the sharp mind you're known for, and you'll find what you need."

Aunt Ro drifts away, and Mr. Cartwright hungrily throws back the entire glass.

Before moving on to the shy girl's mothers, Ro tosses me and Ben a twinkling glance. Maybe I'm narcissistic, but I think her speech to Mr. Cartwright was meant to do double duty for him *and* me. As if I'd ever go near that rose again with a wish in my heart.

One by one, the glasses are divided among the of-age guests. Invidioso to the dark-haired girl and middle-aged lesbian couple (*Ro, your envy radar is a little homophobic*), and Grato is delivered to the French woman and the middle-aged straight couple. Finally, Ro and Paul reach Ben and me with two glasses left—one Invidioso and one Grato.

The winery has become so humid, I have my eyes squarely set on some chilled Invidioso.

So does Ben.

Ro wags her finger, takes the Grato, and empties it into the Invidioso until it's a fine, pinkish rosé. She raises it to her captive audience. "The color of a heart."

Envy *and* gratitude.

With that, she gives Uncle Paul a quick kiss and drains the glass herself in one gulp.

Ben, Mr. Cartwright, and I burst into applause that spreads through the awestruck group. Aunt Ro curtsies in her Sicilian grandmother frock, gleefully accepting praise after such a long day—and a very long five years—of keeping Vero Roseto afloat.

The setting sun casts sharp beams into the window-paneled doors of the winery's shop, a generously sized room with back walls stocked with all varieties of the Wishing Rose label. Next to the register, Uncle Paul mans a small refrigerated counter of jams, artisanal cheeses, and charcuterie. He, Ro, and Ben laugh heartily as they snack on marinated olives. Almost instinctively, the tour has separated into Invidioso and Grato groups. The Grato folk—the French woman and middle-aged straight couple with their sons—converse pleasantly over fuller glasses of red, while the Invidioso group—Mr. Cartwright, the lesbian couple and their shy daughter, and the sullen, dark-haired girl—chatter over their glasses of white with a more relaxed air.

I'm on my way over to Aunt Ro when Mr. Cartwright and the woman with the butch haircut wave me over. "Team Invidioso!" the woman crows. "We won't bite!"

My stomach drops. They're going to want to gossip about my video, and I'm not in the mood. I'll probably never be in the mood, but my duties today are as host, so once again, it's grab-my-ass-and-go time.

I drag a spare seat over to their bistro table—the view from our window is of the torn-up lawn reaching all the way to the rose garden. It'll do for now. Thankfully, the sunset makes even mud look stunning.

"I'm sorry for my aunt," I say in a low whisper.

"What for?" Mr. Cartwright blurts, almost offended. Similar confusion spreads over the rest of the table.

"You know, she gave all the gays the envy glasses." Quickly, I glance over at the young dark-haired girl. "I didn't mean to imply—"

"I am." The girl laughs, taking another sip.

I roll my eyes. *Ro.* Always stepping in it. "You see?" I ask. "She's honestly really—"

Mr. Cartwright lands his palm softly on the table, interrupting, "I'm going to stop you before you dig yourself any deeper." He grins. "Your aunt is a peach. And whether she realized it or not, she was right."

"We were all just talking," the shy daughter of the lesbian couple speaks up. "I don't want you worried that we're gonna bother you about your Wishing Rose video or . . . anything else you posted about. I mean, I'm sorry about all that, but we're here for the rose. Promise."

I swallow hard. It feels like this girl just took ten heavy bags of groceries off my hands. I slump back into my chair with relief. "Thank you. I've been stressing."

Mr. Cartwright unspools the ascot from around his throat. "But, Grant, you should know, Invidioso was spot-on. Envy is wanting something someone else has. Queer people live with that all the time. It's part of our journey. If you're going to date, you'll have to conquer it over and over."

Exhaustion slaps me like waves on a beach.

Over and over? The envy. The want. The churn. Forever?

My gaze drifts to Ben, who is leaning against the counter

123

with my uncle. Ben's pants ride low, his shirt rides high, and the small of his back appears—muscled, taut, and dotted with hair.

Do I want Ben? Yes. Do I envy his easy charm and unburdened heart? Yes.

There's just one question I can't answer.

"Is it worth the struggle?" I ask, not taking my eyes from Ben.

The others at the table chuckle, but Mr. Cartwright sighs. "You're asking the wrong people."

"Um . . ." the dark-haired girl speaks up. We pivot to her. "My name's Thomasin. I was reading a wine-making pamphlet in the train station." Her eyes dart about the room. "Um, about how the grapes ripen. They have to rot first. They get sweeter as they rot."

"Yes, my dear, I believe they do," Mr. Cartwright says.

"The rot creates sweetness." Thomasin nods as she digs through her satchel. Finally, she smooths out a crumpled scrap of notebook paper and reads, 'Rot creates sweetness like innocence decays. I'm not a grape anymore. I can't ever get that back. But as I rot, I sweeten, and the more pressure you put on me, the stronger I become, until finally, I'm no longer a rotten grape, I'm something very expensive.'"

Finished, Thomasin looks up at my stung, heartbroken face. Her mouth broadens with a nerdy, toothy smile. "I wrote that waiting for my Uber," she says.

As the others quietly applaud, I can't move a muscle.

It's me. A glass of wine mourning the little grape he used to be.

Why is it so hard for me to see my value?

Hours later, the guests have gone to sleep in their East Wing rooms, which has left me without a bedroom while the West Wing's renovation finishes. Ben, my uncle, and I gather in the downstairs parlor attached to the kitchen. This room is just for family, and it hasn't changed since the eighties. Thick brown carpeting, heavy furniture, heavier drapes, and framed pictures of family members cover every surface. Paul lights a fire and opens the sliding door onto the patio to let in a breeze. Crickets and river frogs sing us into a dreamy haze as our long day finally ends.

Paul collapses into an armchair. Ben strips off his damp socks and curls into a ball on the arm of the sofa. He's one sleepy kitty. His eyelids have turned purple with exhaustion. Not me, I'm wired. I pull off my socks, unbutton my shirt all the way, and flop onto the other side of the sofa.

We did it.

A minute later, Aunt Ro joins us. Out of her Mama Bianchi outfit and into her usual bathrobe, she carries in a coffee tray, then shuts us inside the parlor with a folding woven divider. As soon as we're alone, Ro moans like she can finally stop holding a gargantuan rock.

"We did it!" she whispers, collapsing next to her coffee tray.

"You *were* Mama Bianchi," I say, bowing my head.

Ro kisses two fingers at a framed picture of my great-grandmother. *"You boys saved the day."*

"You really did," Paul moans from the chair, his eyes already shut.

"I wasn't gonna give you wine in front of the guests," Ro says, spinning the coffee tray toward her, "but I think you've both earned a nightcap."

Ben bolts upright like he's been stuck with electrodes. He and I lean curiously over the tray to inspect our supposed adult prize: not wine; it's four ceramic teacups, no bigger than shot glasses, lined with silver filigree. The cups are empty except for shaved pieces of lemon zest. Beside them on the tray is a silver Bialetti espresso pot and a bottle of Romana Sambuca. Without waiting, Ro begins mixing. A splash of sambuca over the lemon zest, and a boiling pour of espresso on top.

My heart jumps.

Grandpa Angelo made this all the time. I never got to taste it, but the sambuca bottle always smelled like licorice. Us kids *badly* wanted whatever was in those cups. Ben and I eye each other with excitement as Ro finishes pouring. This was something neither of us have thought about in years, but as soon as it's presented to us, it's all we can think about. Ben wets his lips, and I wet mine.

Wow. Adulthood. We made it.

"Vero Roseto, salud," Ro says, raising her cup. Ben and I raise ours. Paul's cup sits forgotten as hearty snores float from his corner of the room.

Salud, Grandpa.

We drink. Heat, sourness, and bitterness assault my tongue from all sides.

POISON.

Ben and I look at each other, and at the same time, our faces collapse in disgust, our tongues explode out on a *pahhhhh* sound, something close to a retch.

This is DREADFUL.

Full-body shivers strike me as the stinging licorice and burned black coffee rattle my central nervous system. Ben doesn't look like he's having any easier of a time with it. Meanwhile, Ro downs her cup, followed by Paul's. Her eyes shut in ecstasy.

"BUGHHHHH," Ben spits, coughing roughly. "Italians *like* this?"

"NO," I say, revolted. "Ro, this is what you all drank so much? It stinks!"

Ro can't stop laughing. Flat on her back, spent from the day, she shakes, tickled at how nastily she's pranked us by giving us what we've always wanted.

The three of us celebrate our wins for a bit longer until sleep finally takes Ro, and she climbs into the armchair opposite Paul. I shut my eyes for a moment, the nasty licorice liqueur pulling me closer toward sleep. Everything has felt so chaotic for so long . . .

But somehow, today, I briefly forget to hate my life.

I actually might like it. The summer wind. The sound

of frogs. My family portraits. The fireplace. Knowing that I helped turn a day at Vero Roseto into something unforgettable for other people. It all melds into a memory, something from my present-day life that I wouldn't mind keeping. That's so rare.

A soft and cool sensation presses down on my foot. I open my eyes . . .

Ben has slid his bare foot onto mine. Strong, smooth, and tenderly stroking mine.

I don't hate it. What's happening?

I groggily look up at him, and his exhausted, bloodshot eyes sway. Neither of us smile. It's too intimate for that.

"Don't drive home," I whisper. "It's so late."

"Okay," Ben says.

"There's a sleeping bag in the game room. Next to my cot."

Ben's chest rises and falls grandly on deep breaths. He strokes the top of my foot, gently and methodically, like an otter swimming. "Okay."

That's when he reaches over. My back twinges painfully as I tense at the uncertainty of his intentions. But he just laces his fingers into mine. "What are you doing?"

"Nothing. I promise. I just want to know you again."

"Okay," I whisper. Finally, my back relaxes.

Then I do the thing I promised I'd never do. I drop my guard.

CHAPTER 14

THE CURSE

That night, I dream about Vero Roseto. But not as it is, as it was back in my family's glory days five years ago. Well . . . when the glory days finally ended.

It's dark in the rose garden, all except for the overhead shaft of light surrounding the Wishing Rose bush. The garden walls are lush and healthy, and the stone fountains are running, bubbling merrily like brooks. But someone here isn't merry.

I watch Little Me—freshly thirteen—crouch by the bush, gripping one of the crimson blooms in his shivering hand. I wouldn't hit my growth spurt for another year, so the boy at the bush is a short, round geek with braces and not a speck of confidence. He distrusts every thought he has, which is why he's out here in the dead of night in his oversize Thor T-shirt and pajama bottoms.

Every impulse in me—the eighteen-year-old dreamer standing to the side—wants to run up and push the boy away. Maybe to hug him, maybe to scare him. But he's about to make the biggest mistake of his life.

"Please," Little Me whispers desperately to the rose. "I

like Hutch, but I like Ben more, I think. Is it Ben? Please let me know. I want it to be Ben, but . . . I'm with Hutch, so it can't be Ben. Please help me. I feel like shit *all the time*. I don't think this is what love is supposed to be. I just . . . I don't think any of it's love. None of this feels right." Both me and my younger self tremble with an overwhelming, all-encompassing sadness at what's coming next. "I don't want to be like this. I just want my family. I want to stay with my family. I want everything to stay the way it is. Please take this away. I wish—"

"No, you can't!" I shout, leaping toward my younger self. I know what's coming—my wish to be straight, my punishing curse.

I'm going to stop him. I'm going to change the course of our lives for the better. I'm . . .

Standing alone in the rose garden.

Little Me is gone. Run off back to bed to close his eyes, his heart racing with excitement that he'll open them in the morning and everything will make pure, perfect sense again.

"GRANT!" I call out, my voice echoing through the vaulting green walls. When nobody responds, my voice cracks. "I'm sorry!"

I run. In the dream, Aunt Ro is just outside the garden's archway, hiding behind the switchboard that operates the rose garden lights. I see her now. She's in her fluffy bathrobe, wiping off tears and staring at her phone, wondering who to text about this. I drop to my knees beside her and shake her out of her trance. "Ro! Tell my mom what you heard. Tell her I'm in trouble."

Tearfully, Ro just shakes her head. "She'll tell your dad, and that'll scare you off. Remember how he acted when your grandma taught you sewing?"

Impatiently, I grunt, "But he's better now!"

"Not yet."

Of course. This is five years ago. It took Dad a minute to come around . . .

"Then go after me," I say. "Tell me it'll be okay!"

Ro's expression crumbles with anguish. "I can't. I'm sorry."

"But I'm gonna lose Ben . . ."

My aunt is no help. I have to do this myself. I leave her at the rose garden and sprint across the lawn—emerald-green and thriving—toward Vero Roseto. By the time I reach it, night has become a bright, shimmering summer afternoon. The deck is littered with family. Grandpa Angelo is barbecuing (a separate shelf of roasted vegetables just for me). Through the throng of laughing, boisterous relatives, cheering one another with red Solo cups of beer and Grato, I can't find Little Me anywhere—or Little Ben.

Grandpa Angelo, round-bellied and gray-bearded, cheerfully hands me a slice of grilled squash on the end of a barbecue fork. "Fresh off the grill, little man," he says.

The squash is piping hot. The memory of its deliciousness is powerful.

"Grandpa, have you seen me?" I ask. "Or Ben?"

He shuts the barbecue's lid over two trays of wings that still need to blacken a bit more. After a thought, he turns back and says, "Don't worry about that right now. Enjoy yourself." He nods sadly. "This is the last time."

"Last time for what?" Fear creeps into my voice.

Grandpa gestures broadly with the barbecue fork at my family. Almost two dozen people crowd the deck, full of joy and food. "Last time we're all together like this." He turns to me. "Your grandma's inside. Go say goodbye."

No. Not now. Not already.

But I'm not entirely in control of my body. The dream is driving me.

Inside the house, it's daytime, but so dark. No one's put any lights on. The entire parlor is so gray, so depressed. Why is my grandma sitting alone in the parlor? No TV on, no nothing. Just sitting in her bathrobe, hunched over the coffee table, and staring.

"Grandma?" I ask, cautiously approaching.

My grandmother looks so *old*, even though she's only in her sixties. She doesn't look up when she says, "You and Ben, that movie you wanted to go see in town with that Hutchinson kid? I looked it up. They say it's very violent and a little . . ."

"*Gay?*" I recall my grandmother's words with bite.

"I don't think your mom would want me letting you see that while she's away. Especially not with boys like that."

My eyes glisten with furious tears. "Grandma," I say through gritted teeth, "you knew you were dying, and that's the last thing you said to me?"

She doesn't say anything more. She never did.

I ran out on her, angry, and hung out with my boyfriend, Hutch, and our mutual close friend, Ben, despite her attempts to warn me away. By the time I got back, she'd had her heart attack. The thing about death is you rarely get those beautiful exit lines like they have in movies—and closure? Forget it. Sometimes, one of your biggest early supporters says something vaguely bigoted, dies while you're away, and then that's all you're left with of them.

When I turn around, my grandmother is gone. The parlor is brightened, but not the mood. It's now filled with mourners. My family, always so loud, talks in hushed tones. Grandpa Angelo sits alone in his special chair. He's the only one not in black. He wears a hideous brown velvet suit with wide lapels and a ruffled undershirt.

It's his wedding suit. The only "nice" thing he ever owned, my grandma joked.

Grandpa stares at the wall of portraits, not talking with anyone, until Uncle Paul walks over and hands him a plate of antipasti.

I remembered the antipasti. It was easy to make. Grandma had always made the other, more memorable dishes. Who the hell was going to make those now? Aunt Ro would have to learn—she'd have to learn a lot of things quickly.

The fury of my dream won't quiet down. Images of my past and present swirl together into this storm of a nightmare I can't escape. Each room holds a new dreadful thing, and the last room is no different.

In fact, it's the worst. I've dreaded this moment the entire dream.

Thirteen-year-old Ben finds thirteen-year-old me in the kitchen. His shining red hair was longer then, like a lion's mane. He was shorter and scrawnier, too, but still a very pretty boy I would've done anything for. That's why Little Me doesn't argue when Little Ben cups his hand to my ear and whispers, "Let's get some Grato."

I always thought Ben wanted to take my hand when he led me into the basement. He doesn't, but I remember feeling his desire to—if that makes any sense.

Regardless, Little Ben and Little Grant sneak downstairs, and Grown-Up Me follows. Everyone is too preoccupied with the wake to notice or care what two middle school homos are getting up to in the wine cellar.

IL DIAVOLO TI ASCOLTA, reads Mama Bianchi's warning above the wooden door as we pry it open. Years later, both of us would have muscles and strength to open the door easily, but that day we both strained our limp noodle arms to the breaking point. But open it does, and the dark corridor of dusty bottles awaits us.

"It means 'The Devil is listening to you,'" Little Me says boastfully.

"Metal," says Little Ben, impressed. His admiration of me wouldn't last forever.

Ben recovers a bottle of Wishing Rose Grato from behind the wooden cubbies, its cork already popped, and chugs it. After Little Me shares a chug, both boys wince back the bitter, earthy darkness of the wine. Little Me juts out his tongue, and Little Ben shivers horribly. Laughter follows.

Carefully, I enter the cellar. It feels like a horror movie. For the second time this dream, I want to pull my tiny self out of a horrible situation and whisk him to safety.

But I can't stop the truth.

"Grant . . ." Little Ben says, absentmindedly peeling back the Grato label. He's scared, but Little Me isn't—I thought I was safe down here. "Um . . . You know you're my best friend . . ."

"Of course," Little Me says, smiling innocently. "You're mine. My—uh, best friend, I mean."

Little Ben's eyes flit up, and he smiles. "Would you be, I don't know, whatever, like, mad if . . ."

"Mad?" I ask stupidly. In this moment, I thought he was going to tell me he had feelings for me. We'd both felt it. I was dating Hutch, so nothing could happen. But if he asked me . . . If he told me how he felt about me, I'd call Hutch right now and say we have to break up. Hutch is so cute and I like him a lot, but Ben—oh my God, *Ben*—he's the one.

Is this the rose's work? Is this my wish revealing my true love? Just like it did for the others in my family? It can work for anxious little gay boys, too? Maybe I don't need this part of me taken away. If I were with Ben, I wouldn't care if my dad got mad that I'm . . . like me. When I'm with Ben, I feel strong. I feel exciting. Like I'm fun. No one at school thinks I'm any of those things, but these summers with Ben have created a monster: a confident Grant Rossi.

As the bitter tang of the wine works its way down my body, a reckless energy rises. I reach for Ben's wrist—the most intimately I've ever touched him—and stroke my thumb against his skin. He lets out a gasp, and when he sees my smiling, amorous face drawing closer for a kiss, he blurts the truth:

"I made out with Hutch. Sorry. I hope you're not mad, it's just . . . It sort of happened, and then he asked me out, and . . . I said I'd be his boyfriend. I mean, it makes more sense than you and him, right? We both live in town, but you're so far away by the city. Summer's almost over, and you'll be leaving us again." Little Ben smiles anxiously, and he swallows. "You're not mad, are you?"

Little Me removes his hand from Little Ben like he's touched a hot stove.

The color drains from my face and, trembling with anger, I whisper, "It's my grandma's funeral. What's wrong with you?"

"What? Um . . ."

Little Ben, terrified by how rapidly my tone has darkened, pulls himself up as he watches Little Me run out of the cellar. Not only did I have to say goodbye to my grandmother, I also learned Hutch was dumping me in the worst way: by running away with my actual true love.

Grown-Up Me stands in the darkened corridor. Ben turns to me for the first time since the dream began . . . and he's no longer thirteen. He's today's Ben, full of height and muscles and a contempt for me I can almost taste. Ben appraises me with a sinister coolness, the who-gives-a-fuck-about-you energy that was seemingly never part of his DNA as a child, but would become his entire persona after our fight. The snake that was always hiding inside the bunny.

"Are you ever gonna forgive me?" he asks derisively, as if I'm a baby for not doing so already.

"Depends," I say, sneering. "Are you ever gonna apologize?"

"You're so deluded." Ben shakes his head. "I did apologize, remember? I ran after you, and you tore into me in front of your whole family. Ruined your grandma's wake. Nobody knew what the hell you were on about. I begged you to let me explain—I BEGGED—but you just threw me out."

"You hurt me."

"You hurt ME. My coming out. My parents' divorce. My dad's cancer. I needed my best friend, but you wouldn't even talk to me. You're an insecure, grudge-holding *child*."

Tears break down my cheeks as I grab Ben by his grass-stained shirt collar. He struggles in my grip, snatches my shirtsleeve, and pushes me back into the Wishing Rose rack. Bottles clang loudly against each other as Ben and I huff hot, furious breaths on each other.

"I thought I meant something to you!" I shout helplessly in his grip.

"You did! But I don't let boys stick around. Not since you. That's how bad you hurt me." He shrugs. "If anyone gets close, I mess it up on purpose. Haven't you been paying attention?" Ben walks to me, strains on his tiptoes, and cups his hand to my ear. "The rose isn't the curse. We are."

I wake covered in sweat as the dimensions of the darkened basement materialize around me. An ache whines in my jaw until I massage it away. That was a damn marathon.

"The rose isn't the curse. We are." Evil Dream Ben's ominous words still swirl through my mind when I remember that Grown-Up Reality Ben is lying beside me, his sleeping bag unfurled next to my cot. Only he's not asleep; he lies on his back, the bug-zapper blue light of his phone washing out his already pale face into something ghostly. But still, unfortunately, handsome.

Anger fills me as I watch him doom-scroll, gentle guitar music drifting out of his phone. When someone torments you in a dream, it's hard to treat them kindly when you wake, even when they have no clue about the murder spree they just committed inside your head.

The music is sweet, though, and it begins to soften my heart.

In fact, the dream slips away entirely, and I remember what actually occurred between Ben and me just hours ago: we rescued Vero Roseto together, and he stroked my foot while whispering, "I just want to know you again."

I want that, too. But I have to be smart.

We're both cursed now. He dumps people who get too close. When it comes to Ben, closeness creates distance.

"Hey," I finally say. Ben jumps a little and shuts off the light on his phone.

"Sorry," he says from the darkness. "Was the light bothering you?"

"No."

"Ah, the music? I like it on for bed, but I can't seem to stay asleep the last few days—"

"It's fine, I like it. I was having a bad dream anyway."

"What about?"

"I don't remember." The lie sticks in my throat like peanut butter, but I'm not telling him. "What time is it?"

"Two something."

"You really can't sleep?"

"Nah. It's all right."

Ben's acoustic guitar instrumental track fills the silence.

He can't sleep the past few days? Since I've been back? The vengeful beast in me retracts its claws as my heart softens even further.

"Ben . . . ?" In the dark, I reach my hand from my cot to his sleeping bag, and right away I find his arm. Broad, taut, and lightly furry. Almost exactly the way I reached for him in the wine cellar five years ago. "I want you to know I forgive you."

More silence, backed by acoustic guitar.

Finally, his other hand finds me, and a heavy, quiet voice comes: "Just like that?" I'm 90 percent sure I do, but I'm rounding it up to forgiveness because I don't want him losing sleep. When I don't respond, I hear him swallow and then say, "Kind of you."

"I want to get to know you again, too." Now it's my turn to swallow hard; this next part requires another sip of bravery. "I think the best way to do that is to keep things light."

"That'd be cool."

It takes everything in me not to snip back, *"Oh, I bet you do think that's cool! Light, light, light, no burdens of commitment for Ben."* I pat his arm one last time and pull it back. "I think we need to come up with some rules to make sure we keep it light. Ben Rules."

He snorts. "Why not Grant Rules?"

"Because you're the high-maintenance one."

Ben's spitting laughter comes so hard, it's like a sprinkler. "Oh my God, delusion."

It's a good thing he can't see my face because my smile instantly dies, recalling Evil Dream Ben telling me I'm deluded. Well, maybe so, but I'm not spending one more day around Ben McKittrick without guardrails that will keep us from falling into bad habits.

"Ben Rule number one," I say, businesslike. "We don't talk about Hutch."

He laughs carelessly. "Fine by me."

"Ben Rule number two. We don't talk about the past. As far as we're concerned, you and I are just two brand-new people."

"Fine." Ben is sounding more impressed with this system by the minute—and so am I.

"Ben Rule number three. No fighting."

Ben moans with disappointment. "Fighting's the best part."

"Teasing, yes. But you know the difference between teasing and hitting below the belt."

"Below the belt's the best part . . ." he whispers in an exaggerated come-hither voice. The darkness is my friend once again as *my* below-the-belt area responds very excitedly to Ben's teasing.

If I could slap it down, I would.

"Any other rules, boss?" he asks.

"Let's start with three and see how we do."

"Deal."

A compromise Dr. Patty herself would be very proud to see me come up with. Ben was one of our few topics that was always triggering and could never find a resolution. Because he just left my life. Or I left his. Either way, we're here now, and we have a rare opportunity to put this old drama to bed.

As Ben curls over in his sleeping bag and tries to lull himself back to sleep, I make a fourth Ben Rule just for me: *Don't fall in love with him again.*

CHAPTER 15

THE BEN RULES

After two weeks at Vero Roseto, details of my life in Chicago begin to fade, like another life I'm struggling to remember. Did I have a relationship blow up in my face? Was any of that even real? For all I know, I was thirteen, spending my summer at Vero Roseto with my best friend, Ben, until one morning I woke up and we had suddenly aged five years. Everything in between those eras—including our ugly falling-out—is a snippet of my life's video I simply edited out.

All thanks to the Ben Rules.

No fighting. No Hutch.

I kneel at the lip of Grandpa Angelo's vegetable garden and watch Ben slowly rebuild what was once a glorious grocery store's worth of crops and herbs. He works fluidly, like a conductor, moving seeds and fresh pots into deep divots in the earth—with one hand, he plants, with the other he covers with fresh soil. *Swish, swish.* His hands are freckled and veiny, with dirt-stained nails and bandages covering his many gardening scrapes.

How would they feel? His roughness has already touched

my hands, but what would they feel like on the small of my back? Or on the back of my neck as he guides my lips closer to his?

These are the horrible, unacceptable thoughts barging into my brain while I wait with bags of the seeds he's planting next.

However, I'm still obeying the Secret Ben Rule: this isn't me falling in love, this is me gripped with brainless lust.

"Need a break?" I ask, clearing a highly embarrassing crack from my voice.

Snorting, Ben doesn't look up from his work. "Going through puberty again? Nah, I'm gonna keep working."

I unclasp a water bottle from my belt loop and tap his shoulder. "Let me rephrase that: Take a break. You're sweating all over the garden."

His back heaving with a sigh, Ben rolls onto his ass and snatches the water bottle away. "Plants need water."

"Not salt water."

"You been staring at me sweating, eh?" After a long guzzle, he wipes his lips with a damp forearm. He never once blinks—he's like a forest predator. I'm too scared to respond, and he knows it. It only makes him smile. "Sinner."

I scoff, but awkwardly. "You need a doctor. No, like, a team of doctors."

Ben just keeps chugging and grinning. "You can lock me up and throw away the key, doesn't change the fact that you're gonna get nervous when I do this . . ."

Sitting, he drifts his bare knee slowly, confidently, toward mine.

Ben's approaching appendage sends red alert shock waves through my system so strong, I'm forced to stand to get away from him. He roars with laughter. "I knew it!" he says, tossing me his empty bottle, which I fumble catching. While I chase after the stray bottle, Ben picks up a handful of rosemary seeds and resumes planting. "You were always a thirsty little cannoli. Do you have any idea how many times I used to catch you staring, tongue wagging like a dog?"

"*Okay*, okay!" It's all I can say as I huffily snatch the bottle and return to his side.

Dripping with smugness, Ben covers the rosemary bed and starts work on the sage. "You were never subtle, always so easy to read, that's why I love y—"

He stops himself cold, but it's too late.

The word is out.

I gasp with joy, not at being loved by Ben, but by the smug opening I now possess. Hurling myself bodily, I slide between Ben and his herbs like a baseball player stealing home base. My smile is enormous, and Ben—correctly sensing what's coming—looks away in disgust.

"You *what* me?" I ask.

Fuming, he turns back. "Love-*d*. Past tense. Get the dick out of your ear and MOVE—"

He tries to push me out of his gardening way, but I won't

budge. It's my turn for smugness. "What else do you love about me?"

Ben shoves his trowel into the soil and taps his chin mockingly. "Let's see, I love what a ride-or-die friend you are. Love how you show up for me. I really love how much you were there for me when my dad fought like hell to keep me in the divorce until he found out I was gay, then was like, 'Enjoy Scotland!' I love, love, *love* that you're such a hothead, I had to follow you secretly on Instagram because I knew if you spotted me, you'd block me." As my joy sinks, he picks up his trowel again. "Don't know if *love* is the right word, but . . ."

I clutch his hand, rough and damp, before he can plow on with work. We look at each other seriously. "Do you wanna talk about this?"

He shakes his head, as if he's mad at himself instead of me. "No, it would break a rule."

As badly as I want to return to our cease-fire, Ben has suddenly let loose such a torrent of emotions he's been holding back, it would feel criminal to ignore them. But I'm also scared . . . and angry myself. Yeah, I wasn't there in his life, but he wasn't there in mine.

But who's fault is that? I ask myself.

"Are you okay?" I ask Ben.

"Totally." He nods, but won't look at me. "You know what the worst part about looking you up last year was?" I don't respond. He seems to be vomiting information just fine.

Wiping another bead of sweat from his forehead, he says, "I moved back, went into caretaker mode—which makes you feel *amazing* and *sexy*, by the way—and every week, I'd drive by Vero Roseto, and want to come find you and tell you how hard everything was." He laughs at himself. "Like, as if you were there. My brain knew you were gone, but my body refused to get it. So, I looked you up and . . . BAM. Hot. You were supposed to get ugly. That was really rude. But there you were, standing on the edge of a fountain looking like a Disney prince."

Ben chuckles bitterly and scooches away from me toward the next area to be repotted. With a sting in my chest, I know the picture he's talking about. I looked great, but I'd never felt more miserable and lonely. As Ben jabs strongly at the earth, he says, "It made it so much harder to keep hating you."

Strangely enough, this sinister comment fills me with warmth. Laughing, I scoot closer to Ben again. "That's . . . exactly what I thought when I saw you here."

He turns and studies me with narrowed, untrusting eyes that used to trust me. After a long thought, he sighs. "Can I smell your hair?"

My eyebrows shoot up. "Hmm?"

"Your hair. You've always been touchy about it, and it's always so bouncy and pretty, and it's pissing me off. I want to smell it. Let me smell it."

Well, okay. Ben has embarrassed himself enough this afternoon that I'm in an obliging mood. As soon as I shrug, Ben leans in quickly and plants his nose in my curls. He sniffs rapidly, like an animal. His stubbly, muscular throat is bared to me, and it takes inhuman strength not to lunge for him. Once he's satisfied, Ben returns to his pot work as if he had simply asked to see my Pokémon cards.

"Gay ass shampoo," he says, folding soil over the pot. "We're supposed to be working the land, and you trot out here smelling like milk and honey. Dumbass."

Sighing, I roll away and pick up my spare seed bags. "Don't hate me 'cause I'm beautiful."

"That's exactly what I plan to do."

And *that* is why we have the Ben Rules.

As the week continues, our momentary dip back into animosity doesn't return, but it still shows up in little ways. After we finish replanting Grandpa Angelo's garden, my next duty was scrubbing and refilling the pool. As I power wash off years' worth of chlorine scum, which is oddly therapeutic, two B&B guests (two middle-aged women) stroll past carrying hearty glasses of Invidioso.

"Ooh, is the pool opening soon?" one asks, mid-slurp.

"Sorry," I say, shouting over the clattering washer. "Not until Fourth of July weekend."

Frowning, they drift back across the still-unfinished lawn

toward the winery. It's for their own good. We can't reopen the pool until the deck is completely rebuilt, or we'll have people walking their wet feet over the dirty plot, making a mess.

The patio door behind me slides open, and Ben traipses out munching a crustless sandwich.

I roll my eyes. "Did you grab that from the lunch spread? That's for guests."

"Is that any way to talk to a guy who brought you . . . this?"

He pulls a second sandwich from behind his back. I shut the power washer and drop the brush like it's on fire. "Gimme that," I moan, pulling the sandwich with both hands. It all goes in at once. *Chomp.* Too fast to even tell what kind it was, but hopefully Ben doesn't hate me enough to trick me into eating cold cuts.

"Oh, by the way," Ben says, hopping off the pool's patio to the ground where our future deck will stand. "Your aunt says the West Wing's almost ready for guests, but would you be open to spending another week or whatever on your cot? Rose Festival tickets are still booming from that video of yours, and she thinks she can give you more of a design budget if she can, y'know, rent more rooms and keep you on the floor."

"How many tickets have we sold for the festival?" I ask, picking up the pool scrubber.

Ben shrugs. "Dunno. But it sounds like you've got a big show coming. Hope you've been designing." Chuckling, and knowing goddamn well I've been too busy scrubbing pools to design anything, Ben skips off toward the sculpture garden.

Since the rose garden and sculpture garden are still under repair, Ben and I start resodding around the vineyard and winery first. Just beyond them lies the pie stand, which in our heyday was a canteen where tipsy guests could snack their hearts out on a variety of slices. Now it's an abandoned home for hornets. Sadly, it was deemed low priority for renovation, so we'll have to get to it last. Once we finish this lawn, the deck will be next—a repair even more imperative now that the pool is clean. After this weekend, we'll get the lumber and begin to rebuild.

I have been promised that I will only be used as a pair of hands, not a professional carpenter.

Aunt Ro has been protective of me, since every night after we finish working, I return to my Studio Surface tablet to brainstorm designs for the Rose Festival, which is now six weeks away.

Inspiration has been slow. But I'm not telling Ro (or Ben).

Honestly, I haven't been moved to design anything or search for schools because life has just been . . . nice. Treating my relationship with Ben as a do-over was a genius move. There's no use going over all that old crap, and I've been kind of liking hanging out with this hot guy who teases me gently and sort of looks like this boy I used to know. I'm different, too. I'm not that little drama queen with braces anymore.

I'm a big drama queen who has nice teeth, a skincare regimen, and enough sense to keep my thornier feelings to myself for the good of the production.

As Ben grabs another roll of sod from our cart, our conversation starts to become dangerous again: "How many exes have there been, exactly?" Smirking, Ben recognizes my discomfort as I help him roll the sod out like a blanket across the lawn. "Or is that breaking a rule?"

"Not breaking a rule *exactly*," I say, cracking my neck, "but we've talked a lot about my exes and haven't talked about any of yours."

"Ah, so our trauma dumping has to be even steven? Is that a new rule?"

"No." I reach for another roll of sod. "And is it trauma for you? The way you tell it, you've been the dumper every time."

"Hmm, well, you'd know a lot about dumpers." He passes behind me, smacking my ass and making a *sproing* sound effect, before grabbing the sod himself.

"Y'know, this is sort of sexual harassment."

"You're *my* boss, though."

"Oh, that makes it okay?"

"Yeah, if you like it."

"Said every sexual harasser ever."

"All right, get me in trouble then." Ben drops the sod and approaches, grinning. "What's my punishment?"

I smile, warm blood rushing to my cheeks. "Before you

leave, you have to follow through on your flirting."

Ben doesn't blink. I watch a bead of sweat snake a trail down his cheek. "Well, now," he whispers, "that sounds like my boss giving me a sexy ultimatum. And that *is* sexual harassment."

"Not if you never leave." My smile falters. "Are you . . . leaving after the festival?"

For weeks, it's the question that's been knocking at the back window in my mind. The first day I came back, Ben told me nothing else was keeping him here. But maybe that's changed . . .

Laughing, Ben pins the fresh sod in place and begins to roll it out beside our last roll. "Yes, I'm always the one to do the dumping."

Dodging my question, true to form. I should've known he wouldn't make it easy on me. So, with nothing left to do but continue the conversation Ben *does* want to continue, I help him unfurl the sod and say, "Tell me about the one that sucked the most."

"Fabian, no question."

"And who was Fabian?" I silently seethe, picturing a super-model with flowing blond hair and nipple rings.

"German boy. Exchange student." Ben walks backward, unspooling the bright green sod, keeping it carefully aligned with the rest of the lawn. "Tall. Beautiful black hair. Hands like frying pans." He sighs comically. "I woulda married him."

A dart sails through my heart, but I just keep smiling and

guiding the sod as it unspools. "What was wrong with him? Too perfect?"

"Eh, he reminded me of you."

"So, yes, too perfect?"

Ben smiles without looking up. "When I told him it was over, he *really* reminded me of you. Those big, pretty brown eyes all heartbroken." He drops the end of the sod in place, but I'm biting my lip to stop the memories from flooding back. When he looks up again, he's smiling sheepishly. "Started panicking and telling myself, 'Ben McKittrick, what's your problem? Getting a fetish for watching brown eyes cry, are you? You're disgusting.'"

Only with his Scottish accent, it sounds like "diss-goose-tang."

"Hey," I say, reaching across the sod for Ben, but he backs away tensely.

"I broke a Ben Rule, I know, but . . . I really don't know why I did that to him, poor guy." He slurps back water. "You think I'm cursed, too?"

"No," I say without hesitating. I try not to remember Evil Dream Ben telling me the rose isn't the curse, he is—well, *we* are.

"Liar." Ben laughs nervously.

Laughing, I take a water break so Ben doesn't see me blush. Whenever I feel this warmth behind my cheeks, I know they're turning as rosy as St. Nick, and I don't need him needling me about it. When I finish chugging, a stream dribbles down my lip like it's my first day drinking liquids. Ben grazes a finger under my chin to catch the runoff.

"Sloppy Sally," he says.

Despite our so-far platonic friendship, Ben still surprises me with tiny touches like this. Sniffing my hair. Poking my cheek. A hand on my back when he's squeezing past me.

When Ben's fingers come near me, my skin fizzes like I'm holding an ice cube too long.

Always shocking, never relaxing.

Yet every time his touch leaves, I count the minutes wondering when it'll happen again.

This isn't good for me. Being anything more than friends with Ben isn't good.

While it's been nice getting to know Grown-Up Ben, my affection levels are getting dangerously high, in violation of Secret Ben Rule number four: no falling in love again. And it sounds like Ben has as much to work through on that front as I do on mine. Light and sweet is what will work for us.

The following evening marks the end of an era.

At dusk, Uncle Paul and his small team of guys dig up the six crumbling topiary sculptures from the sculpture garden. The swan, the wolf, the rabbit . . . they may be dying and so overgrown they'd long since lost their familiar shapes, but they've been on the grounds since Mama Bianchi laid the first bricks of Vero Roseto.

Ben, Aunt Ro, and I build a bonfire on the garden grounds

where my parents took their engagement pictures (speaking of bonfires). The flames reach as high as the walls surrounding the Wishing Rose, kicking and dancing at the sky in a beautiful funeral pyre. One by one, we watch Uncle Paul hurl the dying sculptures into the fire, and each time he does, the flames dance higher and Aunt Ro whimpers a little softer.

She quietly cries into a ball of tissues, and I fight my own tears as we watch our family's history literally go up in flames.

I know what she's feeling. Did she fail her family?

She didn't. She kept it going as long as possible.

The enormous fear feeding the flames of my tears, however, is the uncertainty that maybe the rest of Vero Roseto will join the sculptures on the pyre soon enough. And if that happens, *I* will be the one to blame. The festival has already sold hundreds of tickets, but is that enough to keep us going? I'm afraid to ask Ro the number she needs. And if they do come, what kind of show will they be seeing? I haven't done something on this scale since my ex . . .

The second my last scrap of confidence is about to leave me, my gaze follows the wolf sculpture in the flames. The biggest of all the topiary creatures, the wolf stands massively in the fire, its outstretched claws whipping around as it burns. It almost looks as if it's dancing, the bonfire around its base as wide and dangerously elegant as a dramatic ball gown.

"No way . . ." I whisper, reaching for my phone. Ben is the only one to notice as I open the Notes app and begin feverishly typing my revelation.

"What is it?" he asks, sliding so close to my shoulder, I can smell his divine body spray.

"The sculpture garden." I turn to him, my eyes wide. "I know what to do. They'll be alive. Living sculptures wearing gowns made out of roses. We'll get models. Maybe they can even dance."

The smoldering remains of the wolf reflect off Ben's face in the dark, but he's definitely smiling. "Sounds complicated."

"Have we met?"

Laughing, Ben clutches me happily by my neck and pulls me close, affectionately but platonically, like my straight brother loves to do. Still, it's nice to have Ben's affections again. And it's even nicer to feel hope that maybe all of this isn't headed for the bonfire just yet.

CHAPTER 16

THE RETURN OF THE ROSSIS

The following week—the week of Fourth of July and five weeks until the Rose Festival—Hell descends on Vero Roseto in the form of a "delightful" surprise. My brother and sisters are popping in. Well, some of them. Aunt Ro invited my three oldest siblings to bunk in the East Wing (once again kicking me to the basement) and stay for the local fireworks. She pitched it as a family reunion, but really she's enlisting additional free labor to get this deck rebuilt.

I know Ro. She's always running two cons at once.

When the children storm in, Ben and I are cooling off in the kitchen. Hollering and slapping walls, three toddler boys with inky-black hair race inside, followed by a quieter, similarly dark-haired boy of five, who walks in and waves politely. "Hi, Uncle Grant," he says. "We saw six trucks coming here and three tractors."

"Hey, Angelo," I say, stooping to wrap a hug around my nephew. Little Angelo eyes Ben warily, too young to realize he's a friend of the family. "That's Ben, my friend. The tractors are heading to the grape orchard, but those trucks?

They've got *sooooo* many planks of wood on them. Me, Ben, your mom, Aunt Traci, and Uncle A. C. are gonna build a deck so we can all watch the fireworks this weekend!"

"A. C. too?" Ben asks with a hint of fear as he rummages through a box of Triscuit crackers. "That'll certainly be interesting."

The last time Ben was around my oldest brother, he was closeted like me and the air was thick with A. C.'s clumsy gay jokes. A. C. has massively chilled out, but this *will* be interesting. As usual, Ro doesn't give people a heads-up on who they're collaborating with on projects. She just throws conflict-heavy people together and yells "Surprise!"

She'd make a great reality show producer.

"There's gonna be fireworks?" Angelo asks, tugging on his fingers.

Somehow, I've upset him.

"He doesn't like fireworks," my sister Kimmy says, rubbing a firm, loving hand on her son's shoulders. Kimmy is twenty-eight, as tall as I am, and dressed in a plain pink tee with basketball shorts drooping past her knees. She's sporty, with strong shoulders from a lifetime of winning volleyball championships, and her dark hair is piled high in a messy bun.

As Kimmy lands a hearty kiss on my cheek, she waves to Ben, who is shrinking into the corner by the fridge as Angelo's wilder brothers sprint back into the kitchen, this time with toy lightsabers.

"Memorial Day," she explains, "our neighbors were shooting off these damn explosions—just *real* cannons. Shook the whole house. The German shepherd next door's roaring, crying, hates it. Angelo, eh . . ." Kimmy hands her son a baggie of green pepper slices, which he anxiously gobbles. "Well, he didn't like it much either. Can't seem to get him excited about the Fourth."

"Little man, don't worry," I tell Angelo. "These fireworks won't be anywhere near us, and they're put on by the city, so they're more like the ones you see at Disney." Finally, the boy looks up from the table, a hopeful smile forming. I wink at Kimmy.

As the former Most Sensitive Boy in this family, I am sympathetic to Angelo's inner plight, which if he's anything like me is turbulent. Especially since—like my mom with my dad—Kimmy married a redneck who does not understand his lovebug of a son one iota.

The flurry of entrances doesn't stop as my second-oldest sister, Traci, runs me over with a hug. Traci, twenty-seven, dark blond, and muscular in a white tank and khaki pants, is every child's favorite aunt. Angelo and his brothers drop what they're doing to throw a hug on her, but when she sees Ben by the fridge, her mouth drops.

"BEN?" Traci asks, racing to him. "I gotta get on my *tiptoes* now?! You were so little. Ro warned me, but I didn't want to believe it." Ben and Traci laugh together as she refuses to break apart the hug. "This is so unacceptable, ahhh!"

Maybe this visit won't be all bad.

Finally, my brother, A. C.—the oldest Rossi child—lumbers inside carrying his toddler son.

It's a Big as Hell family, and this isn't even close to all of us. I'm the baby—and I *mean* the baby. I'm five years younger than the next-youngest kid—something A. C. would later throw in my face. I was the "Band-Aid baby" who was supposed to hold together my parents' flop marriage—their last-ditch attempt to make it all work—but surprise, babies don't function like that.

As Kimmy and Traci hug each other, Ben taps my wrist. "I'll leave you all to it," he says. "Gonna let Ro know everyone's here."

"You can just text her," I say, struggling to hear him over the chattering.

"Nah." Ben's eyes flick briefly—angrily—toward A. C.

"He's better now. Let's just say hi."

"He's not my brother, and I don't feel like it." Ben shrugs, lobbing another Triscuit happily into his mouth. "And what do you mean, he's *better* now?"

Glancing over Ben's shoulder, I spy A. C. still in the middle of roughhousing with his wild pack of nephews. Still, I lower my voice. "No more jokes."

"What a saint. Y'know, when we were little, there wasn't a dirtbag comedian he wouldn't defend like they were your mam. Did he ever apologize?"

"Basically."

Ben's eyes narrow as he munches, lost in thought. "You've

been kicking me in the nutsack all summer over our thing, but you're cool with your homophobic brother over *basically* an apology?"

He's got me there, but A. C. is benefiting from his crimes being more indirect and, frankly, constant. I clear my throat. "He supported me when I came out."

"That's what people are *supposed* to do, sweetums."

"Well, how was he supposed to know we were gay when he was making those jokes?"

"Because you were a . . ." Chuckling wickedly, Ben holds up a limp wrist.

"No, I wasn't." I playfully smack his shoulder. "You were."

"No." He scowls. "I was?" I shrug. "Okay, I'm sorry you're too scared of your brother to take as hard a line with him as you do with everybody else, but that's between you all. Leave me out of it. Kisses!"

I can only sputter petulantly as Ben skips out through the parlor, throwing a peace sign A. C.'s way as he vanishes. Damn Ben! He's comparing our situation with my thing with my brother and, like, not to be rude to my family, but the reason I'm angrier at Ben is because he really mattered to me back then and my family . . . is nice, but there's a lot of them, so keeping an emotional distance from one of them just isn't as much of a problem as it was losing Ben.

Having watched Ben leave, Traci creeps toward me, her eyebrow arched, and whispers, "What's going on there?"

"Nothing," I say. It's not until this moment, my shoulders slouching with disappointment, that I realize I wish there was something to report.

Two bearish arms—each the size of a log—clamp around my chest and hoist me in the air. As tall and built as I am, A. C. still has size on me. Nearing thirty, A. C. has a full black beard, receding hairline, and a stomach as round and hard as a boulder. "BABY BRO," he cries, deadlifting me as I fling my legs in the air helplessly like Woody when Andy is looking.

My nephews applaud A. C.'s antics as I regain my balance in a room that's spinning. "You got me," I chuckle.

"Was that Ben McKittrick I saw running out?" A. C. asks. Not wanting to get into it, I smile and nod. A. C.'s eyebrows shoot up. "You two, uh . . . ?"

Disappointment once again pummeling my chest, I shake my head. "No, we're just fixing the place up together."

A. C. nods, his narrowed eyes computing. "He wasn't leaving fast 'cause I got here, was he?"

I wince. There's no point lying. A. C. is as shrewd as me and Ro.

Pain crosses my brother's face. "Shit," he whispers, trying halfheartedly to laugh. "I was that bad, huh?" Wincing again, I shrug. "Any chance you could . . ."

"Apologize for you?" I shake my head.

A. C. nods, accepting his penance is not yet complete. I don't even know if an apology will cut it. Ben is a much more physical person than an emotional one. If their bad blood is going to stop, they'll probably have to fight it out. It worked for Ben and me, wrestling in the rose garden and hurling mud at each other.

That night, while Aunt Ro fries up chicken cutlets and bread patties for the family, the kitchen explodes with joy. The guests spread across the East and West Wings leave out their used room service trays, and I bus them. As I bring down the trays, I pass my quartet of nephews (three rodeo clowns and one gentle soul, Angelo) playing action figures by the laundry flap in the hallway. Angelo carefully sets Hulk and Doctor Strange along the flap's edge, teetering on the brink of a fatal plunge down the laundry chute.

Smiling to myself, I leave them alone to create their own memories of Vero Roseto. As I descend the stairs, Ben is waiting on a step halfway down. Still in his damp gardening outfit, he crosses his arms and observes the boys playing.

"You're right, you know," I whisper. "About A. C."

Ben doesn't look away from my nephews as he smiles. "Of course I'm right."

"I promise, I'll say something to him."

"Aw, don't, I was just being a daffodil." He shakes his head, something weighing heavily on his thoughts. As I inch closer, his shoulders tense. "If you're in a good place with your brother, don't make waves just for me."

"But I want to."

"Remember, I'm not sticking around." The air between us thickens as an invisible hand crushes my insides. He's already said it so many times before, but things have changed. Haven't they? Plus . . . I'm not sticking around either.

Ben watches me pitifully, dark circles forming under those shimmering eyes. "Do it for you. 'Cause if things go bad in the family, and I'm not here . . . I don't want to be the bad guy again."

I must've really let him have it back then. Was I that much of a beast?

With nothing more left to say, my and Ben's attention drifts back to my nephews on the landing. Next to the laundry chute flap, the twins whack lightsabers at their lined-up action figures, and down they go.

"That's why we're doing this, you know," I say, tapping my elbow to Ben's. "Rebuilding everything. It's so we can keep the house and let them have everything we had."

"What did we have?" Ben asks, smiling sadly. He shakes his head. "Nobody'll ever have what we had."

My heart moans at the thought.

"Nobody," I agree. Without thinking, I land a kiss—soft and brief—on Ben's ear. Intimate, not romantic.

There's no Ben Rule against little kisses!

I leave Ben on the stairs. Each step away from him hurts. We were doing so well as adult friends, no acknowledgment that anything was ever anything between us. Now anger is flooding back alongside the lovely memories.

I'm so tired of holding on to this baggage.

But every time I want to let go, it's like my hand is fused to the handle.

CHAPTER 17

A SPARK, THEN SMOKE

Two days into the reconstruction of the deck, what was once a high-spirited endeavor of music and inside jokes has devolved into silent, tense labor. The outer frame is already complete, along with three sets of stairs—a left one going toward the winery path, a right one going toward the swimming pool, and a grander, central one going toward the rose and sculpture gardens. All that's left now is to fill in the top of the deck and "pretty" it, but that's tougher than we thought. This deck wraps the entire East and West Wings, which means it's full of irregular angles, which means irregular beams. The Fourth of July is a few days away, and then my siblings go back home.

Good for my sanity, but bad for the job.

With Uncle Paul and his carpenter friend from Valle acting as foremen, Ben, Traci, Kimmy, A. C., and I drill, nail, measure, and cut what seems to be a never-ending supply of gray-stained lumber. The high sun, as fierce as knives on my skin, makes everything worse. The heat has literally been turned up on all preexisting conflicts, and among this tiny group, there are shockingly many.

Ben is still mad at A. C.

A. C. is mad at Ben and me for holding him to the dumbass jokes of his past.

Kimmy is mad at me for making a snide remark about her husband, who should be out here doing this shit instead of me.

I'm mad at Kimmy for using the Wishing Rose to bind herself to such a libertarian hick, who I *know* is already being clumsy with the feelings of his oldest son, who I am *sure* is queer, and who I *know* will be intentionally steered away from seeking advice from his gay uncle, because that's exactly what shithead straight parents of gay children do.

And Traci is mad at all of us for making this such a chore when she could be downstairs trying to score a jackpot on the slot machine.

This is the exact same group that—less than a decade ago—enjoyed one easygoing summer after another together. Now we're all snippy grown-ups, half of us watching the clock until Aunt Ro returns with wine.

"Hold the work, please," Uncle Paul says, a damp washcloth resting on his head. We all instantly, happily oblige. My triceps scream as Ben and I set down our impossibly heavy two-yard-long beam. The weight finally off my hands, I pull off my bandanna and wring out an inch of sweat into the grass. Ben fans himself with his hat as Paul visibly struggles to tell us something. "We don't have to do anything over . . . but most of the bolts we're working with are wrong."

Traci and I moan the loudest, while Ben, A. C., and Kimmy retreat into grim silence. My fingertips are beet red from hand-threading these bolts, and they've been wrong the whole time? Making a deck is like an IKEA project came to life just to strangle you.

"Better to catch it now," Paul says, "but I *am* gonna need one of you to go to town and pick up the correct bolt order."

"I'll go," Ben says, gingerly hopping over the deck frame. My siblings revolt en masse, but Ben just shrugs. "You know where Slava's Hardware is? You know how to get him to knock off twenty percent? Any of you have an ass this cute?" He spanks himself, and it indeed *boings* like a cheap mattress. "No to all three."

I slump dramatically over the deck frame and say, "I like to think that my ass is also—"

"Close, but mine's stronger." Winking, Ben disappears down the rear entrance for guest vehicles, finally getting what he's wanted for hours—to be rid of my family.

Now on a forced lunch break, Traci sprints inside to try the slot machine again, and Kimmy follows her to give Ro a break from the kids. Paul digs two bottled Pepsis from a cooler and hands them to me and A. C. Icy slush from the cooler drips down my arm so pleasantly, I don't even want to drink it yet. A. C., scowling behind his thick beard and bucket hat, downs his in one.

"Gents," Paul says, "you two gonna be nice? It's not good

for brothers to hold grudges. Once they start, it's hard to stop."

"I'm fine," A. C. says at the end of a soda belch. "Your gardener's got the attitude problem."

"Hey," I snap. "Ben's been looking after this place longer than any of us have, and if it weren't for him, we'd be selling off our entire family history right now."

"Fellas . . ." Paul says with a hint of warning.

I don't care. I'm supposed to be looking at European design schools right now, but instead, I'm drawing doodles of installations for the Rose Festival because A. C. and the rest of this family sat by and watched this place turn to piss. What would've happened if I were already overseas? If my last relationship had worked and I'd stayed in Chicago? If *anything* had gone right for me?

I'd be listening to Mom cry on the phone because Ro just hocked another heirloom.

Ben and I might have a shaky cease-fire with each other, but I'm not going to let him get dragged when he's the only one of us kids who gave a shit about Vero Roseto when it mattered.

A. C. flexes and puffs his chest like he's king of the wilderness. As if that's going to intimidate me. I straighten to my full height and flex, leaner but still able to drop him like dirt if that's what's needed.

"I thought you hated that guy," A. C. says.

"You don't know anything about that," I say.

"I remember you at Grandma's wake, hollering your guts

out at him. And when he left, I remember you telling us to never mention him to you again."

Breaths come shorter and sharper through my nose. My heart rate triples. But still, I don't blink. "You are stepping on something you don't know anything about."

"You were middle school dweebs. How complicated could it be?"

"Do not minimize me."

A. C. steps closer, jabbing a large finger at my sternum. My breath halts altogether, but still, I don't flinch. "Our grandma was dead. Everyone was grieving. And we had to stop to focus on your middle school bullshit."

My throat closes completely. The sun's knives push deeper into my skull as a headache consumes me. Sweat dances with my growing storm of tears. Next to us, Paul doesn't speak or get in the middle. Whatever is happening, it has to happen, and he knows it.

"You called me a Band-Aid baby," I say through gritted teeth.

"What?" my brother asks.

"Band-Aid baby. When *I* was dealing with losing my grandma, and my best friend, and my boyfriend, you thought it would be a great time to remind me that the only reason I *exist* was because Mom and Dad were trying to fix a broken marriage with a baby. You minimized me, you minimized my existence, and when they got divorced anyway, you blamed me for not being enough to keep them together."

A. C.'s nostrils flare open and closed, rapidly, like an animal. "I was upset."

"Or maybe you're just an asshole who runs his mouth when he should shut up." My jaw clicks with tension. "Maybe *that's* why Ben didn't buy your apology. Because he knew what I was too much of a pushover to admit—that you aren't sorry for your jokes at all. That you have no concept of our pain or your role in it."

"I *am* sorry," A. C. spits, more frustrated than anything else. "But you gotta work with me—"

Now my finger pokes his sternum. "I don't gotta do a goddamn thing."

I exhale loudly. Paul and A. C. say nothing. I quickly glance behind my shoulder, where the rest of my family watches from the parlor's screen door. "Uncle Grant's yelling," one of my younger nephews say as Ro hauls him away to the kitchen. Traci, Kimmy, and little Angelo remain, staring with fear stitched onto their faces.

I almost give in. I almost let A. C. off the hook and tell him it's okay, just to lower the tension. But Angelo's face stops me.

If I'm right about him, he needs to see this. He needs to see me hold the high ground.

Turning back to A. C., I ask, calmer, "Do you even know who Nick Hutchinson is?" My brother's blank reaction tells me what I already know. "No? Hutch. He was my boyfriend that whole last summer. Lived in Valle. Probably still does.

He was a friend of Ben's. He was my first kiss. First every-thing. Did any of you even have a clue?"

A. C. shakes his head. "You weren't out yet. Everything was a secret."

"But there were *clues.*" I slap my hand into my palm for emphasis. "There are always clues. I had a girly voice and so did Ben. Don't tell me none of you talked about it. Spotting baby gays is a national American pastime. So, what you do when you sense that is two things: create a welcoming envi-ronment and be aware of who we're sneaking out to go see. Homophobic bro humor and total indifference to our lives is not it. So, I'm sorry it happened at the wake, but I was a kid with a really hard secret who was going through an *obvious* breakup, which is middle school nothingness to you, but to me, it brought me a depression I still can't get rid of."

I thrust my arm in the direction of the rose garden. "Every-one in this family found their true love magic because of that rose. But when I had problems with Ben, who could I tell? None of you people. I had to tell the rose! And who did Ben have? His parents split. We were all gone. He didn't even have me! He had it so much worse than me, and I had it *bad.*" I throw my arms up, exhausted. My breaths shudder with help-less rage. Finally, I whimper, "Why couldn't any of you see us?"

Leaning against the deck frame, I clutch my chest to steady my breathing.

Oh God. I talked myself in circles.

I overdid it. The truth all came out, and I overdid it.

If nothing else, I just wanted to show Angelo a gay person could be strong and speak their truth. But all he probably saw was some scary, unhinged, lonely guy.

Just don't cry, Grant. Don't faint and don't cry.

I swig my bottle of Pepsi, which has turned lukewarm.

"Have you gotten that out of your system?" A. C. asks, his shoulders still pumping with heavy breaths. Weakly, I nod. Then he pulls me into a powerful hug. "I'm sorry, little buddy."

It's not his usual non-apology. It's from the gut.

Behind us, the screen door opens. Traci's tennis shoes land hard on the dirt as she leaps from the patio door through the open deck. Kimmy follows her, and she helps down Angelo. All of them, including Uncle Paul, swarm me. Tiny Angelo weaves around his mom's legs to find me. With a mop full of curls identical to mine, he smiles—a front tooth missing— and I melt.

If I'm right about him, he just got a great all-clear signal from his family.

Half an hour later, when Ben returns from town with the new bolts, he finds a refreshed and revitalized Rossi family. On sight, A. C. raises him a cold bottle, crowing, "Hey, there he is!" My brother throws a chummy arm around a highly uncomfortable (and confused) Ben. "Buddy, when you were growing up, I was a prick. There is no excuse, and I'm sorry. And to be totally honest, since my brother came out, I haven't gone a single day without remembering what I said. And every time I remember those little jokes, it hits me like an icicle *right here*." Still in A. C.'s iron grip, Ben watches my brother jab at his sternum. "Right here, Ben. And I feel it for you, too."

"Thank you . . . Uh, keep it up." Beyond baffled, Ben squirms out of A. C.'s arm, lobs the new bag of bolts to Uncle Paul, and approaches me chilling alone at the edge of the deck frame.

"What's going on with A. C.?" he asks, scooching next to me on the beam.

Smiling, I guzzle more freezing pop. "You missed a blowout fight. Him and me."

Ben's eyes widen with fiendish glee. "I MISSED IT?" he whispers. "Who won? And what about?"

"That'll teach you to run off. I won. And it was about you. Well, me. And, I guess, us. He started in on you, and . . . I lost it. It came rushing back to me, how scared you were when I told you to leave my grandma's wake. I know I . . . hurt you, and left you alone with your dad, who sucks."

"Mm-hmm, my dad, who sucks."

"And then you had to move, go through all that alone. Anyway, I let him have it. Nobody shit-talks you but me."

For a long time, Ben doesn't react, and I don't say anything either. Sometimes, apologies are best when you just put it out there and let it cool like a pie right out of the oven. Finally, he bites his lip and asks, "You fought for me?"

On a cleansing inhale, I reaffix the bandanna around my

sopping curls and say the words I never thought I'd say to Ben in a million years: "I want to start over. Forget the rules about bringing up our past. I can't hold on to it anymore." My jaw tenses on a sharp swell of guilt and hope. "If I only got you around for a few more weeks, I want you and me to start over for real."

A grin finds Ben. He stares at me as if he's waiting to make sure I don't take it back or say "JK!" I watch him, my own hope rebuilding. Finally, he slips his hand inside mine and whispers, "Gay."

I smile. This isn't a fleeting touch, this is his hand gripping mine and not letting go.

Jackpot.

The next day, we complete the deck. The day after that, the city inspector clears the deck for occupancy. The day after *that* is the Fourth of July, and the new deck's furniture fills with my family and new B&B guests while the kids swim. "Oh, what you've done with the deck is gorgeous!" says an older Black woman, sipping wine with Aunt Ro. "I used to come here every summer with my kids until they were grown. It's been a few years, I think, but I remember this deck looking its age. It looks fabulous!"

Ro clinks her glass to the woman's. "I'm looking my age, too. How do I get looking fabulous again?"

Spitting laughter, the woman clinks her glass again. "Please!"

Before the sun begins to set, Ben and I go to the basement to find Uncle Dom's pantry of illegal fireworks and low-key military explosives. After thorough internet research, we determine the best way to dispose of such things is an overnight bath. In the morning, we'll wrap them in towels and dump them at the local solid waste disposal.

It feels good to get rid of things that are no longer serving us.

We save some smoke balls, black snakes, and TNT snappers. My nephews shriek with delight at the snappers—even Angelo, who earned a bravery badge when his uncle Grant helped him hold fire in the palm of his hand with that snapper. Down goes the small white bulb, striking the new deck with a *snap!* Angelo screams, followed by gales of laughter as he begs me to let him do it again. While my littler nephews ignite coils of black snakes, Angelo chases them through the clouds of orange fog belching out of the smoke balls.

As soon as the twilit sky turns violet, blasts of colorful fireworks explode, far in the distance over Valle Forest. Later that night, Aunt Ro and Uncle Paul haul out stacks of old, physical photo albums, each flip of the page bringing gentle memory-filled sighs or gales of roaring laughter. The biggest laugh comes from looking at the pictures of Grandma and Grandpa's anniversary party. I was ten—Ben was there. And there was Grandpa Angelo in that *hideous* brown velvet suit with the wide lapels and flurry of ruffles. He looked like a stuffed Thanksgiving turkey with those frilly little booties.

"Hey, I liked that suit!" Ben argues, laughing with A. C.—something I thought I'd never see. "Angelo said he was gonna leave it to me. I wanna file a complaint. Ro!"

"Don't look at me! Nobody knows where it went," she says, deep into a bottle of sambuca with Traci. "If it was up to me, I woulda burned it."

"I'm gonna sue."

"Go ahead! All I got is Vero Roseto, and it's a dump!"

As everyone boos Ro, A. C. smacks Ben's shoulder to get his attention. His cheeks are flushed red from Grato. "That garden looks brand-new. Just the way it used to after planting. You made it look exactly the same."

Ben smiles sheepishly. "Yeah, I remembered what it looked like."

"From *memory?*"

"Yeah, Angelo actually gave me some tips that summer. He was cool."

As Ben gazes at the ground, looking lost in a flood of memories, I'm struck silent remembering my dream. Grandpa Angelo's wedding suit, his anniversary suit, the suit he wore to my grandma's wake. The only reason he wasn't buried in it is because no one could find it after he died. Apparently he wanted Ben to have it, but where did it go?

"*Enjoy yourself,*" Grandpa told me in the dream. "*This is the last time we'll be together like this.*"

Terror striking my heart, I glance around at my nephews,

my brother, my sisters, my aunt and uncle . . . and Ben, and I realize if I go far for school, this could be the last time for us all over again. Next to me on the deck, I slip my arm around Ben's waist and pull him into a side hug—and to my ecstasy, he lets me.

CHAPTER 18

THE SECRET RULE

Mama Bianchi's pie stand is a small canteen behind the former sculpture garden, just before the Vero Roseto property gates that lead into the dense thickets of Valle Forest. In the declining last few years, the neglected pie stand has become a vermin lair, so it needs a severe cute-ening. While I vacuum cobwebs from the corner, Ben leans against the pie stand's windowsill.

Things are getting . . . easy between us, and I like it.

A few days have passed since the Fourth of July, and miraculously, I don't regret relaxing the Ben Rule about ignoring our past. If anything, it's been a relief letting go of this anger. And not a moment too soon! The Rose Festival is in exactly one month, so I really should be focusing on developing more ambitious designs for the gardens. I've already got mounds of sketches up in my room for my living sculpture garden concept. Six models will replace the topiary animals, and each one of them will wear a gown crafted entirely of different roses and flowers. It's a great start, but I still don't have any idea what to do with the Wishing Rose garden.

Honestly, I've been avoiding it. Not just because of the memories, but because . . . I don't know. Hanging out, talking to Ben, and vacuuming rat shit is more relaxing. If I'm designing, that leads me to think about the future—about schools, about leaving Vero Roseto, about saying goodbye to Ben—and as soon as the festival is over . . . so are we.

"Got a question for you, if that's all right," Ben says, leaning across the windowsill like a pushy customer.

"Since when have you asked me permission for anything?" I ask, grinning.

A mischievous glint catches his eye. "Your curse. How many boyfriends would you say it's snatched away? I know about Hutch and Micah, but who else?"

It's a testament to the power of the Ben Rules that he could ask this question after a month of my being here, and it doesn't sting anymore. I shut off the vacuum and casually lean against the pie stand's daily offerings sign while I think out loud:

"There was Dylan Lee. Really good singer. Just these beautiful eyes, *oof*, they cut right into me." An awkward sigh stops my roll. "Realized he wasn't over his ex, and they got back together. Ruben De Soto was before him. We hooked up over the holidays. Just a painfully cute guy. Lots of piercings. He liked making these big plans. All he talked about for weeks was bringing me over to meet his family. I said it was too early, but he kept *digging* . . ." For some reason, I can't stop laughing at the memory. "When I finally said yes, he stopped texting. Just . . . gone, baby. Then I saw on his Instagram, he got together with this guy. His best friend."

Ben isn't relaxed anymore. He straightens upright and stares at me, gently.

"You don't need to do the pity thing, it's okay," I say, truly, honestly numb to these stories after so many retellings.

"I'm not pitying, I'm listening."

"So, you're probably sensing a pattern. Micah—got together with his best friend. Ruben—with his. Dylan—his ex. There's a few others before them, same sitch." To keep the peace, I keep up Ben Rule number two and don't mention Hutch, my first boyfriend who ditched me for his—and my—best friend, Ben. "They all had other guys waiting in the wings. They enjoyed my attention and then . . . something about me was just too scary, I guess. Not scary, maybe just . . . a lot." Laughing nervously, I pick up the hose again. "I swear, I tried to act as normal as possible for them. I tried."

"Maybe they saw someone acting." Ben *really* doesn't do pity, after all.

I fire up the vacuum, and the whir is so loud I have to shout like a reporter standing next to a helicopter. "People don't want real. They say they do, but they want real and fun. Not real and needs meds."

Ben doesn't blink. He shrugs and casually asks, "Do you take any meds?"

Once I've sucked up another trail of pine needles from the pie stand's floorboards, I cut the vacuum and face Ben. His face is open, nonjudgmental. With all my strength, I don't look away. "Lexapro since sophomore year. But I've been on and off it."

"How 'bout now?"

"Off."

"Why?"

I shrug, and that's the truth. "I thought I was better, so I stopped. Then I was not better, but I didn't feel like going through the sleepiness of the side effects again."

"And now?"

"I've been thinking it's time to make that call to Dr. Patty."

"Dr. Patty sounds cool."

"She is." On another vacuum *slurrrrp* of a cobweb, I grin at Ben. "She *hates* you."

"Well, fuck her." Boyishly, Ben grips the windowsill and hoists himself inside the pie stand. Sweat pins a dark red curl of his hair to his ear, and it just might be the cutest thing I've ever seen. Without another word, he wraps me in a hug, and I can't tell if I hate it or need ten thousand more. We haven't progressed beyond these friendly touches, and I'm not sure if we should. Even if my body is begging for the *other* thing.

"Thank you for telling me the truth," he says, breaking the hug. "And not being a fake bitch again."

I would scream, but it catches in my throat and becomes a laugh. "Anytime."

"You know, I had a Dr. Patty." I shut the vacuum without thinking twice and turn to him, imaginary popcorn in hand. "Dr. George. He thinks you suck."

"Is that right?"

Ben blinks first. "No, I never had time to bring you up. Only saw him a few times after my parents divorced."

"Why didn't you stay in it?"

"Dad stopped paying."

My smile drops. Matt McKittrick has been and will always be that rat. Still, Ben seems to only get more cheerful as he socks me in the shoulder. "Don't worry, I soaked him for a gym membership. Getting hot was great therapy."

I would kiss him, but my Secret Ben Rule is still in effect.

Besides, Ben and I have enough to worry about creating this festival. Now that the deck, lawn, pool, and vegetable garden are renovated, all Vero Roseto needs is the centerpiece: the rose and sculpture gardens. All month long, guests have been paying pilgrimage to the Wishing Rose and purchasing a hybrid (at a premium). There's already been two surprise wedding engagements the morning after a stop in the garden.

"Not that much of a surprise," Ben mumbles as later in the week, he and I join Mama Bianchi on her latest wine tour. One of the guests is a townie straight couple from Valle with their teenage son, whom Ben and I have nicknamed "Demon Twink."

Demon Twink is tall, blond, and tanned white, with a swimmer's build.

Everyone's basic nightmare, but Ben and I have spent the last month in a sex-free zone of teasing, tiny touches, and watching each other change out of our sweating shirts, so we are going to look at the pretty boy and hopefully release some of this tension later, alone (and separately) in the downstairs basement.

Demon Twink stays on his phone the entire tour while his white, middle-aged suburban parents are "selected" by Aunt Ro to receive Grato, which delights them.

Ben and I don't care he's on his phone. It allows us to hungrily track him through the crowd like two wolves spotting a fawn.

Who knew some low-stakes, low-expectations thirsting would be everything we needed?

If Ben and I were a couple, we'd take this energy from Demon Twink and unleash it on each other upstairs in my room . . .

Shit. He's seen us.

Demon Twink glances up, and Ben and I jerk our heads away simultaneously. When I glance back, Demon Twink laughs quietly to himself, makes full eye contact with me, and winks.

Ah. Serotonin. I thought I'd lost you.

"Get his room number," Ben mutters in my ear.

"No, no, no." I swat his shoulder. "I'm not doing anything with that."

Ben arches his eyebrow. "Just browsing?"

I'm not at Vero Roseto to browse. I'm here to help Aunt Ro save the place, heal my baggage with Ben, and then return to my real life. I wish it were that easy. That night, while I'm washing off my day in the shower, I don't think of Demon Twink. I replay Ben's hug in the pie stand. That tough little punch on my shoulder. That gleam in his eye.

I want to take care of him, but I can't. I can barely take care of myself.

But that doesn't stop me from dreaming.

CHAPTER 19

TWIN CURSES

The next morning, Vero Roseto's popularity gets another shot in the arm when a glowing review of our B&B and winery publishes on *Holiday*, which is evidently an enormously trafficked travel website in the UK. Our old friend Mr. Cartwright came through! Ben, Ro, Paul, and I huddle around our coffees in the kitchen and flip through the review, calling out our favorite snippets:

"'Mama Bianchi's showmanship alone is worth the price of admission,'" Ro gasps, delighted, as Paul massages her back.

"'The family that owns Vero Roseto still lives on-site after three-quarters of a century, bustling around you like delightful characters in a fairy tale,'" he reads.

I read, "'The romantic and magical myth of the Wishing Rose is irresistible to even the biggest skeptics. Don't miss your wish, but be warned: they do come true.'"

Oof. Hearing Mr. Cartwright echoing the warnings in my rose video reminds me just how seriously I've been taking this whole rose curse thing for so long. The longer I spend with Ben, the sillier that superstition has seemed. Still, superstition is good for business. Since that article was published, we sold over a hundred more tickets to the Rose Festival, which is bringing us dangerously close to a thousand.

"'And don't miss the local gardener,'" Ben reads with mock surprise. "'What a piece of ass!'"

"Oh!" Aunt Ro balls up her coffee-stained napkin and lobs it at him, which he ducks.

"*So* annoying!" I laugh.

"What?" Ben asks. "I'm flattered and humbled and . . ."

"All right, a toast!" Ro raises her mug to Paul, Ben, and me, and we join her. She takes a moment to say anything, and I know why: Italians (and especially the Italians in this family) are very, very jinx-phobic and careful to phrase their toasts so as not to accidentally doom themselves or the family in a monkey's paw–type situation. I mean, I've based my whole romantic life around such an error in wish-phrasing judgment. Finally, having decided on a path forward, she says, "To the four of us. We're doing good. Keep it up."

"KEEP IT UP!" We cheer, clinking mugs.

With his one review, published only four weeks before the festival, Mr. Cartwright has strengthened our myth. And the expectations.

The pressure isn't new to me—in fact, pressure is where I thrive (professionally, not romantically). Unlike previous times I've put on a large, anticipatory show, I'm not going to follow the internet chatter on this one. That's the last thing I need.

That afternoon, Ben and I take a walk to the back of Vero Roseto's grounds near the pie stand. Here, where the high trees make you feel insignificant to nature, Mama Bianchi had built an ivory gazebo with a swinging bench. Happily, Ro kept this maintained over the years.

"Thank God this works. I don't think I'd have the strength to rebuild a gazebo, too," Ben says, swaying beside me on the bench, his leg draped carelessly over the armrest.

"Please!" I agree, sketching an outline of the rose garden on my tablet. The gazebo turned out to be a perfect brainstorming spot, with full views of both the rose garden and the freshly mowed plot where the sculpture garden will be reconstructed. The Wishing Rose is concealed behind high green walls, which used to feel like a magnificent, fantastical realm when it was covered in snarling vines and blooms. It was important that they were removed once they rotted, but something just as fantastical will need to take their place.

And I only have a few weeks left to make it happen.

The labor involved in design and creation looks less impressive than the construction of a deck, but it can be just as draining. I delete sketch after sketch while Ben peeks over my shoulder—never offering feedback, just calmly watching, his eyes bright with amazement. Every once in a while, he'll mutter, "Wow," and when I delete it five minutes later, he whines, "What was the matter with that? It was gorgeous."

"But it's not right," I say.

"If you say so."

My ex and I used to create art together, and the back-and-forth of our brainstorming was exhilarating. Do I want this for me and Ben? I want him to feel like I welcome his opinions, because this reconstruction is just as much his as it is mine. But it's hard to tell what he wants, because Ben's waters run deeper and calmer than anyone I've ever been with.

Except I'm *not* with him!

God, I could smack myself with this tablet. What I've grown with Ben is intimacy, not romance. Complicated, abiding friendship love, not romantic love. It will be more lasting in the long run, even if it's not what I grew up wanting.

On my tablet screen, I've drawn and redrawn the Wishing Rose bush a dozen times. What could I do with that space that's fantastical, but different and new? Something that speaks to me and Ben. Our mud fight replays in my mind. Laughing with him again, freely, for the first time since our dreadful fight at Grandma's wake. The streams of water hitting him as he danced in my spray. The fountains, which Ben said not to fill because still water brings mosquitoes. Memories flutter, all the way back to the origin of my curse. All the tears they caused.

My eyebrow lifts.

Water. It's all about water.

Running water from the fountains. Cleansing sprays. Streams of tears from wishes that didn't go right, or wishes that ended a lifetime later in a funeral home, surrounded by grandchildren.

Invidioso e Grato. Love can't be appreciated until you've known the pain of being without.

"We need to surround the Wishing Rose with a fountain," I say, my heart racing with new ideas. Ben straightens against me, unseated as I lean deeper into my tablet, my electronic pen tracing streams of bright blue across the ground. "The fountains won't be those old-fashioned stone ones. We'll build a running river through it, kind of like a Zen garden, and it'll lead to the Wishing Rose. We'll put underlights in the river to make it reflect against the walls."

My hand whirls across the screen until the doodle is complete.

Two large streaks of blue run down from the rose bush. Ben makes an interested sound. "It looks like the Wishing Rose is crying."

"Exactly." My voice is clear. Energized. "It's love. Happy or sad, you always pay in tears."

"That's metal as hell." Ben snatches my tablet to get a closer look at the new concept. He turns to me, blinking heavily. "Who's building that?" Guiltily, I sputter laughter into my hand. "Aw shit, *me*?! Forget I said it was good."

"Nooooo! You and me together!" I thrust a tickle fit into his belly, and he squirms on the bench so much, it bounces on the gazebo's hinges.

"Okay, okayyyyyy! Stop tickling, I don't like it."

Instantly, I throw up my hands in surrender.

As Ben's laughter settles, he faces me, folding his legs on the hanging bench. "Since we're friends again, can I ask you something?"

Yes, you can kiss me.

"Sure," I say, shrugging as carelessly as I can manage with this much care in my body.

My heart has decided to stop beating until it knows how Ben will proceed.

I've been here before, deep in the bowels of the wine cellar, the Devil listening, waiting for my hand to fall lovingly on his wrist before he destroys me a second time.

"Is there something wrong with me?" Ben asks. I expel a wheezing laugh. "Don't answer yet! I'm just . . . you know how much I've dated and how quick my relationships are over."

"Well, I just assumed you were trying not to get tied down before you went back to Edinburgh . . ." My breath slowing, my eyes drift up. "Right?"

"Maybe. I don't really know what I want after this. Tending these grounds has been the biggest gardening project I've ever had to deal with. Maybe . . . if my dad's health stays all right . . . Going back might be the best place to keep up my skills?"

There it is: the future. Ben's thinking about it, and I have to, too.

The summer will be over soon, just like all those beautiful summers before they ended, and I have to be ready with my next step, just like Ben will be ready with his.

"But back to the guys thing," he says, tapping his lips. "It's like . . . when I'm with someone, and it's going fine, he's cute, we're vibing, but then . . ." Ben tosses his hands. "Meh. Two or three dates later, maybe four, he starts bugging the shit out of me, and my interest just floats away."

Ben turns his attention to the chain-link cord holding up our bench. He plays with it instead of looking at me—even though my eyes are far from judgmental.

On a pained laugh, he says, "I keep hurting people. It's like I can't stop. I *want* to get serious. I want to keep liking someone, but I can't. Then I see someone I want again and . . . the cycle starts all over." Shaking his head, he finally looks up. "What kind of person does that, knowing they just mess guys up?"

Now is not the time for touch. Or for romantic mixed signals. It's time for connection.

"You're not a bad person," I say. "You're just . . . not feeling it."

"It feels like I've got a curse, too."

I don't laugh. I know how serious it is to feel this way. "I'm cursed to never find someone who stays, and you're cursed to always leave."

He smiles weakly. "Good thing we're friends, then."

"Yeah." The word "friends" should feel like a hundred arrows to my chest, but there's a new lightness in me—a balance—where this doesn't upset me. Ben and I are rebuilding, slowly, like Vero Roseto, and soon, who knows? Maybe something happens.

Maybe he's the one who stays. Maybe I'm the one he stays for.

That whole last summer, I was with Hutch, but my true connection was with Ben. I just didn't know Ben could've liked me. Until suddenly, he was with Hutch.

Ben taps my ankle with his shoe. "So, you don't think I'm some lost cause monster?"

My usual desire to hurl shade doesn't come. Instead, I shake my head. "All relationships go away . . . until they don't. You wouldn't tell me to give up, would you?"

"Oh, you should give up."

I sweep his legs off the bench. "Aaaaaaasshole! I take it back! Monster. Beast."

Laughing, Ben throws his arms around me so quickly, I have to lift my tablet so it won't get crushed. My ex–best friend—now regular friend who's sort of flirty—rests his shimmering red head on my chest. Muffled, he says, "Thank you. I've been holding myself back for a while, but all this talk about taking chances and blah, blah, blah mushy stuff was starting to make me feel like . . . like I needed to start fresh, too."

I squeeze him tighter.

One day it will happen.

We both need time to rebuild, that's all. And when it happens, I could get my fairy-tale ending after all. I had the boy this whole time, from when we were kids. The failures, the rejections, the curse . . . All that was just to keep me free, so when Ben was ready, I'd be here.

The tears weren't meaningless. They served a purpose.

That night, after the last Mama Bianchi tour, the B&B guests settle in to watch the stars on the deck. I stand in the parlor, watching the view—and the guests—behind the screen door. A smattering of elderly couples clink glasses of chilled Invidioso, while the other couples enjoy full glasses of Grato. Demon Twink swims gracefully through the pool as the night lights turn on, casting flickering shadows of blue against the garden walls. Just as they will in the rose garden when we finish my installation.

"How long is Freddie going to be in that pool?" asks Demon Twink's mother. "This view! He's missing it. We have a pool at home."

"Kris, take it easy," her husband says, leaning across chairs to peck her cheek. "We wanted a nice staycation, so let's try to just enjoy it."

I snort to myself. Valle townies trying to break up their doldrums. Vero Roseto really is back to its glorious roots.

Aunt Ro sneaks up behind me. She's recently changed out of her Mama Bianchi frock and into a bunchy magenta sweater. She sighs happily and watches the stars. "I can't believe we're actually doing it," she says. "The view from this door has been depressing for years, and now people are paying us to look at it!"

"Next stop, Rose Festival," I whisper, nudging her. Her smile falters. "Don't worry. Ben and I came up with some exciting stuff today. Just gotta track down a few more places where we can buy the installations, but I promise you're gonna be blown away."

Beaming, she tugs my earlobe. "You and Ben together again."

"Ahh, slow it down—"

"Okay, okay—"

"One step at a time—"

"I know! It's just nice. I like it. Keep it up, you two."

"Yes, ma'am."

After Ro returns to the kitchen, my smile doesn't last long. Ben crosses the deck, but doesn't turn toward me in the parlor. He keeps walking . . . toward the pool . . . toward Demon Twink. Freddie. Ben kneels at the pool's edge, and Freddie breaststrokes toward him, his long, swimmer's legs pushing him gracefully.

Demon Twink emerges like a mermaid, torso out, arms folded along the pool edge as he gazes dreamily—blue eye-edly—up at Ben.

"So, uh, I've been thinking about what you asked this morning . . ." Ben says. My ears prick to catch every syllable. "And, uh . . . here. Call me."

Ben produces a scrap of paper. Freddie takes it slyly, a smirk crossing his handsome face. "Glad you changed your mind. I'll call you tomorrow, Rose Boy."

"Ben."

"Ben."

Freddie places Ben's number under a neon-teal beach towel and then pushes himself from the edge in an elegant glide.

Horrific realization crashes over me. Ben wasn't asking about his curse because of me. Some townie guest hit on him, and he wanted my permission to make his move.

Ben prances away from the pool and down the deck, looking every bit like the trickster he is. Before disappearing, he turns back to me at the screen door and flashes crossed fingers.

Smiling, I show him my own crossed fingers.

Wish me luck.

Luck. I wouldn't know it.

In the parlor, another oil painting of my great-grandmother—strong, imperious, and hiding within the petals of the Wishing Rose itself—laughs at me.

The curse is permanent. You can try, but alone is what you asked for. Alone is what you get.

CHAPTER 20

BED & BREAKFAST
& BETRAYAL

The following morning, I choose villainy.

This entire summer, I've been saying that Ben McKittrick charms you until you drop your guard, and that's when he sticks you with a knife. I didn't listen. I let Ben and A. C. and Uncle Paul and Aunt Ro and a million other people who act like they're therapists convince me how unhealthy it was to hold on to my baggage. How juvenile I was. How sad.

What they don't understand is that my baggage *protects* me. It isn't baggage, it's a boundary.

As I dash down the East Wing stairs for breakfast, I pause under my great-grandmother's portrait. Mama Bianchi—the iron-willed matriarch whose magical rose showers blessings of love to everyone in her family except for me. I sneer at her. I want to slash that portrait like I scratched out my own face from the Art Institute magazine. My heart hurts with a blackened, charred pain.

This *place*! Why did I come back here? Why did I trick

myself into thinking it would be good to face all this bullshit again: my family, the rose, *Ben McKittrick*.

Even in Chicago, even as I was finally building a new, powerful identity away from these people, this *smallness*, Mama Bianchi's curse—the curse of *Ben*—found me. That's why I never could blame my exes for dumping me. It's almost as if they never had a choice.

Ben. Ben again.

Playful tapping. Tickling. Nuzzling. Wrestling. Reminiscing. I liked it because I thought this meant something, but it was just a way of getting me to drop my guard. After our huge falling-out, Ben needed my foolish, puppyish devotion again, or what good could I be to him?

Now he's going to do the same thing to this poor townie, Demon Twink.

Well, it's time to course correct. If I can't be the hero of my own fairy tale, then I'll be the villain everyone thinks I am, because I won't be anyone's helpful stepping stone ever again.

Leaving Mama Bianchi's portrait with another death glare, I continue toward the West Wing parlor, where the buttery scent of freshly cooked waffles greets me. The guest-facing cousin to Aunt Ro's old-fashioned East Wing kitchen, the parlor is the coziest room in Vero Roseto. A handful of guests eat breakfast at a smattering of round, rustic tables beside a roaring fire. Other guests have taken large mugs of coffee to one of the many cushy armchairs next to the latticed windows that look out onto the vineyards. Along the walls, bookshelves offer mysteries, true crime, and book club picks—both Oprah and Reese.

My heart lifts when I spot him, all alone, eating a waffle: Freddie—the Demon Twink. It's late in the morning; his parents—like Ro and Ben—must've risen early and already eaten.

See? I haven't embraced villainy for more than an hour, and fortune is already smiling on me.

Quickly, I make myself a waffle in the self-serve cast-iron skillet, pour a cup of black coffee, and approach Freddie. His pool-blue eyes widen. Like every guest, my Cursed Wish confession video is probably the reason he's here.

Good Grant would have cowered under this knowledge, but I'm Evil Grant, and nothing will weaken my heart again.

"Mind if I join you?" I ask, already setting down my food.

"Sure!" he says, scooting his plate to make room. "Was having a boring morning anyway. My folks left at six for a forest hike."

I groan sympathetically and devour a big slice of waffle. "So. My gardener friend tells me he's very excited to get to know you."

Freddie's mouth drops open. "So you *do* know Ben real well?"

Laughing, I slurp my coffee like a Viking guzzling mead. "Oh, I know Ben. We grew up in this house."

"Did you two ever . . . ?" Freddie leans in curiously.

Momentarily stunned, I remember that I'm Evil Grant, not

nice, bullied, pushover Grant. Lies come easily. "That was a long time ago. I moved on, but we stayed close. I probably know him better than anyone."

As I carve out another waffle slice, I catch Freddie scanning me warily. Will he take my bait?

Ask me, bunny. Ask me how well I know that beast.

"What's he like?" Freddie asks, and my heart smiles. Three roses—jackpot.

Laughing darkly, I lean back and down the rest of my coffee. "Ben McKittrick . . . Well, he's not afraid to cry. *Loves* talking through his feelings. Don't let the tough groundskeeper look trick you, he's much more at home staying in, cuddling in front of an old movie. Doesn't even really like hooking up."

"Really?" Fascinated, Freddie leans closer, pressing his slender hands to his cheeks.

"Yeah." I wince, thinking up as many lies as I can. "He couldn't really keep up. I just wasn't able to give him what he wanted. In fact, I wouldn't try doing anything with him until, like, the fourth date. He likes to make sure he's *really* with someone special first."

"Got it. Wow." Thrown for a loop, Freddie just nods and checks his texts.

"Yeah, that's our Ben. Great guy." Sighing happily, I finish the remains of my waffle. "Really looking to get into something serious, you know? Plant some roots."

"Totally." Freddie is growing quieter by the second.

"That's what you're looking for, too, right?"

"Absolutely! I mean, I'm open to that."

I narrow my eyes. This isn't good enough. I need one more thing about Ben, something to scare this bunny away for his own good. He's only going to get trampled if I let this go on, and this poor kid won't be expecting the pain like I was when the Ben Truck hit me.

"He told you about Scotland, right?" I ask.

Freddie brightens. "Yeah, his accent is cute."

"No, like, you know he's going back there?"

The boy's smile weakens. ". . . When?"

I shrug carelessly. "Don't know. He's always talking about it. His mom's back there. He's just sticking around to help with the Rose Festival, but then . . ." I throw up my hands, and Freddie's smile vanishes. "I'm sure for the right guy, he'd take you with him. That could be a fun adventure, right?"

"Right . . ." he says breathlessly, glancing at his mug.

I don't think happiness has ever come as easily before I turned villainous. More people should look into this, it's solid therapy.

Yet when Freddie sips again, his face seems to change. No longer smiling and sweet, he hardens his glare into something hateful. "Do you think I'm stupid?" he whispers.

"What?" His voice is so dark, the room temperature plunges thirty degrees.

"You're making up stuff about Ben just to get me to break off our date." Freddie leans closer, his voice lower than ever. "I saw your rose video. I felt bad for you for what happened, even when my friends thought you came off really angry and toxic. But they were right. You're just . . . broken, aren't you?" An invisible dart pierces my chest as the room darkens around my periphery. A nasty sneer comes over the boy. "I bet nothing ever even happened between you and Ben. But you wanted it to, right? This is pathetic jealousy. I see right through you."

I've gone blank, like a robot switched off. Grant Rossi is currently unavailable.

"You don't know me" is all I can squeak out.

The rage swarming my body gives me strength enough to finally stand. Without another word, I hurry past the other guests reading books by the fire before running into Uncle Paul. "Oh, Grant, you get breakfast yet?" he asks. "We're closing up the griddles."

"I'm fine," I grunt, charging past him, out of the West Wing and into the entryway. I can already feel the storm building in me. I need to get to my room as soon as possible.

But the universe, as always, has horrible plans.

Under the portrait of Mama Bianchi, I collide with Ben, whose work tank top is already stained with grass and sweat. "Sorry there," he says.

"Your *boyfriend* is at breakfast," I snarl.

Ben laughs uneasily, instantly clocking my darkness. "Cool, well, one step at a time on that. I'm gonna snag some waffles."

My hands shake with rage just looking at him. This boy, constantly living in blissful innocence about the boundless ugliness of this world. My jaw trembles as I growl, "You're too late. Paul's closed up the food."

"Ah, really? I had an early morning, I'm starving."

"Then STARVE!"

I run before I can see Ben's reaction—or, more importantly, before he can see my tears—but I know he's shouting at me to come back. My voice sounded so ugly. I hate my rage. I don't want to be a villain anymore. I shouldn't have yelled like that. I'm ugly, I'm jealous, I'm pathetic, I'm a monster, just like everyone's always said.

The rose isn't the curse.

Ben isn't the curse.

I am. It's me. It was always me.

Those boys left because they sensed something was very wrong with me, and if I don't push Ben away now, he'll get swallowed up in my curse next. He deserves anything else but that.

I bound up the East Wing stairs, two at a time, three at a time, more beast than boy, and don't stop until I reach my room. I throw the door shut with a thunderous slam that rocks the walls of Vero Roseto like the cheap sets of a high school play and then lock myself inside. Unable to catch my breath or stop my reddening hands from shaking, the tears break like a typhoon. Guttural, animal sounds escape my chest as I sob and slide to my knees.

Standing is impossible.

Thinking is impossible.

Everything is pain.

No one is rooting for you, Grant.

"I didn't do anything," I moan into the floorboards, writhing in agony.

Knocks come on my door, but my head is filling with so much fluid, I can barely hear who's calling my name. As if I would answer.

Slowly, I crawl underneath the bed until I'm completely hidden. I want my sleeping bag. I want my life back when I would lie here, side by side with Ben without knowing that was the happiest I'd ever be. I wish I knew then it would never get any better than that era. I would've enjoyed it more.

Some villain I turned out to be, crying in a ball under my bed.

I ignore the desperate knocks from outside.

I'm not moving, not for anyone. No one would understand what's wrong anyway. I'm the only one who knows how easily a bunny can bruise a beast.

CHAPTER 21

ORIGIN OF THE BEASTS

Laughter from outside won't stop spilling into my bedroom. It's ruining my staring at the abyss. What I stare at changes every few hours—the other day, it was the curtains. I saw a hot gardener outside those curtains once, and it ruined me. Yesterday, it was my jacket, slung over a rocking chair in the corner. The jacket is black vegan leather with a hand-stitched pumpkin across the back—its vines are identical to the ones Mama Bianchi carved into the entrance of Vero Roseto. I made that jacket. It got me into my Chicago design program.

It got my ex to notice me on the train when we were just strangers.

Every time I look at it, I don't see me, I see my squandered promise.

Today, I stare at my grandma's old Singer sewing machine on the writing desk by the window. She brought design into my life. She guided me, even if she didn't always choose her words right about my gayness.

I need to get my hands sewing again. I need the tactile.

An odd heaviness, more powerful than gravity, pulls me

deeper into my bed. I haven't left it since that horrible break-fast days ago. After a while, Ro, Paul, and Ben stopped knock-ing and trying to coax me outside like I was a frightened cat. Now they leave trays of food outside my door like they would for guests, and as of yesterday, I started eating again. I only leave to use the bathroom, and everyone has correctly intu-ited that they aren't to use that window of opportunity to corner me. Like Mama Bianchi, I occupy the house, but I am neither present nor corporeal.

I'm not alone, though. I'm here with my sublime terror, a terror which grows more powerful with every second I spend in this room, a terror of knowledge that I came to Vero Roseto to escape my problems, but that I've somehow become more lost than ever.

So lost I'm unable to see the road anymore.

Hilariously, this terror has one enemy, one chunk of Kryp-tonite that keeps it at bay: when I eat a sandwich. Ro's paninis, stuffed with Grandma's bread patties and a tangy smack of tomato, and suddenly the road becomes a bit more visible.

Why is a sandwich so powerful?

Either way, I'm grato. Today is better than yesterday. I try not to doom-scroll too much on Instagram. Eshana texted me, and I responded with some pleasant niceties—I've scared her enough this year, and she needs to be able to live her life without being on Grant Watch twenty-four seven.

After finishing the panini, I fix my hair, smooth my bed-sheets, and open a Zoom link on my phone. The one good thing I did the day everything fell apart was email Dr. Patty. In my darkness, I was shocked she even remembered me. My low point triggers are always invisibility and self-worth. Who am I to be remembered? But in Dr. Patty's infinite goodness, she welcomed me back without judgment and with (thank GOD) an opening in her schedule.

"Good afternoon, Grant," Dr. Patty says on the video call. She's in her seventies, white, with frizzing, wild silver curls. She looks like my grandmother did in her better years. She's draped in sherbet-colored scarves like some daffy, beloved art teacher. Dr. Patricia Asp (call her Dr. Patty) brings the sunshine crashing into the storm clouds in my brain.

"Good afternoon," I say back, already wiping a tear. Her presence is just that welcome. In the picture-in-picture window, I see my unshaven reflection and hiss like Dracula in a mirror. "I look awful, sorry."

Dr. Patty chuckles amiably. "You are beautiful. Now. It sounds like we've got some catching up to do." We spend most of the hour catching up on my summer: Vero Roseto's problems, the high stakes of the Rose Festival, telling off A. C., and . . . Ben. At his name, she brightens. "Ben. *The* Ben? There? How do you feel about that?"

My smile fights against a swell of tears. "I missed him so much. And it's been so nice, and we were getting better, but then . . . I don't know what he wants from me. It's making me feel so flooded, and I just want to relax around him, but I can't. Maybe if we'd done this a few years ago, I'd be able to calm down, but it just feels like too much has happened. I can't trust him. And I don't know if that's a him problem or a me problem, or both, but I just know that I can't." My lip quivers like a leaf weighted down by a spring rain. I can't look up at Dr. Patty, who stays quiet. The soft crackle of the Zoom's silence fills my room. "It doesn't matter anyway. In a few weeks, the festival is gonna be over, and he's gonna leave for Scotland. I don't know where I'm going."

"You're not going to design school?" Dr. Patty asks, concerned but very gentle. "I know that was in your plan."

I sniff loudly. "Yeah. Still is. I just . . . lost track of time."

Stuck in the past is more like it.

"If it still is your plan," she says, "I think sending some applications in would be a good way to take your mind off this Ben thing, don't you? Maybe it'll help you calm down enough to see him with more clarity. Two birds, one stone?"

Dr. Patty understands everything.

Brightness rushes into my chest at the possibility that I *can* organize myself out of this mess. It's what I do best. Well, it's what I *did* best, but I can get back there.

We set a time to talk again later in the week (there's still so much more Ben to cover), and she renews my script for Lexapro. Brightened, but not repaired, I continue to camp out in the room. However, it stops becoming a prison and is more like a safe cocoon. I can't open that door again until I'm sure I'm strong enough to fly out of here like a gorgeous monarch butterfly.

Two days pass. In that time, I stumble on a few design schools abroad, mainly to check how late I could submit a portfolio. Milan. Paris. London. All of them feel so . . . far. Not physical distance, but in the way they extend my grasp. I melted down in Chicago, am I really gonna go be a designer in *Milan* without self-destructing? Ro's paninis won't be able to find me there.

After sending off a few emails, I give up the hunt and return to my abyss staring.

The laughter and splashing from the pool outside reminds me I want to stay right where I am for a while. I've heard laughter and splashing in this room before—it's a nostalgic sound—but I know it's not my siblings and cousins outside. They've grown up. Those times are gone.

Everyone has moved on but me.

Not anymore.

I peel off my baggy gray shirt and let my chest breathe. In the floor-length mirror, the reflection of my chest confirms my brain is a liar: I'm still hot shit.

The Singer turns on with a startling rattle, and it rumbles against the old writing desk like knuckles. With two swift *snips*, I shear off my shirt's stanky sleeves, and another few *snip-snips* removes the collar and most of the chest. Gradually, I feed thread and cloth into the Singer.

Rattle-rattle-rattle.

My grody shirt disappears inside its gears, but my hands

remember exactly how to do this. I don't think about Ben, or my exes, or how much I think I belong in the deepest, darkest dumpster forever; in fact, I don't think at all. My hands do.

My eyes sharpen.

The room comes into full clarity.

And after a few minutes, the shirt exits the Singer as a fresh tank top with the biggest Italian Tits McGee plunging neckline I could manage. A smile slowly returns. Whatever I am, at least I'll look hot.

The moment I shut off the Singer, a knock shakes my door. A thundering cop knock.

A spike of fear drives through my chest. Oh my God. Aunt Ro called doctors. I withdrew too much, scared her too badly, and she's called people to help. Scrambling to the door in nothing but my pajama bottoms, I pull on my new tank and start pacing in place.

What if I just grabbed my stuff and ran? I can go back to my studio in Chicago and be a bummer there. I won't get meals, but at least people will leave me alone.

"Grant, can you hear me?" Ben's voice comes gently through the door.

My anxious pacing stops. "I'm fine, Ben."

"Not what I asked. Can you hear me?"

"Obviously!"

"Grant, I don't want to have this conversation through a door, but if you're not gonna let me in, that's what I'm gonna do, and everyone downstairs is gonna hear it."

"Jesus Christ," I grunt, yanking open the door. My agitation leaves me when I see how handsome Ben looks: no gardener work clothes, freshly showered, ruddy hair styled in a slick little bounce, and a hunter-green coat with a wool collar. And I look like a drowned rat with visible nips.

"Hey," I say, not meeting his eyes. "You look like you're going on a date."

"Well, I'm not," he says with a hint of anger. "Let me in?"

As soon as he's inside, I lock the door. He stands stiffly, not taking a seat. I approach slowly, my back hunched in shame, and defensiveness comes pouring out: "Look, I'm really okay. Every once in a while, I get like this, and I just need to be alone for a few days and then I'm fine." When he doesn't respond, I confess, "I'm so sorry I yelled at you. There's no excuse."

He sighs, as if he wants to be angry but can't. "How are you feeling now?"

"I'm fine, I told you."

"You slammed this door so loudly, paintings fell down. Ro and I heard you through the door for hours. Talking to yourself. Crying." Ben's hard eyes soften, and he touches my elbow. The gentleness makes me flinch so hard my body spasms. "You're saying this happens a lot? When you're in the city . . . and alone?"

Humiliation burns my neck, cheeks, and ears. It's everywhere. I can't believe I let myself be seen like that, especially by Ro and Ben, who care about me but who—for different reasons—I don't want knowing how intense I can get.

"I take care of myself okay," I say, puffing my barely concealed chest.

Ben doesn't blink. "I don't think you do. You don't have to feel this way."

I nod, unable to look at him. "I called Dr. Patty, and she wrote a new script for Lexi."

"Lexi?"

"Pro. Lexapro." I roll my eyes. "Gay."

"GAY." He snorts. "Okay, great, I'm proud of you. When's it ready for pickup?"

I pick at my nails. "Yesterday . . ."

"Then it's ready!" Ben doesn't drop his energy for a beat before tapping my shoulder—not affectionately, but to make sure he's got my attention. "I know what that twink said to you. It's over. It was never really on, but just know . . ." He makes a cutting motion across his throat. "I'm sorry that happened. You know I never would've allowed that if I was there, right?"

"I know. You're a good guy, Ben. And I'm . . . not." I wince back a stabbing pain in my chest. Guilt. "I brought it on. I said shit, lies, to make him not interested in going on your date." I can't stop shaking my head. "Movie villain behavior."

Ben nods, restrained as ever. "I heard about that, too. Want to tell me what that was about?"

Scoffing, I throw up my arms. "You don't know?"

He smirks. "I know, but I want to hear you say it. I think I've earned that."

Looking into Ben's eyes, while he looks this perfect and I look this goblin-esque, I mutter, "I was jealous, and I wanted to date you."

Victorious, Ben thrusts both arms to the sky. "FINALLY, YOU ADMIT IT."

"Don't get smug!"

"How long have we known each other?"

"Ten years."

"I have waited *ten years* to hear you admit this shit."

I roll my eyes. "You have *not* been clocking my crush since we were eight."

Chuckling, Ben grips his head. "Your problem is you think you suffer in silence, when in reality, every day with you—from back then to now—has been one big Italian opera. You have many talents, but hiding what you're feeling isn't one of them."

I jab his chest. "Did you come up here to make me feel worse?"

"No." He snatches my finger and holds it. He steps closer, until we're inches away. "I have the day off, and I want you to come with me into town to meet someone for coffee. Not a date, an old friend. You owe me. I should be kicking your ass more about your snake behavior, but I think Demon Twink punished you more than enough. Shower up those tiddies."

Ben flicks one of my highly visible nips, and it wakes me up. All right, so he still wants to hang out with me. Good enough for now.

An hour later, I've scalded off my depression skin with a hot shower, dressed in Uncle Paul's all-black server outfit (Ben insisted I'd want to look as good as possible), and driven into Valle with Ben to pick up my prescription and meet his old friend. The quaint village lies in the hollow between two massive forests. Everything is tailor-made for tourists and staycationers: bookshops, antique stores, fishing gear shops, and cafés. Everything you'd need to while away your hours in your rented cabins before it was time to return to the lake.

Ben parks outside Smalley's Bistro, a cozy spot with exposed brick and even more exposed ductwork. Before exiting, he turns to me, anxiety tattooed on his face—a rarity for Ben.

"What?" I ask.

He licks his lips uncertainly before answering: "Just know I would've waited to do this until later if we didn't have the Rose Festival to get back to."

"Waited to do *what*?" I glance around. "Is this a hit? Are you gonna kill me?"

He smirks, confidence flowing back. "I'm not gonna kill you until I get paid through the summer. Meet me inside."

Ben runs inside to meet our mystery guest, but before I

follow him, I give myself a quick glance in the rearview mirror. Blemish-free, bouncy curls, dimples for days. I emerged from a three-day depression hole less than an hour ago, and I'm still gonna be the cutest one in the room.

Who else but me? I can do it all! Lowest lows, highest highs.

Okay, babe, well, we're gonna see about that, says the Lexi bottle chilling in my pharmacy bag.

Yet from the moment I step inside the café, I realize yes, this is a hit.

Ben waits at a table next to a breathtakingly handsome boy who is eagerly awaiting my arrival. The short boy has light olive skin, accentuated by his Day-Glo yellow tank top, a swoop of jet-black hair, and a bright smile with two prominent front teeth like a chipmunk. A cutie I could recognize a mile away, even though the last time I saw him was five years ago. Unlike me and Ben, he's barely grown an inch.

Nick Hutchinson.

Hutch.

Ben brought me to see Hutch, the boy who dumped me via my best friend by *revealing* he was dating him, all during my grandmother's wake.

"Grant!" Hutch yelps, running to meet me.

I freeze like it's a police raid. The little guy can only reach my chest as he wraps a hug around me. It's brief but terrible. I'm being attacked by a terrier. "It's been forever, oh my God!" Hutch gasps, his voice noticeably more fem than when we were younger. He pulls me to his table, where he's got an extra to-go latte waiting.

While I glare daggers into Ben, who stays smugly quiet, an amped-up Hutch continues to mouth diarrhea about his life: "I'm moving to LA, can you believe?! I've got singing classes lined up, but this guy already messaged me saying he has a modeling job for me! I was like 'WHAT? Okay, creep,' but then I googled him and he's totally legit, so I don't know, I might *do it*? I just feel like I have to take every opportunity, you know? Gah, I'm blabbing."

I chuckle uncomfortably. "How many lattes have you had?"

Laughing, Hutch grips my wrist. "Two!"

"Listen, Hutch—"

"Oh. It's Nicholas." Hutch's sunny expression darkens, as if I've broken some serious etiquette by calling him the nickname he once demanded we adopt.

Ben and I exchange hard glances before I continue: "*Nicholas. I*—"

Hutch drums excitedly against my arm. "I cannot believe you're back! We thought you were gone, gone, gone, big city, red carpets—I have been so inspired by you, by the way—and then I saw your *video*." Hutch presses a hand to his heart. "I had no idea I had that kind of impact on you."

Hellfire erupts behind my irises.

His impact on *me*? That was Hutch's big takeaway from my "I convinced myself I could wish away my gayness, and it destroyed my mental health forever" video.

"Ben, why am I here?" I ask quietly.

"What?" Hutch asks, grinning as if he didn't catch that.

"Nicholas, sit," Ben says, waving for his attention. Hutch doesn't oblige. We're all standing around a table while he sips his iced latte and waits for Ben to say what's on his mind. As do I. "I'm going to tell Grant how you and I got together in eighth grade."

Hutch's eyes widen in fear. "You said we weren't gonna."

"Yeah, well, now we're gonna. Grant's processing a lot and deserves the truth. Plus, wouldn't you like to start your new LA life with a clean slate?"

Hutch can't look at either of us. "My slate is clean."

"Hutch."

"Nicholas."

"Sit!"

We both listen this time. The tension in the café thickens as Ben stares into Hutch's soul. I don't speak. I'm not even angry anymore. My curiosity is too high that there's a previously unknown piece of the Ben–Hutch puzzle they've been keeping from me all this time.

Finally, Hutch rolls his eyes. "Whatever, it's not a big deal. It's ancient history. We were kids . . ." Then his eyes find mine. His smile drops. He must have seen some deeper wound in me that he wasn't expecting.

Slowly, beneath the table, Ben's hand slides onto my knee, and my heart finally slows. He looks at me, and in a rarity for him, there's no smirk this time. No twinkle. Ben is looking at me with softness, vulnerability, and genuine affection. It's more than my nerves can handle, but I don't look away.

After all, Ben has been hinting this whole summer that I "got the story wrong" between us, and he wouldn't have gone through all this trouble to bring Hutch back into our lives if there weren't *something* new to tell. But what could I have missed the first time around?

"Grant," Ben begins slowly, biting back a deep, quiet pain. "When you visited, you and Nicholas hung out—and eventually became boyfriends—but I already knew him from school. But you and me had gotten so close, it never felt like I was the third wheel."

Hutch snorts. "Felt like *I* was the third wheel . . ."

"Shush." And Hutch listens. I just stare at Ben, trying desperately to picture Dr. Patty's warm, inviting face urging me to listen, to hear Ben out, not to listen to my inner demon telling me to cuss them both out and run back to Chicago. As Ben rubs my knee, he continues: "But each time you left, each time fall came around, it hurt. Hurt us both." I glance at Hutch, who nods, seemingly against every fiber of his being to admit such a thing. I return to Ben, whose face is still vulnerable and open. "When you came back to Vero Roseto that last summer, and you started actually dating Nicholas, I got depressed. Things were really bad at home, like you know, but really, I was already dreading you leaving as soon as you came."

"I dreaded it, too," I admit, biting back the words *And I'm dreading this current summer ending!*

Ben sucks in a deep breath, a brave breath. I hold mine. This is it. "One night, you were busy with family, and Nicholas and I hung out . . . I told him how I was feeling about you leaving. After we talked for a while, he asked if we could make out, and we did."

I squint with a twinge of frustration. "Okayyyy, but I know this already."

"Oh, do you? Do you know everything?" Ben asks, somewhat snippily, before turning on Hutch. "And what did I say when you asked me to make out?"

"I was thirteen." Hutch laughs. "Who knows who said what?"

But Ben does. Recalling the incident with brutal clarity, he leans across the table and whispers, "I asked, 'What about Grant?' And you said . . ." Ben waits for Hutch to say something—anything—but my original ex is clearly clueless or refusing to damn himself in front of me. So Ben completes the picture. "You said, and I quote, 'Grant dumped me. It's over.' Then you said, *very shadily,* 'Oh, he didn't tell you? I thought he told you everything.'"

I spin on Hutch, my nails digging into the wicker chair. "You WHAT?"

"And then he stuck his tongue down my throat," Ben finishes.

Forgetting my delicately coiffed hair, I grip my curls with

both fists and try to process the unprocessable. Hutch lied to Ben about us being broken up to get with him, then basically forced Ben to break up with me for him.

Hutch can only sit there, sucking down his iced latte as if the faster he's done, the faster he can scram out of here. "I really thought the three of us were just gonna catch up," he says, texting someone else furiously. "Maybe hook up or something. Guess not." He finally sets his phone down, his eyes genuinely vulnerable. "I lied! I was a horny kid! Okay? I'm sorry. I'm a different person now. Plus, you both ended up tall, so you got your revenge."

The room vanishes. Everything disappears except me and my new knowledge. This whole time I thought Ben stole my summer boyfriend, just before I was going to break up with him for real and ask out Ben. This whole time . . . I've been hating Ben McKittrick, and he's only ever been a friend. It was Hutch all along.

That's what Ben wanted me to hear so badly.

Minutes later, with everyone out of the hanging out mood, I hug Hutch goodbye and sincerely wish him well on the West Coast. Strangely, my anger can't and won't attach to him. He's right. We're all different people now, and that drama feels so far away. So why do I feel it more intensely when it's Ben? Because at the time, five years ago, I handled my disappointment abysmally. I didn't ask questions. I didn't give my best friend the benefit of the doubt. I made my assumptions, and then started roaring my lungs out at him at my grandma's wake. I hurt his feelings as bad as I possibly could, and then refused to talk to him.

The problem *is* me.

Once Ben and I are alone in the parked car, I take his hand— not intimately, but as a friend. "I abandoned you, didn't I?" I ask carefully.

He squeezes my hand, his jaw angrily set. "You did."

"You've always had my back, haven't you?"

"I have."

"I really messed up." I squeeze his hand. "It all went down that year. You, me, Hutch, your parents' divorce, my grand-parents. All of it."

Ben nods heavily. "One bomb after another took us all out." He wets his lips. For a moment, I think he means to kiss me—but he stays in the driver's seat. "I know you've got demons, I know that. But I'm not one of them."

My hand feels too weak to keep holding his, but I refuse to drop his first. Through a throbbing, swimming headache, I say, "I'm sorry. I hate myself."

"I don't want that." Looking sick, Ben pulls my hand to his lips. It's so loving and so nice, it burns my heart. I don't deserve it. I don't deserve any of the memories we've made this summer. It's been up and down, but now that I know the truth, all I can think of is how much more fun we could've had if I hadn't been so busy hating him for a lie.

"So, what do you want?" I ask.

Ben bites his lip, as if what he's about to say requires

inhuman courage. "I feel the same way you feel about me, always have."

It's what I've dreamed of hearing my whole life, but now that I've heard it, everything feels broken.

Ben calms himself with steady breaths and then looks at me squarely. "You've got Ben Rules, but I have some Grant Rules, okay? Grant Rule number one: You can't think I'm your enemy. You can't make bad assumptions about me. You tried to snake my date away from me instead of just owning up to what you felt and *fucking asking me for what you wanted.* That was a bad move. The only reason I'm not angrier with you is that you've kicked your own ass enough this week."

Gathering a brave breath, I nod. "What's Grant Rule number two?"

He smirks. "How 'bout you try mastering rule number one for a while first?"

My mouth opens, but no sound comes out. He's right. All I can do is nod.

A few minutes later, we arrive back at Vero Roseto, but Ben idles the car outside the arched entrance with the carved rose vines. It's his day off, and both of us need to process the last hour for a bit before we jump right back into fixing the rose garden. He leaves the car idling and walks me under the arch. The air is sweet with honeysuckle. The frog song in the river behind Valle Forest has never been more symphonic.

The lowering sun catches Ben's auburn hair, and it's more than fiery, it's like the sunset itself.

"Thank you for not running out when you saw Hutch," he says. "Thank you for hearing me out and believing me."

"I'm sorry it took me so long," I say.

He smiles sadly. "I knew you'd need him there to really believe the story."

"No—" I reach for his hand, but he slides gently away.

"It's okay, I don't blame you. We're rebuilding trust. It won't be overnight."

My hands drop to my sides. There's no use denying it. It did help a lot to hear Hutch's confession. Would I have believed Ben if it were just him telling the story? Probably, I'm not a monster, but the little voice in my head would've found it convenient that Hutch has been the villain all along, and poor, sweet bestie Ben was cruelly led astray.

We lost five years because of this lie. It's almost too awful to comprehend.

"Today was a great first step, for you, me, and Lexi," he says, taking my hand. "Because I needed all this truth out in the open before . . ."

I swallow hard. My hand goes limp in his. "Before what?"

Without warning, Ben McKittrick brings himself close, grips a handful of my curls, and does what I should have done five years ago in that wine cellar. He kisses me.

His kiss fizzes inside my head like freshly poured ginger ale. The taste is sweet, with a hint of the caramel bullshit he drank in the café.

Then it's over. A quick kiss, not the prelude to a make-out session.

"That was a sample," he says, winking. "Your aunt is losing it over this Rose Festival. We gave you your space because you had a rough one, but we're four days behind, and we *need* you. Are you gonna help?"

I glide my tongue across my bottom lip, still tasting that bite of caramel.

"Depends," I say.

"On what?" he asks.

"If I can kiss you again."

Ben's eyebrow arches as he returns to his car. "It'll be more fun if I make you earn it."

I hate him so much. But now, finally, for the right reasons.

As Ben drives away, I smile, realizing something else: He knew to drop me at the archway. He knows I like to run the gravelly path all the way up to the house. He knows me better than anyone. Supercharged with more strength than I've had in years, I take off toward Vero Roseto's front porch like a jungle cat. I've never run faster.

CHAPTER 22

MY EX LOVED SHIT LIKE THIS

The next few weeks at Vero Roseto are disorienting. Everything appears to have gone back to normal: Aunt Ro doing Mama Bianchi wine tours, Ben maintaining the grounds, and me upstairs drafting sketches for the festival on my tablet. Between sketches, I start auto-sending applications to design schools across Europe and the UK. My biggest swing is University of the Arts London. Their reputation is impeccable, their website is top-notch, and . . . it's only a handful of hours from Edinburgh.

Am I coldly strategizing for my future? Yes. Is it healthy? That's for Dr. Patty to decide.

Everything feels different in a post-kissing-Ben world. My heart's greatest desire for the last billion years has been fulfilled, and I'm supposed to just go on with my life as usual?

Yes, dummy.

Ben doesn't do relationships, and I no longer do the thing where I let my career dreams get entangled with boys I like.

We kissed, but we're not dating. Maybe we'll have some fun, but it's better for me if I keep things simple and . . .

disappointing. Maybe there's no great love story here, just a sweet epilogue to a great friendship before I start my life over.

But I want Ben. As my digital pen crosses over my tablet, all I can think about is that caramel-sweet kiss (and wondering when the hell it's going to happen again). I want Ben, but I have to be smart. This whole situation will be mental health quicksand for both of us if I don't step around it correctly. Besides, Ben and I have too much work to do for the festival, and our situation (whatever it is) can be a highly disruptive force.

"I appreciate you being so honest with me about becoming intimate with Ben," Dr. Patty says during our virtual session (our fourth so far). Unlike the other times we've talked over Zoom, I'm showered and dressed in something other than pajamas. Despite her affirming words, Dr. Patty's brow is wrinkled with worry. "And I'm relieved to hear that he was not as *duplicitous* as we once thought."

"But?" I ask.

"But nothing. I think you're a smart boy who's aware of the pitfalls of getting closer with someone who's been so much baggage for you, so I don't need to remind you to be careful."

A numb, heavy weight settles over me. "Him leaving?"

"There's that. But that's just geography. The real issue is trust. In our first session, when you were so desperate, you told me whether it was his issue or yours, you felt you couldn't trust him. Now, you may have learned some new truths since then that alleviates his guilt, but . . . you said his issue *or yours*. And trauma, based in truth or not, leaves scar tissue. If you are going to keep this boy in your life"—I launch forward in bed to correct her, but she's way ahead of me—"whether you date him, whether you build a life with him, or whether you are just casually kissing him this summer . . . you're going to have to deal with your scar tissue. You lost him, you lost Hutch, you lost your grandparents, you lost your big family summers, and you felt abandoned by your family's myth—which is really about feeling abandoned by your family—all in a single moment." Dr. Patty raises a finger to the camera, her creased eyes filling with compassion, and I hold my breath. "Your life changed overnight, and it was so disruptive, you were so vulnerable, that you felt you had to become a new person just to survive. That's a lot for a thirteen-year-old. It's a lot for anyone."

I cursed myself.

The kid I was, the person I was becoming before the events of that summer happened . . . he died. A beast took his place. He wore my face, but he lived with a new anger that grew and grew until it became his whole identity.

On the bed, I mop tears from the corners of my eyes with tissues I now keep handy on the side table. Dr. Patty's expression softens. "I'm not trying to bring you down, Grant," she says. "I'm so happy you get this second chance. You've been *such* a serious grown-up since you were thirteen, and I've wanted to see you be a boy again so badly. But for years, Ben McKittrick was the face of your pain. And that might not go away quickly. So, whatever you two do . . . treat him carefully."

I want to.

Five years ago, I gave in to my hurt and lashed out at Ben before he could explain. If I had just let him explain, the truth would've come out right away, and it would've saved Ben and myself years of bullshit. The problem is me. This time, I'm going to be strong. I'm going to trust.

An hour later, it's noon: my daily date with Lexi. The white pill lands on my tongue, and I chug her down with a full glass of water. She's such a good friend—no matter how long we go without talking, she's there for me when I come back.

Shaking the bottle of Lexapro, I slip it back into the medicine cabinet and tell it, "Love you, see you tomorrow, honeyyyy."

In the few weeks I've been back with Lexi, I've been sleeping more than I'd like. Having so much work to do and being this tired has been frustrating, but the calm she's brought back to me has been worth it. It'll probably take another week before I really feel the effects, but just the idea of being in control again has been like an electric charge.

And so far, I don't need to worry about the sexual side effects. The mere memory of Ben's toughened fingers grazing my cheek has kept my junk in a constant state of heaviness. It feels like I'm walking around with a chunk of alabaster stone in my jeans.

Now that I've completed the self-work portion of the day, I continue into the next part of my journey: creative self-expression. It's time to actually construct the living sculpture gowns I've sketched. The festival is in early August—almost two weeks from today—and Team Vero Roseto has to wrangle materials for my "crying rose garden" installation, resod the sculpture garden's chessboard pattern, and build the flower gowns.

Thanks to my post-Patty confidence, I finally let Eshana see my designs. One at a time, I text her screenshots of the six gown sketches, each one featuring a different flower: red roses, white roses, lilies, magnolias, hydrangeas, and tulips.

SCREAAAAAAAM, she replies. I haven't seen a Grant Rossi design in months! Gawd, I have missed this! I hearted my faves!

Lying facedown on my bed, I quickly swipe through the pics to see which ones she's hearted. **Babes,** I text. **You hearted all of them.**

I LOVE ALL OF THEM, YES. Grant Rossi is back in business!!

Strength returns to me with each passing moment I talk to her. I type feverishly: **And it'll be simple to assemble! The flowers will be installed on light wire frames, and the models just slip inside it, like a cage. Biggest problem will be installing irrigation tubes throughout to keep the flowers all fresh and dewy, but my uncle Paul is pretty confident with plumbing to make it work.**

Cool cool, Eshana texts, getting into business mode. Lemme know if you need models. Irene and Coco and Luisa from my Art Institute show would drop EVERYTHING to do something 'grammable like this.

Flipping over to my Notes app, I jot down the models' names. Thank God for them. Putting this show together so quickly is going to need all the help it can get.

The next day, after compiling the full list of supplies I'll need for the gowns and garden installations, Paul breaks the bad news to me: Valle won't have everything we need. Some of these supplies, like the water filtration systems that'll create a river around the Wishing Rose, can be assembled from Slava's Hardware in town. But the living sculpture gowns are trickier. The tubing must be custom-made to hide inside the silhouettes.

When I was designing at the Art Institute, finding materials was easy, but now there's no choice: I have to go back to Chicago. I'll need the half-body mannequin forms from my studio, and the rest of the materials can be rented from city shops.

"So, when do we leave for the big city?" Ben asks over lunch. He, Ro, Paul, and I huddle around the kitchen table, ravenously devouring food so we can stick to our overwhelmed schedules. Blessedly, Ro made macaroni pie, which is amazingly gobbleable. Like all Italian dishes, it's just pasta, cheese, egg yolk, and gravy, this time in cube form, like a Rice Krispies Treat of spaghetti.

"Ah, I can go alone, you're busy," I tell Ben as I gulp another square whole.

"You can't go alone," Ben says, eating his own square in one bite. "It'll take you twice as long without help."

Anxious acids roil through my stomach, threatening to

send back everything I've just eaten. "Well, I'll need the truck for it, so why don't you come with, Paul?"

Uncle Paul mops his sauce-stained mustache and shakes his head. "Can't do it. The Rose Festival isn't just Vero Roseto. We're the last grand finale stop on the tour of other homes in town. I have to make sure everyone is still participating. We've had a lot of drop-offs the last few years because our festival . . . you know . . . started to be nothing special."

He eyes Ro warily, like maybe he shouldn't have been so blunt about her past festivals.

After a stung moment, she shrugs and takes a hit of Grato red wine. "You don't need to be so polite. My last three festivals have been shangad."

Paul scoffs. "They were not shangad."

Ro downs the rest of her glass. "Shan! Gad!" She makes the sign of the cross. "If Mama Bianchi saw what I've done."

"What's 'shangad' mean?" Ben asks.

"Tacky," I say. "Cheap. Poorly done." I glance at Ro. "Sorry."

"It's true!" Ro bused her plate to the sink. "I run Vero Roseto like a boss, but I can't put on a show. People can't do everything on their own. And neither can you, Grant, so take Ben to the city with you. End of subject."

Both Ro and Ben instantly catch me struggling for a way to say no.

As Ben's eyes narrow, I realize this is not a great way for us to heal our situation. My shoulders slump as I embrace an embarrassing truth: "We'd have to go to my studio, and it looks out of control. I didn't clean it before I hopped a train out here on a whim—on a spiral. I'm not . . . my best self in that city, and I have no idea how I'm gonna act when I'm back there. Ben, you've dealt with a lot of me already."

At the sink, Ro watches me. So does Paul. Ben calmly walks over and grazes my chin: "Little Italian boy, you're so dramatic. Thank you, but I've seen worse, and you're gonna be okay. Now let's hit the road."

I *hate* him, but I can't stop smiling. Those fingers on my chin. Those little touches.

Life could be so easy if it were just him and me here. But I know our futures are going different places. If I pour more hope into this, it's just going to be worse when it ends. When whatever is going on between us gets ruined by my curse—or his. These little touches can't mean anything more.

On the same whim that brought me to Vero Roseto in the dead of night, Ben and I decide to just kill the day and leave immediately. The stores we're renting from don't close until seven, so we can round everything up, get on the road, and be back in Valle before it's too late.

We stop to gas up just as the Valle forests end and long, blank cornfields begin. "I'll get it!" I say, hopping out of the passenger seat to reach the pump before Ben can open his door. While I fill up Paul's dinged flatbed truck, Ben laughs. "What are you being so nice for?"

I shrug. "It's just gas, no reason."

Yes, just pumping gas. Certainly not me trying to make up for years of unwarranted asshole behavior.

However, Ben's suspicions really come alive when I come back from inside the gas station with Snapple Apple and a box of Junior Mints. His absolute favorites from when we were kids. He takes them with narrowed eyes and says, "Okay, please just make fun of me or something. I can't take this Nice Robot Grant."

"What?" I say, trying to sound innocent as I buckle myself in. "Snacks for the road!"

Ben doesn't blink. "Okay. I'm watching you, but you better start acting rotted again soon."

I hold up three fingers (*scout's honor!*), and with that, our journey to Chicago begins. The drive is three hours through mostly woods and cornfields, so while I busy myself with my tablet designs, Ben listens to the ancient radio. He jumps around through a lot of static, but eventually lands on a death metal station he's pretty happy about.

When that becomes too much noise for me, we chat. Even though we've spent the whole summer catching up, our new, romantic-adjacent dynamic has spread a sugary glaze of *importance* on these stories.

"So, here's a rotted question for you: How long were you and the great *Nicholas Hutchinson* together?" I ask, resting my feet on the dashboard.

"Four weeks," he replies, rolling his eyes as if it were the most annoying era of his life.

"You two ruined my goddamn life over a four-week fling?"

"You let your goddamn life get ruined over a couple of middle schoolers?"

"Fair." Chuckling, I reach over to flick his ear. He hisses and elbows me away.

"Anyway, you'd know that already if you hadn't unfollowed us both."

"Didn't unfollow you." Ben glances over, confused. My joy deflating slightly, I pick at a cluster of dirt under my nail. "Took a social media break for about a year. Just deleted everything. Dr. Patty's orders. It helped a lot, and Lexi did the rest."

For a long minute, Ben drives in silence. The country road flies by in a monotonous but pleasing hum. "Didn't know we messed you up that bad—"

"It wasn't you." I pet his leg, which is something I hadn't planned on doing, but I need to make myself clear. "Not you. Okay? Just a soup of my brain chemistry and family stuff. This . . . misunderstanding with us, it was just the spark."

Ben nods, satisfied but looking miles away. "So, this Dr. Patty is really mother, huh?"

"Oh yeah!" I drum my hands against my knees. "My mom rankings go: Ro, Dr. Patty, Melissa McCarthy, then my own mom."

"Ouch, Mom."

"She's good! The other three are just better. My mom never . . . *got it* with what was going on with me, and after a while, she started getting impatient."

A fresh surge of guilt courses through my chest at how flippant I've been about Mom, who has eight kids and four grandkids to wrangle, but whatever, it's not my fault. If she wanted things simpler, she should've given birth to a lower-maintenance kid.

"My mom got *so* much better once she left my dad," Ben says.

"Divorce is weird. Like, when mine split up, I thought it would calm everyone down, but they just got more . . ."

"More what?"

"MORE."

Laughing, Ben reaches over to smack my chest. I wince at the exquisite pain. The tiny touches are starting again, but the longer we spend in this car, the more I crave them.

"You said you came out during their divorce?" I ask Ben, remembering our tense chat weeks ago when we were replanting Grandpa's garden.

Ben nods. "Best thing I ever did. Unmasked my dad as a creep, got me a one-way plane ticket to Edinburgh, and my mom went into hyperdrive rainbow support mode." He throws back his head luxuriously, taken by some beautiful memory. "Grant . . . She bought me so much shite that year."

"Damn you." Lowering my feet from the dash, I turn to Ben, eager for details. "Tell me everything."

Rapidly, Ben counts items on his fingers against the steering wheel. "Designer shoes. Imported cable-knit sweaters from Sweden. Whenever they put out a new iPhone, I got it. Personal trainer sessions five times a week." He flashes his taut bicep, his shirt material straining to contain it. "Eyebrow threading."

A guffaw rips out of me. "Stop."

"*Blue* contact lenses."

"Shut up—" But the word "up" gets strangled in my wheezing laughter.

Smiling smugly, Ben snaps his fingers. "Laugh all you want, miss. Those next few years, I got dick on dick on dick."

"I'm happy for you," I groan. "I got Dr. Patty."

"Don't mope. My dad got sick, and the party was over. It was like he *knew* we were having too good a time, and he manifested the cancer."

I just let him talk. Ben sounds like he hasn't shared these heavy caretaker woes with anyone, probably not even his mom, and she *hates* his dad.

"But hey," I say, making spirit fingers over my face. "Brought you and me back together."

Laughter escapes Ben in an exhausted moan. "I forgot, what a blessing!"

As we fall back into comfortable silence, I smile, letting my eyes travel over Ben's strong, unshakable beauty as he handles the unfamiliar truck with ease. His hint of reddish scruff that, if I lived in a different, simpler universe, I would want to watch become a powerful beard someday.

After several hours of midwestern country landscapes, our drive becomes industrial—following a long stretch of highway leading toward the outline of the Chicago skyline. As soon as I spot the familiar towers, an odd calm sweeps over me. It's not the PTSD trauma bomb I was expecting. I'm strangely relaxed, like all my months away at Vero Roseto cleared my head enough to allow the many positive memories of the city to return.

Ben slaps my knee. "Need me to strap you down?"

"What?" I ask, thinking, *Yes, please.*

He grins slyly. "You made it sound like just being in the city would turn you into a werewolf or something."

"You are *so* obnoxious!" I burst out laughing, and joy stays with me the rest of the drive.

Hitting up stores before nightfall is easier said than done. We collect the wire frames and bolts of fabric for the dresses in the garment district, but by the time we finish our scavenger hunt for the tubing, pumps, and miniature spray nozzles needed for the interior irrigation systems, it's a race to closing time. Even when complicated feelings come up with Ben, I'm too busy to linger on them.

But it's *so* cute watching Ben, out of breath from dashing around the store, fight through his accent as he tries explaining to the stunned cashier that he's looking for "nozzles," and not "nuzzles" or "noodles."

I laugh so hard my guard briefly slips, and a horrible thought invades my mind:

Ben would be such a good father.

Oh, goddamn it, where did that shit come from? I was doing so well!

These awkward feelings only intensify when it's time to hit up my studio. I almost got away with Ben not seeing inside. We have this huge flatbed, and I thought he'd have to wait double-parked while I ran up to get the mannequins. But the universe laughed, and for the first time in history, there's plenty of parking on my block.

At least I picked my mountain of clothes off the floor before I left.

The room is dark, but my three mannequins—half-body forms on metal pegs—are bunched together neatly right when we walk in. Of course they're neatly bundled; I've barely touched them since my last show.

Ben scans my simple studio, which I never had time (or energy) to decorate or do anything notable with. He shrugs. "This is what you were worried I'd see? Just a messy room?"

He's right. There's nothing scary here. I walk through the space cautiously, like I'm a paranormal investigator hunting for ghosts. Maybe that's what I was afraid he'd see—some *Grudge*-like specter created from the endless bad vibes I've poured into this place since I moved in.

Then I see it on the floor beside my bed. My stomach twists like a wrung-dry towel.

The magazine.

The one I hurt my feelings with whenever I get how I get. The Art Institute magazine with me and my ex as cover boys on the red carpet of our debut show. The show that would be my last professional high in almost a year. I kneel to pick it up and stroke the cover . . . and the frantic pen scratches I used to carve out my face. My deluded smile. I left my ex's picture how it is—he wasn't the problem.

All of it was me. Partly for giving up on Lexi, and partly for letting down my guard and mingling boys with work. I can't make this mistake again. These pen scratches are too serious.

On a pained sigh, I stand and walk the magazine over to Ben. "Since we're sharing," I say. "Since I'm healing and not avoiding the tough parts, I want you to see what I was afraid you'd see."

Ben doesn't judge. He accepts things as they are. Carefully, he runs his fingers over the pen scratches, and I watch his eyes shimmer with tears. "Grant . . ."

I don't snatch the magazine back. My feet remain firmly planted, my chest out proudly as I show him something I planned never to show anyone. "I'm not who I was when I did that. I wouldn't do it again. I regret doing it. It's my only copy, and there aren't any more, so my memories of that show— the best work I've ever done—will always remind me of how crazy I am."

"That's not nice." Ben glances up seriously.

"Yeah, but it's the truth."

"It's not." He lobs the magazine onto my mattress. "And your best work is ahead of you. You've still got this festival. And then after . . ."

"After . . ." We don't have to say it: after the festival in two weeks, I'll pursue designing somewhere else, somewhere most likely not Edinburgh, which is where Ben is most definitely returning to.

After. Horrible word.

Gazing deeply into my eyes, Ben reaches for my shoulder . . . but his hand lands on the back of my neck. He strokes it lovingly, and a coat of fizzing, beautiful energy courses down my limbs. Slowly, he navigates his hand up, sinking his fingers deep into my curls. He massages and tugs and never looks away . . .

Bzzzzzzzt!

My back jerks in surprise as Ben's phone and mine go off at the same time. Our spell briefly broken, we glance at our new text message, sent to both of us from Uncle Paul:

> Gentlemen, you've worked so hard for us all summer instead of just getting to be kids one last time. We are so grateful, but you deserve a night off. Don't get back on the road when you're done. Ro and I booked you a hotel at the Mayflower downtown. Find a garage for the truck. It's on us. Have a good time.

This is the nicest—and most manipulative—thing Ro has ever done.

She wants Ben and me to shack up, and she wants it to happen *now*.

To keep me here? To ensure a successful festival? Because she loves us?

I want what Ro wants, but even though Ben was just being so affectionate with me, I have to stay focused and not stumble down a rabbit hole falling in love with my childhood best friend just when I'm starting to get my shit together again! Ben and I will enjoy the nice hotel for the night, have a slamming breakfast, and then get back to work.

When we arrive at the hotel and flick on the light, my stomach drops. It's a pretty hotel—nothing fancy, fairly basic and old-fashioned—but there's one giant problem.

"There's only one bed," Ben says, raising his eyebrows devilishly.

Indeed, there is. The king-size bed waits for us, like a big, quilted invitation to fuck.

"Ro," I groan. "The old *there's only one bed* trick?"

Giggling, Ben kicks off his shoes and cannonballs onto the bed. "I love when that happens in movies."

I scoff and slide out of my shoes. "Oh, my ex loved shit like this. Romance novel shenanigans."

"Talk about your ex again, I'm getting so hot." Ben can't stop chortling as he tests the bed's springs, which sound creaky as hell. He spreads across the covers and looks back over his shoulder at me in a *very* suggestive pose.

ENOUGH! I want to scream. But I settle on a restrained, more dignified:

"Hey, what is this?"

"What's what?" Ben asks, peeling off his socks—slowly, and making constant eye contact. I better stop him before he gets serious.

Standing in the entryway, balled-up fists perched huffily on my waist, I ask, "You *want* something to happen? Because I thought we were focusing on the festival."

And I *thought* you didn't want this to turn into a relationship. But I can't say that yet. That's an intense card to play, and if I play it now, the answer alone could topple me, Lexi be damned.

As Ben silently wiggles his toes and unbuttons his flannel top, an ominous weight grows in my jeans. I'm not ready. I want this, but I haven't had meaningful sex in way too long. I don't think I'm ready. I've hooked up with plenty of guys since my last ex, but this would be sex that *matters*. It has importance, prominence, and weight. Weight that fills my jeans like a damn bowling pin with each second Ben lies there, summoning me with his eyes.

"We've worked on the festival enough," he says, flapping his hand. "Here."

It's so commanding, like I'm a dog. I hate it, but goddamn it, I love it, too.

Glancing anxiously at the bathroom next to me, I rake my fingers through my curls and say, "I think I'm just gonna sleep in the tub tonight, I—"

In a flash, Ben launches off the bed and gallops toward me.

He throws a strong, muscular arm between me and the bathroom doorway. His chest, visible beneath his half-unbuttoned top, heaves as he eyes me not like my old friend. That boy is nowhere to be found in his face. This boy's eyes are wild. He brings himself within a centimeter of my lips.

His breath is hot.

I don't argue, nor do I want to.

Ben whispers, "All summer, I wanted you to get out of your head, forget about all our stuff and whatever more's coming, and just be *here* and *now*. You showed me today you could do that. You're finally in the moment. And it makes me want to *take you*." His lips are closer than ever. "It doesn't have to be serious. You've always wanted this. I've always wanted this. What if this is our last chance? Do you really want me to leave, and you never let me do . . . this . . ."

He grips my belt loop with his pinkie and starts tugging down.

We can do this. This isn't a relationship, it's a sexy situation.

It's friends with perks. It doesn't have to be complicated. We both want this, and I'd be silly to turn it down over what *might* happen. Ro and Paul are right. Ben is right. We've worked so hard—not just on this festival, but with all the struggling he and I have gone through over the last five years.

We want it.

We've earned it.

Let's go.

My lips quiver as Ben closes the last incremental gap between us. Our lips finally touching, I whisper, "Take me."

And as he turns off the lights, he does.

CHAPTER 23

THORNY FOR YOU

It helps that the lights are off.

Not that I'm not liking being in bed with Ben, because I really am, it's just . . . disorienting? No, that's not the right word. It's a lot. My head is making so much noise, my self-consciousness is at an all-time high, and I'm just so grateful that my face can process these thousand different emotions without Ben having to see how overwhelmed I look.

What am I feeling? Let me count the ways.

I've had sex since Micah—but this is the first time where the stakes have been high. These might be even higher, because it's *Ben*. With Micah and Dylan before him, they were so inexperienced, my stress was more about making sure they felt safe, comfortable, and turned on. With Ben . . . he's got more moves than me, so I've gotta bring my AP-level skills. Not only that, but some major brain wackiness is also happening, because I've never touched Ben like this before. We were kids together. We slept in side-by-side sleeping bags and played with Nerf guns. Now my hands are peeling a shirt off the taut little rib muscles of some dude's body—and you're telling me this is *Ben*? Impossible. The heavy warmth I feel rising against my leg is Ben's *dick*? The last time I hung around Ben this much, the word "dick" would've made us giggle like hyenas.

The very idea that I'm holding Ben's toughened, grown body against my own is so ludicrous I have to stomp down the laugh rising in my throat.

It's almost too much to comprehend that *I* have a grown body. Lately, when I've been hanging out with Ben, my brain remembers being little, scrawny, and childish. Yet his strong hands are swirling down my broad back and destroying that childlike image. His palms grip my thighs firmly but carefully, like I'm a clay pot he's molding. But when his fingers find my waist, I flinch, like he's touched a fresh scrape. My waist has gotten softer since the last time a boy held me.

I don't mind getting bigger. I know I'm beautiful—I'm just not ready for my body to change.

Everything's changing.

Ben is starting to look like a man. Our adulthood is coming, but I'm not ready. I don't have college figured out. I can't live on my own without spiraling. For fuck's sake, I can't even get over my eighth-grade boyfriend. Everyone is okay moving on but me.

You're not a kid anymore, Grant.

You're not the Band-Aid baby.

You're not the star Instacouple boyfriend.

You are Grant Rossi, a handsome young man who has fought many demons but still finds the beauty in life.

Like beautiful, all-grown-up Ben.

Light from the city cuts inside our hotel's fifth-floor window, painting silver around the edges of the darkness. I can't see Ben's face, only the outlines of his high cheekbones, dimpled chin, and strong nose. Gripping his bushy hair, I pull his lips to mine. They're the only part of him that's soft. Everything else is hard, rough, or bristling with hair.

Ben climbs on me, squeaking the cheap hotel's cheaper bed springs, and lowers himself onto my lips again. As he kisses me, his breath sweet, his spare hand reaches across my chest and draws circles around my nipple.

I inhale a quick gasp, and he pauses.

"You all right?" he moans, his Scottish accent growing stronger.

"Just surprised me," I say breathily. "When'd you get moves like this?"

He chuckles darkly and his hand grips my shorts again. "When'd you get an ass like this?"

I moan happily, enjoying his hand there, until he slowly moves it up, swirling over my stomach. Instinctively, my body tenses, and he notices again. "You okay?"

"Fine!" Except my words come out tight and falsely chipper.

"Liar."

"It's nothing, just ignore me." My body turns rigid against his, everything is stiffening except my junk, which is deflating. "I'm just . . . sensitive. I got bigger this year."

Ben lowers himself to me, nose-to-nose. "I know big boys who would give you a smack on the tit for calling yourself fat."

He flicks my nipple, but this time, it's not sexy, it's boyish teasing.

Laughing, I squirm underneath him. "Stop! I didn't say fat, I said *bigger*!"

"They would still smack you in the tit! You are a buff young homo. Okay, so your tummy's out of bounds, got it. Anywhere else?"

"No." I smile, easing comfortably into him. The sounds in my head finally quiet. "Ben?"

"Mmm?"

"What if this is it? The Rose Festival ends, and we don't see each other for another five years?"

Sighing, Ben rolls off of me, plopping his head next to mine. He pinches my cheek, and a rush of warmth enters me. "I don't know what you're trying to get me to say," he says, "but I don't plan on letting it get that long again."

I brush my nose gently against his. "Yeah?"

"I like that you still want me in your life."

The room falls into a crackling silence, broken only by the loud whir of the hotel air conditioner. I kiss him quickly. "I don't ever want you out of my life again."

"I missed you, Grant. It was . . . really fucking hard watching your last relationship over Instagram. Watching this happy, grown-up Grant I didn't recognize be so loved. All those people seeing you how I always saw you."

Memories of my ex—and our all-too-public relationship—tighten my throat. Instagram lies. It makes everything look happier than it is.

"And how did you always see me?" I ask.

In the dark, Ben's chest rises sharply and falls shallowly against my shoulder. He's tense. Emotional. "Just a magical guy," he says. "My parents used to fight so much, I felt like such a piece of shit. Like I didn't matter because I couldn't stop them. Like my family was just fucked, and that I'd be fucked, too. But then hanging out with you, it was all right. You made me so calm. Then I went and . . . lost you. I wasn't calm ever again after that."

My cheeks are burning hot, and I don't want to cry on him in such a vulnerable position, so I pull him into another ferocious kiss. He kisses back just as powerfully, and then when we separate, I press his forehead to mine. We breathe each other's hot breath.

"I wasn't happy in those pictures," I say. "Not even once. I couldn't be calm with Micah. I tried so hard to hold on tight to him, I don't even know why. But I know when I lost you, I stopped being me. I didn't realize it until we started hanging out again, but I've been in a goddamn coma for five years. It's like I can finally be me again." I smile, even though I'm sniffling back tears. "But turns out the real me is still super chaotic."

"HELLO." Ben roars with laughter, his shoulders bouncing

against mine. He pokes my chin and snuggles closer. "Well, whoever you are, I'm glad you're back. I won't lie, even though I knew how busted up you were after your breakup . . . I was hoping this would happen, you coming back. I thought about messaging you a million times."

"I wish you had."

"You were so angry at me . . ."

I nod, collecting a deep, knowing breath. "I was out of my mind last year, I probably would have blocked you. We needed Vero Roseto."

Ben's fingers stroke behind my ears, and he stares at me, his eyes shining like crescent moons in the city light. "No more scratching your face out of pictures, okay?"

A powerful blanket of shame lowers my head as I nod. He saw my weirdest, most serial-killer behavior—my thorniest thorn—and it only made him want to help me more. Ben and I really are different people now, and that's a good thing. We're not kids anymore. With each passing day this summer, Adult Ben and Adult Grant have emerged from our childhood ashes like phoenixes.

"Thank you for seeing me," I whisper, and we fall asleep in each other's arms.

CHAPTER 24

ELECTRICITY MEETS WATER

Two weeks pass in a heartbeat.

The Rose Festival is a few days away.

Ben and I have graduated from a sexy situation to a very exciting sexy situation. The word "boyfriend" hasn't been uttered, and we aren't affectionate and kissy around Ro and Paul—but they paid for our hotel room, so they're clearly not clueless. Neither Ben nor I are comfortable defining this damn thing at the moment, because I'm so ungodly busy with the festival, and beyond the festival lies a horrible, uncertain future without Ben!

Whew.

"Sex with Ben?" Dr. Patty gasps in our sixth video session. Now seated at my sewing desk instead of the bed, I wince.

"It was really nice," I confess. "He was like a different person, or no, *I* was like a different person. Well, not a different person, it was like I was me, finally me, the me who's moving on, the me I'm gonna be in the future who's got his career together and can be with a guy without overthinking, and—"

"Grant," she giggles, readjusting her powder-blue necker-chief. "I'm happy for you."

I smile, my eyes brimming with tears. "He was always on my side."

"Do you think, perhaps, the others were on your side, too?"

I inhale sharply. Dr. Patty always knows how to shank me.

It's my turn to pay Ben's positive energy forward. After my session, with forgiveness on my mind and weight on my heart, I sprawl across my bed, suck in a deep breath, and dive into Micah's DMs. My fingers are shaking and my sweat-slicked palm can barely hold the phone, but to calm myself, I hold my pumpkin-embroidered jacket. It always reminds me of Micah.

I was wearing it when we met. We were on a train and had been flirting so much, we forgot to tell each other our names. We got separated accidentally, and I'd left the pump-kin jacket behind. Somehow, using only clues from the things in my jacket, he found me again. It was so romantic, I thought it broke my curse wide open.

Do you think, perhaps, the others were on your side, too?

Ben, Micah, Dylan, Ruben, on and on . . . maybe they always were.

I linger in my ex's DMs, not writing a thing, but I shouldn't stay long. I'm just extending an olive branch. He didn't cheat. He didn't lie. He felt his heart moving toward somebody else, and he did me the courtesy of ending things truthfully. Should we have stayed friends? Maybe, but I was incapable.

Stop blaming yourself, Grant.

It helps to have a little vision of Ben pop into my head whenever my thoughts turn down a bad alley. Ben doesn't like me because I'm an easygoing, untroubled person. He likes me because I'm finally being honest with myself. He also likes the *hell* out of my body. Sex with my inexperienced exes often left me feeling in charge. It was exciting, but I was really just helping young bunnies discover brave new worlds—but with Ben, he makes my body feel like the brave new world.

My ex's DM window is a challenge. I haven't messaged him since before our breakup. In fact, the last message sent was me sharing a post from the Art Institute account where we were about to do our show—the show where he broke up with me. As it happens, the anniversary of our show (and breakup) was yesterday. It's also the anniversary of Micah getting with his new boyfriend. Navigating that anniversary post was like walking across hot coals.

My last message was an overenthusiastic **TONIGHT'S THE NIGHT!!!**

Three exclamation points *and* all caps. A year later, I'd be making fun of Ro for using both in the Vero Roseto ad. Did I change? No, I haven't, but maybe then I thought fake sunshine would help me keep my boyfriend.

Dr. Patty calls it "my representative." We all do it, bringing a sanitized version of ourselves to a new relationship. It's technically us wearing a happy mask so we don't frighten this new person away. Typically, our representative starts to fade around month three to six. That's when the real us takes back control—the insecure us, the angry us, the us that farts, the us that doesn't like our partner's friends or family, the us that admits we actually don't like rock climbing.

Sorry, New Partner. Don't like this version? Too bad you're already invested!

It sounds like we're tricking and trapping people, but everyone who engages in a relationship does this subconsciously. We want to be liked. We need to be loved.

My exes only ever saw my representative. A charming, adventurous, trusting, understanding, enthusiastic boy. The one time they ever met the Real Grant was when they were dumping me.

The cursed boy who always knew this was going to happen.

The boy who refused to text back for any reason.

The boy who *will* ice you out if you reject him.

Like I did to Ben.

Never again. My first order of business in breaking this cycle is an invitation.

Hey there, I message my ex. I'm going to make it a single, unbroken statement so he doesn't have to ask follow-up questions or engage in conversation if he doesn't want to. **It's been too long. I hope you've been all right! Congrats on your anniversary. Anyway—thank you for sharing my video. It really helped my family's B&B. This place means so much to me, so**

thank you. Speaking of that video, this weekend is the Rose Festival at Vero Roseto. It's my first time putting on a big show since our thing, and I wanted to extend an invitation to you, if you're free or interested. It would be nice to see you again if you can make it.

I hit Send, close the app, and shut off my phone.

There—that's enough growth for one day.

We finally complete Vero Roseto's reconstruction when Ben and Uncle Paul rebuild the sculpture garden's trellis. They erect several free-standing pillars, connecting them with beautiful, draping canary-yellow fabric—a unifying color for the festival, I determined. It's light, airy, summery, and perfectly offsets the vibrant red roses.

I stroll through the sculpture garden, which Ben has resodded with alternating types of grass—lighter and darker, so it resembles a chessboard once again. It's stunningly detailed work, but Ben just magicked it into reality as if he were picking up nails from the store.

Later, just after midnight in my room, I squeeze a pair of pliers until my hand is red. The wire girding spills down from the half-body mannequins I brought from Chicago, but the shapes aren't behaving. The living sculpture that's going to be filled with lilies has a wide-hooped ball gown silhouette, which I thought would look cute because that shape is usually so rounded and lilies are sharp, piece-y little buggers. However, this particular piece of chicken wire refuses to bend to my will.

Cross-legged on my floor, eyes blurry from staring at these cages all day, I take a deep breath, relax my grip on the pliers, picture the curvature I want, and then pull . . .

It works!

The rigid wire leading down from the corset loosens into a smooth bend, giving me the wide arc I need to fit the fluffy petticoat underneath for the model.

"YES!" I cheer, flopping onto my back and dropping the pliers loudly.

Aunt Ro, lingering outside my open door, peeks in. "What was that?" she asks.

"The pliers," I say, not moving. "You can come in and snoop, Ro."

The door thrusts open on a *creaaaaaak*, and she storms into the room. "Wow," she gasps, brushing her palm against the wire silhouette. "So this is all gonna be filled in with flowers. I don't believe it." Then her hand finds the corset around the mannequin's waist, and she darkens. "Don't know if I love corsets. A bit old-fashioned . . ."

"Ro, please," I say, crawling up to sitting. "It's late. We can have your TED talk on reductive feminism in the morning. This corset isn't a lady prison. Gowns with this big of an undercarriage need the girding of a corset, or the model won't be able to move. They'll throw their back out carrying the thing."

Casting me a sour look, Ro cinches her robe and sweeps toward the door. "La-dee-dah, thank you for mansplaining."

"It's not mansplaining. You said something wrong about my work, so I'm explaining."

"And now you're mansplaining mansplaining!"

"Okay, my apologies." Standing, I guide my aunt out of the room. "Good night, Sister Suffragette." As I shut the door, she curses me under her breath.

The next morning, Paul, Ben, and I finally move the six wire gown structures down to the sculpture garden, where we install the custom irrigation pumps within the frames. After the pumps are in place, Ben and I spend an unforgettable—and oddly quiet—day assembling the floral patterns into the gown frames. It's just the two of us, the birds, and the frogs along the lake. The flowers are mostly preassembled onto platters that contour to the dress dimensions, but Ben's job is to fill in the gaps and make the vision seamless. It requires delicate work, but his toughened hands manage it beautifully.

He loops a red rose stem around the wire like he's hanging an ornament on a tree.

While he works, I press the platters of roses flush to the wire frame to keep a uniform line. As Ben loops the next stem—and the next—his hands come closer to mine until they touch.

I watch him work. He's so careful.

Finished, Ben looks up. I'm staring. He knows I was.

"You all right?"

Don't go to Edinburgh. Stay here, and I'll stay, too. We can be happy here.

"Nothing. You're just doing a really good job," I say, praying he doesn't catch me lying.

Ben shrugs. "You and dresses, me and flowers." He snorts. "Five years ago, I thought our whole fucking lives were gonna be about Nintendo."

Giggling, I kiss his ear, and he kisses my nose.

It's so easy. Falling in love with him would be so easy. If I just bend the Secret Rule a little . . .

Finally, each gown's flowers are in place—the silhouettes are as different as the flower selections. Half of them are massive pieces with flowing trains. But the most special of all is the red rose, shaped in the formfitting cocktail dress of a lounge singer. She's my heartbroken diva.

The loneliest and loveliest of the flowers. Bursting with mystery.

That afternoon, Eshana texts me that she's locked in another two models for the living sculptures. Sadly, she's at her limits with people who can make it happen. There's still one spot left—for someone small and slender who could make the rose diva come to life.

Well.

I know a tiny diva hungry for the spotlight.

Continuing my forgiveness tour, I offer Hutch the role, which he gleefully embraces. Hutch, Ben, and I—torn apart by a rose, or so I thought—will be healed by a rose.

I'm just *so* operatic like that.

The final thing the sculpture garden still needs is the

protective tent. The sun can be merciless, and Uncle Paul says we've got summer storms rolling our way this weekend—just in time for the festival.

Aunt Ro and I order him never to mention storms to us again, and we go on pretending nothing was said. As for the tent, I'll have to check if Uncle Paul can get it in canary yellow, or at least see if we can drape the color over it. A similar canary curtain conceals the arched entrance to the rose garden next door. That curtain, I sewed to be twice as thick. It's heavier, so it requires guests to literally push their way inside.

A magical barrier between worlds.

Maintaining the mystery of the rose garden is key.

When I part the curtains, Ben is waiting for me. He stands atop a ladder, trimming stray branches from the fresh garden walls with hedge clippers. We redressed the walls—once thick with vines—with hundreds of roses, bound intricately to latticework dyed green to make it invisible against the garden walls where we hung them. We've created a paradise away from the world.

Because that's how I see it. The world—the future, and anything beyond the next few weeks—is my enemy.

Now comes my moment. The centerpiece. The big finish.

Long into the night, I create the artificial riverbed surrounding the Wishing Rose bush. "You've done enough," I tell Ben as I set up my station of bandsaws, sheet metal, and rivets. "Put your feet up, and I'll take it from here."

Grunting, Ben plops down, his back against the garden wall, and opens another iced tea. "Will you quit showing off? We're out of time, and I'd like to sleep at some point, right?"

I kiss the air, and he kisses back.

An hour later, his fun, jabby comments die off as I cut row after row of sheet metal—thin gutter walls, ten inches high—and lay them into the soil Ben dug earlier. The gutters cut like two veins through the garden leading to the Wishing Rose bush, which is surrounded by an already installed oasis pool that I'll have to connect to my new artificial river gutters.

Blissfully, my thoughts leave me again as my hands take over. They know exactly what to do. Exactly how much metal to shave off the top of the gutter wall, exactly how curved the end piece will need to be to create a perfect flush with the curved, basin-like oasis.

I'm back. I'm in my art again, and this time I'm not letting the rush I feel slip away.

With a flash of a hammer and a drizzle of sparks, I seal the gutters to the oasis pool with rivets, and all the while, I catch Ben staring. Whether it's at my metalwork or at my wet bicep, who's to say? But my boy's transfixed.

"Who knew you had that kind of salt in you, dressmaker?" he asks, brushing a cold can against his cheek as he stares like a leopard.

My chest heaves with how much strength it took out of

me to seal the riverbed to that oasis, but still, if it's got Ben looking at me like that, then I'm smiling.

"Let's get this baby wet," I say, hopping from my knees to my feet.

He joins me. "Thought you'd never ask!"

Now that the hoses are connected behind the oasis pool, Ben activates the faucets, and a mighty, Biblical flood races to fill my installation. In under two minutes, it's complete. Water flows continuously around the oasis and through the rivers, and the rivers circle back to the oasis. Constant flow—no mosquitoes here. The rivers create two powerful, separate streams.

It worked. The Wishing Rose looks like it's crying.

Is it crying because the love the roses bring can be unrequited—or because even if it's a match, it will end someday? I'm a thornier soul, so I believe the latter.

Ever since my night in the hotel with Ben, as happy as I am, I can't shake this demon.

Will he leave me for Scotland?

Will I leave him for somewhere else?

Where is life taking us after the festival is over?

"Hey, you," Ben says, walking over for a kiss. He slips off his cap to run his fingers through his hair, flattened at an odd angle by too much hat time. Nuzzling my cheek, he turns to take in the rose garden with me. "We made her into something."

"You did," I whisper.

"We did." Ben's voice taps into a pocket of annoyance. I'm downplaying myself again.

"Now we're going to see her look *really* special." I walk back to the switchboard beside the archway and rest my palm against all four toggles. Ben crosses his fingers. We haven't tried this yet—the lighting grid was only installed this morning.

Grimacing, I flip everything at once.

Sapphire-blue light fills the cavern. Not only does the Wishing Rose's faint, magical spotlight illuminate, every footlight we placed along the rivers and oasis ignites. Blue as a Caribbean beach, dotted with cool white lights to soften them. It's summery, but it also could be snow. The white and blue look like a pattern of icy snowflakes covering a window.

Ro could keep these and give winter tours.

My heart races. Oh my God, I've got to show her.

Ben covers his mouth and stares at me. The biggest smile of my life explodes.

More than that, this installation is us. I'm passionate and unpredictable, like the lights, like electricity. Ben is calm, deep waters. Water and electricity—volatile and beautiful.

It's almost too perfect.

That evening, I'm reminded exactly how *too* perfect it is. Ben and I lounge on the sofa in the East Wing parlor, a fire blazing, his legs slung over my lap as he dicks around on his phone. Still no response from Micah. Which is totally fine. He probably doesn't want to get into all that with me again. I didn't make it easy on him. And to come out three hours for such a not-easy time—it makes sense. I'm disappointed in myself, but it makes sense. Still glad I reached out, though.

While I'm drafting a post reminding folks about Rose Festival details, an email pops up. The University of the Arts London. One of the schools I emailed during my spiral.

Tension grips me like a bear, but I don't make any sudden movements. Something inside me says not to let Ben know something just happened. I glance up, and he's still blissfully scrolling.

With a trembling thumb, I open the email:

> Dear Mr. Rossi,
> Thank you for inquiring about admission to the University of the Arts London's design program. While we're at capacity for the fall, we will gladly consider your portfolio for the winter term. Please submit any relevant materials by the end of the month.

The end of the month—this month.

It's not too late. My portfolio is waiting for me outside in the gardens.

Like a child being pushed on a swing, I soar into the air, my hope freshly renewed that my talents could still be needed and wanted by a top program. But like a swing, I hurtle backward with a dizzying churn.

If I go, would Ben follow? Is that asking too much?

London and Edinburgh are about four hours from each other. That's not so bad, right?

Not much farther than the drive between Valle and Chicago, and that distance was more than enough to hide Ben from me for the last five years.

Did I repair a damaged relationship—one of the most important of my life—just to lose him all over again? The parlor's portrait of Mama Bianchi gazes at me with a cruel reminder:

The curse is still in play. The curse *is* me.

Worse than before, I have so much more to lose now.

CHAPTER 25

NIGHTMARES RETURN

That night, I dream again of Vero Roseto.

But not as it is, as it was. Not even as it was in my childhood, but on the day the last brick was laid in 1945 at the end of World War II. In the dream, I leave my bed and go walking into a sunny, misty afternoon. I'm wearing luxurious satin pajama bottoms, champagne colored with a violet pinstripe. I'm bare-chested except for the expensive silk robe flowing openly behind me like a cape while I stroll the grounds in a serene haze. The house is empty but lived-in, as if everyone vanished, leaving behind their knitting and loaves of rosemary bread cooling on the stovetop. The scent of fresh paint is everywhere.

The walls are blank, though. That's the biggest difference.

No memories yet, no family pictures. Not even a family yet, but there will be. I'm filled with certainty about that much. Romance, children, grandchildren, an empire. It's all coming.

"Is anyone there?" I call out, to no response. "You don't know me yet, but I'm your family."

When I emerge outside onto the deck, the crisp newness

of the wood makes me smile. The world has turned black-and-white, like an old movie, but I'm in color. Somewhere, big band music plays, faint and ghostlike. It's disorienting, but somehow, I know where to go:

Straight ahead, to the rose garden.

When I cross the lawn and pass under the archway, I see the first speck of color that isn't me—a young woman stands by the Wishing Rose bush. Her collared farm shirt, tied in a knot above her belly, is as screamingly red as the rose she's holding. Her hair is raven dark. Her cheeks are round, cherubic, and pretty.

It's my great-grandmother. The original Mama Bianchi.

Only it isn't her, it's me. I'm dressed as her: long black hair, crimson lips, and in sensible, feminine work pants. It's me, but I know it's really her inside. I'm so lovely.

As I approach Mama Bianchi, the vines that once smothered the rose garden walls pulsate and shift, as if they're living tentacles. My silk robe billows in the growing wind, the cape-like hem somehow longer than before. I am commanding and elegant, and so is Mama Bianchi. We are worthy opponents on a battlefield. Our meeting has an adversarial energy I can't explain.

She's been expecting me.

When she looks up, she extends a rose. "Want to do the Lindy Hop?"

I shake my head. "There's no time for that."

Sadly, she nods. "I'll wait here for my husband, then."

"He's not your husband yet. He's overseas."

Mama Bianchi chuckles and smacks my shoulder playfully. "Do you really think I'd build all this if I wasn't sure he'd be my husband?"

My great-grandmother gestures beyond the garden archway. It's true, Vero Roseto was her handcrafted love letter to an impossible man. Was it faith in him that drove her to invest this much in an uncertain prospect? Or was it delusion? Overhead, the big band music changes to the melancholic Duke Ellington song "(In My) Solitude." Piano and brass notes fill my heart with heaviness.

There's no way I'll ever have an ounce of that kind of faith in a guy.

I scowl at my great-grandmother, my robe flapping like a flag in the windstorm. "Your rose is ruining my life! You made up this whole rose myth, and now everyone in our family thinks it's the only way to find true love!"

She smiles—it's my smile. And a happy tear falls. "I have a family?"

"Yes! And I'm part of it. You die when I'm six, but you keep controlling our lives." My chin trembles, but I refuse to cry for her. "I need you to take back your curse. I'm in love with a boy, and I can't lose him again."

Her hand—my hand—black-and-white except for brilliant, scarlet nails, grazes my cheek. Her eyes—my eyes—fill with pity, the kind you have for someone sick. "My roses don't curse."

"They do," I whisper pathetically. "I can't be Ben's boyfriend if you don't take it back. Something's going to happen to ruin it. I need him in my life. Please. And *yes*, I'm with a boy!" My heart shakes with rage inside my chest. "That's why I wished on your rose to make me different. I wanted what the rest of you had! You didn't make space for *me* in the rose myth!"

Gently, Mama Bianchi pulls me into her arms—my arms—and cradles my head. I've never hugged myself before. It's nice. As she pets my curls, she whispers, "I didn't make space for you. My father didn't make space for me. My husband didn't make space for me." Her tone intensifies into an ominous growl. "*Make* me make space. Show me what you're worth. I showed them and turned this filthy sheep farm into Vero Roseto—stone and clay and vines and myth. Roots so deep they can never be pulled out. This is the moment my family began, not when my husband came back from France. If I didn't show strength when I had it least, I would have never trusted it. Show *me*. If you say there's a curse, break it yourself."

Mama Bianchi releases me from the hug and drifts away with her rose.

"Wait!" I say, my robe whipping violently. "I need your help!"

Under the archway, she turns back. "Yes, you do. But all you've got is you."

She leaves. I chase her.

"Wait! I can't lose Ben! I can't hurt Ben!"

When I reach the archway, Mama Bianchi has already traveled to the patio. She smiles—my smile—and waves the rose. I follow, sprinting as she disappears inside. But when I reach the patio, she's already at the top of the East Wing stairs. She waves the rose, and I chase her again. But when I reach the stairs, she's already walking inside my room.

I burst inside the room, furious. "Hey!" I shout, but once I'm inside, I look out the bedroom window and see Mama Bianchi back outside on the lawn below, waving that goddamn rose. "Wait! WAIT! WAIT!"

It's dark in my room, except for a small touch lamp turned to the lowest setting, which is as bright as a candle flame. I sit straight up in bed, staring at the window where, moments ago, I screamed at Mama Bianchi. My chest is slick with terror sweat, and for some reason, I'm still hollering, "Wait! Wait!" to an empty room.

Except it's not empty.

Someone is dabbing my shoulders and head with a cool cloth. Frantic hands try to dry me off before pulling me into a fierce hug. Whispers come: "It's okay, Grant, stop it, you're awake, you're here, you're okay."

"*What?*" I ask, not fully awoken. "No! No. N—"

"You're dreaming," Aunt Ro says, her concerned voice far away but traveling closer. When I turn, I finally see her. Not me in Mama Bianchi drag. No black-and-white house. It was just a dream, but it was so vivid. Ro, wrapped in an oversize nightshirt, smooths my hair with a trembling hand. "Grant, you were screaming. Are you okay?"

"Ro . . ." I say, grasping weakly for her. My entire body is quaking. I don't think I've ever felt this scared. My heart won't settle. I think I had a panic attack.

Anxiety won't release its stranglehold, even when I'm unconscious.

"Ro," I say, clarity returning. "I can't hurt Ben. I'm not stable enough to be what he needs. I can't do long distance. I just can't. I'm not strong like Mama Bianchi."

"What?" she asks, sleep-deprived but desperate to understand.

"If I lose him again . . . My curse . . ."

"HEY." Ro snaps her fingers loudly. My spiraling attention collects and obeys her command. "There's no curse. There's no myth. It's just a rose, Grant. I'm sorry we fed you this dumb story, but it's just a story, that's all. It's not worth destroying your life over. Or losing a boy like Ben. Or waking up screaming, honey. I'm so sorry we did this to you."

Her hug swallows me again, but I scramble out of it. I feel unhinged, like I need her to understand something primal about me. "It's not you, I did this. I made myself sick." I wince back a splitting headache. "The curse is real to me. I know myself, I'm gonna end up doing something that scares Ben or pushes him away." Now the tears come. "He can't know I'm still messed up—"

"Grant." Ro hands me a travel pack of tissues from her pocket. I dab at my eyes as she strokes my leg above the covers. "Loving someone means they have to see your vulnerabilities. They see what you don't want other people to see. Do you know the gross things your uncle does? Do you know the scary shit I say to him sometimes? No. That's knowledge for him and me alone. You are *human*. This isn't anything I haven't seen before. Ben's seen you more intense before. Remember your grandma's wake?"

I moan unexpectedly. "I tried to wish away one of the most important parts of me. What's wrong with me?"

Silence crackles in the empty bedroom as Ro considers my question.

I lace my fingers behind my head like a long-distance runner, willing my breaths to slow.

Finally, Ro looks up, her dark features hardened in the low, flickering light. "Grant, when are you gonna give yourself a break, huh? I promise, you're not the first boy in history to make that wish. And by the way, *everyone* regrets the dumbass things they wished for when they were thirteen. I wished for a *third* Reagan term. You know why? Because I didn't know a goddamn thing, and the planet is lucky that wishes are just make-believe. Wishes are intentions. They are you. It's all just you. You want to mess things up with Ben? They'll be messed up. You want to make it work? I believe you can do it. The rose is just a token of your intention."

Mama Bianchi's dream words find me again.

You say there's a curse, break it yourself.

But in the dream, I was Mama Bianchi. This knowledge is already in me.

"Thanks, Ro," I say. "Sorry to make you philosophize in the middle of the night."

Chuckling, Ro stands from my bed, her eyes glistening. "It's God's punishment on me for letting you make that wish. I should've told you *that night* you didn't have anything to worry about."

I smile weakly. I don't know if that would've been comforting or frightening, to have someone so close reveal that they heard everything—that they knew what I was trying to bury.

"God's punishment, huh?" I ask, smirking. "A minute ago, you said there's no such thing as curses, that we're all masters of our own intentions or some garbage like that."

Without missing a beat, Ro waves me away. "For you, there isn't. For me, there's mystical punishment."

"Nice talking to you, Ro."

We blow each other a kiss, and she returns to her room. I lie awake, the touch lamp's low light still flickering like a candle, and I wonder exactly how much intention I really have in this situation. Do I want this to work with Ben? Yes, but there are more things to consider than a relationship.

What if school in London works out?

What if Ben really would be happier in Scotland?

What if we do long distance, and I see him on Instagram with another guy . . . and then I make bad assumptions again?

I don't know if I've done enough work on myself yet to be stable for him.

What if Ben and I are meant for each other, just not right now? I want to be healthy enough to treat him the way he deserves. I have to figure out this curse on my own, without the pressure of letting down Ben.

Could we split up and find each other again a third time?

If my great-grandmother could build Vero Roseto for a man that she didn't know could really show up for her, then I can have faith that Ben and I will work out someday.

Just not now.

CHAPTER 26

TI DESIDERIO

At the end of a long week, Ben and I find ourselves with a free afternoon for the first time since . . . ever. But that doesn't necessarily mean there's peace.

After two months of nonstop planning, the Rose Festival is tomorrow.

My living sculpture gowns are finished. The fountain at the Wishing Rose is running. The grounds look even prettier now than when we were kids. Vero Roseto has been successfully rebuilt, but I can't shake this horrible sinking feeling that an unexpectedly beautiful chapter in my life is about to close.

Like a rose, this summer bloomed bright, but after tomorrow, everything will start to decay.

Today is the last bittersweet day to enjoy what Ben and I have grown together.

In the basement, on the "good kid" side without all the scary doors, Ben and I sit cross-legged and sift through boxes of memories. At least ten cardboard cartons sit stacked on top of one another in the cupboards next to the children's books and board games. I run my fingers over an inscription on one of the boxes, written in green Sharpie in childish cursive: HALLOWEEN.

The O is colored like a jack-o'-lantern.

"I wrote this!" I say, admiring my fine illustration. Ben pops open the lid, and just as we remembered, it's filled with children's costumes. The ratty, gray Rapunzel wig. A wizard's cloak stitched with patterns of silvery stars. A Jason hockey mask with fake blood smears. A headband that makes it look as if you have a machete going through your skull. We paw through the contents like it's a time capsule—Ben and I never got to spend Halloweens here, but my grandma kept this box of costumes for us to play with year-round.

"Speaking of costumes . . ." Ben says coyly, leaping up. "I finally got my outfit for the Rose Festival sorted. Wanna see?"

"Immediately!" I pop up, accidentally kicking the Halloween box as I go.

"Eyes closed." Ben reaches for my cheek and gently shuts my eyes for me. As Ben spends the next minute loudly rummaging through the games closet, my heart won't settle. I'm actually nervous he's going to look too handsome, and it'll make leaving him even more excruciating.

But when he tells me I can open my eyes, my worries are soothed.

He looks awful!

Ben McKittrick, the handsomest man for miles, wears the most hideous outfit that's ever existed: a brown velvet tuxedo the exact shade of a UPS truck. The undershirt is ruffled and frilly. The lapels are 1970s wide. And a matching brown ribbon tie, extra fluffy.

It's Grandpa Angelo's wedding suit! We thought we lost it.

"STOP," I say, covering my mouth. "Where did you find it?"

"He gave it to me," he says proudly. "Before he died. Told me to keep it somewhere safe so it wouldn't go into the coffin with him. He wanted it still bothering everyone after he was gone."

"Why'd he give it to you? When . . . ?"

Ben's smile freezes. "You mean how did I end up with the suit Angelo was wearing the day you banished me from Vero Roseto for a thousand years?" Struck silent, I have to nod. Ben shrugs. "Guess he felt bad for me. I hid it in the Halloween box. Figured nobody would go looking there, since everyone but us was grown up, and you and me were history."

My jaw hangs open, speechless.

"So, as punishment for convicting me without a trial," he says, patting those truly awful lapels, "I'm going to wear this and mortify you at your festival." Giggling, he spins in place. "This was so big on me when we were little, but it actually fits now."

The fit is impeccable. The brown jacket is so bunchy, and Ben's chest is so prominent, it looks like he's wearing an IKEA dresser.

"You and Grandpa were the same size! I don't believe it!"

I say, unable to remove my hands from my mouth as I stare helplessly at the train wreck.

Ben twirls again. "Angelo and me were both tiddied out!"

"Nope! We're not gonna talk about my grandpa's tiddies, *thank you.*" Ignoring me, Ben seductively smooshes his pecs together. "Okay, that's it! You're going down!" I leap up and pry the jacket off him as he smacks me away. Before I can pull his arms from the sleeves, Ben twists backward to kiss me.

I kiss back, but each time I do, I hear the toll of grim funeral bells.

Gong.

Soon, Grant. This will all fall apart so soon.

"And your sibs are coming, too," Ben says. "They're gonna *freak!*"

"Totally." My thoughts still miles away, I laugh hollowly.

Ben sighs wistfully. Good—he didn't notice my sudden darkening.

I reject your negativity, I tell myself. *I hate you, Grant. You've stolen every nice moment from me.*

My mind says nothing back. It simply plays a little movie from the future: a movie where I'm at school in London, my hands trembling as I try to load my sewing machine. They're trembling because I've just seen Ben's Instagram of him and his ex in Scotland—and they're no longer exes.

It's all *so* possible, and in the little movie in my head, I spiral and block Ben. But then I change my mind and unblock him, but he's already seen my block. He's furious. He's yelling at me about how he knew my love for him was fake. Then he blocks me.

I never see him again.

In the reality of the basement, Ben—covered in smiles and my grandfather's ugly suit—pulls out another box. I inspect a row of Nancy Drew books on the shelves behind me, but this is a ruse to brush away a tear while Ben isn't looking. After a cleansing, centering breath, I return to him. The box is filled with photo albums—some are ancient and frilly, detailing my great-grandmother's marriage, my grandparents' marriage, my aunt's marriage, and obnoxiously, my parents' doomed marriage; each of the albums' covers are emblazoned with a rose and the phrase TI DESIDERIO in gold filigree script.

Ti desiderio.

I desire you.

An invisible hand wrings my heart like a sponge as I try—and fail—to picture Ben and me in our own Ti Desiderio rose album. The image won't conjure in my mind, not even for pretend. A thick brain fog prevents it from manifesting.

Ben flips through my grandparents' album with a faint, dazed smile. "Angelo was so cool. He always made me feel like I was part of the family. I worked in his veggie garden with him once, and he told me that marrying into this family was tough. The Bianchis are hard to crack, and you're close-knit, so it's real easy to feel like an outsider. He said that's why you all need a magic rose to prove you belong with someone, because you only listen to higher powers, not your own hearts."

Okay, drag me, Grandpa.

But he was right. Actually, he was *too* right.

I blink, and a serene clarity spills over me. I reach for Ben's bare knee and stroke its fine, light fuzz. "Why did Angelo tell you that?"

Ben smiles, but can't meet my eyes. "I think he knew."

Wave after wave of emotions smash me against the rocks in my head. "I thought . . ." I suck in a pained breath. "I thought he didn't know."

Ben chews his lower lip and keeps staring at the album. "We always think we've got 'em fooled, don't we? C'mon, Grant, I was around so much. People saw. And . . . after I lost you, I feel like he was trying to help me stay a part of the family."

Vero Roseto has more spirits in its walls than just Mama Bianchi guiding the fates of her descendants. Angelo has his say, too. He was a cool-headed, understanding builder and farmer, bound by love—not a rose—to care for the wild Bianchis. Like Uncle Paul. Like Ben. Like my dad, who found the responsibility too heavy.

Will Ben join Angelo and Paul? Or will he end up like my dad? Too weak to fight after too many hard years.

The next album isn't any kinder. It's newer, hardcover, some kind of shiny plastic vinyl made by Shutterfly. On the cover is a picture of the entire family at one of our barbecues on the deck. Everyone is there. SUMMER 2018, the cover says in a rainbow-colored font.

"I've never seen this," I say, opening the booklet immediately.

"Me neither," Ben says, crowding in closer.

Shoulder to shoulder, both of us young boys again, we pore through our old memories, each photo as fierce and poison-dipped as an arrow: Ben and me setting off Roman candles with my siblings; Ben and me with our faces painted after the Valle street carnival; Aunt Ro scream-laughing as Uncle Paul carries her piggyback through the parlor; Grandpa picking tomatoes from his garden; Grandma tickling my nephew, Angelo, who was just a newborn then.

Maybe this album is treating Ben nicer than me, because he can't stop smiling.

Aunt Ro must have compiled this. She never showed anybody. Did she just make it for herself? Was it so bittersweet that even she had to stash it away with all the other dusty memories?

The next pages answer my question.

In the photos in the back half, my family poses in black suits and dresses. Grandma's funeral. Next to these, in an oval frame, is a portrait of my grandma on her wedding day—gorgeous and dark-eyed in a white veil. Surrounding the frame, Ro has added rose stickers. This was the picture they used on her casket.

With a pulling at my heart, I remember the chaos of that

day. Fighting. Tears and blame. Me against Ben. A. C. against me. Mom against A. C. Dad against Mom. Aunt Ro against Dad.

In the history of the world, I don't think a family has ever gone from perfect to shattered so fast in a single moment. At least, not of their own self-inflicted wounds.

Grandma would have healed everything. She would've stopped us. But she was gone.

These pictures burn worse with my new information, that it was a misunderstanding based on Hutch's childish lie and my own belief in my curse. I was so frantic at the idea of losing Ben too that I made sure I'd lose him for good. How does that make any sense? If I'd just handled it better, the confusion would've cleared, and he might have been back in my life so much sooner. Ben wouldn't have had to lose my family when he needed an intact home more than anything.

In the basement, today, Ben lovingly plays with the curls on my neck. I shut my eyes on another painful throb.

I have to be strong and do this for us.

"Ben, I can't lose you again," I say weakly, my neck collapsing in shame.

"Hey." Ben swirls his hand across my back. "You're not gonna."

I wriggle free of his touch. I can't let his sweetness stop what I need to do. Ben clocks what I did—he flinches and scoots away, his eyes narrowed in fear. Lightheadedness sweeps over me, and I grip my chest to feel my heart—it's beating erratically fast.

"What I did to you was awful," I say.

"I don't care about—" Ben starts to say desperately, but I cut him off.

"This summer has been a dream. But, like, a dream that doesn't feel real. Like I'm gonna wake up in my bed in Chicago, and I'm gonna have dreamed the whole thing. It's making me out of my mind . . ." I keep my hand on my racing heart. "The summer's ending. The festival is gonna be over. We're going separate places, and we need to get real about that."

Ben laughs nervously and readjusts his cap. "So, what, are you firing me or dumping me?"

Finally, I let myself look at his eyes—eyes that are already heartbroken before I say the terrible words. "We can't do this right now. Be together."

Blood drains from Ben's face as he turns as white as a corpse.

The basement turns silent. Not even a mouse dares to scurry.

"You're serious." Ben's voice shatters me. Not angry, just calm and so, so tired. "After all this? That's it?"

Ro's pleas from last night try to reach me, but my cursed mind is stronger: *Hurt him now, or I'll hurt you both so much worse later.* Sorry, Ro. I know myself, and I'm doing this to save Ben from me.

I fumble my phone out of my pocket to find my UAL email. "The school I'm applying to is in London. I have to get my career back on track—" Ben stares helplessly. "If we did long distance, and it blew up again, it would kill me."

"It would kill *you*?" Quietly, Ben pulls off my grandfather's suit and returns it to its felt hanger. "You're worried *I* would blow it up, so you thought you'd blow it up first. I got that right?"

I don't need to speak to give Ben his answer.

He stands perfectly still—terrifyingly still. "Are you in love with me?" he asks.

"Yes."

"I'm in love with you." Ben slips off his hat and slowly rustles his hair. Everything he's doing is so calm, so *not* surprised at what's happening. "You know that Grant Rule I have? I made a second one. Never told you about it. It was 'Don't fall in love with this dickbag.'"

I don't mean to laugh, it just comes out. But Ben isn't laughing, so I quickly explain: "I had a secret Ben Rule, too! Don't fall in love with this jerkoff."

Blessedly, he cracks a smile. But it isn't comforting. It's a tired smile.

"Well," he says, shutting away the horrible suit in the game closet. "I don't know how you could be in love with me when you're already in love with someone else."

"There's nobody else!" I reach for his hands, but he takes a giant step back.

"I was referring to the lifelong romance between you and your drama." Ben slips his cap back on. "And there's no way I'm joining that threesome."

Sighing, Ben drifts away toward the stairs. I reach for him again, but again, he dodges. Halfway up the stairs, he stops, and hope slips back to me.

"Grant," he says, his back to me, "I'm not stupid. I knew this was gonna be hard. I just thought you'd trust me this time around, like I was gonna trust you. I thought we were worth trying for, for real. Sucks you don't agree."

There have been many insults traded between me and Ben over the years—some playful, some not—but his final insult is so true, so diabolically correct, such a sonic blast, that I'm numb.

I was afraid to lose the game, so I knocked over the board and stopped playing.

As I watch him leave, the only thoughts that come to me are *ti desiderio.*

I wish for you, Ben. But I don't do wishes anymore.

CHAPTER 27

THE EVIL EYE

The Rose Festival is finally here, so I truly couldn't have picked a worse time to break up with our gardener. The grounds don't need much tending, though, as Ben had placed everything perfectly last night.

But as usual in this family, nothing runs smoothly.

"We're getting rain," Uncle Paul shouts from the parlor. He presses his face to the sliding glass door and gazes hopelessly at the greenish clouds forming ominously over Valle Forest.

At the kitchen island, Aunt Ro—already dressed in Mama Bianchi's Sicilian peasant frock—eyes me sourly before returning to her plate of cold bread patties. Slumped next to her in my dress blacks, I roll my eyes. "Oh right. I made it storm."

Ro calmly sets down her mug. "You put the evil eye on us. It's been a summer of nothing but *mule* labor, and you go pissing off the one person who helped us." She lobs a set of keys noisily onto the table. "I found these this morning—his house keys—and a note. Ben's quitting. He asked me to mail his last check."

Lexi is really pulling her weight today. I might be exhausted, but the pain of Ben's instant departure floats mercifully in the distance. It still hurts like hell, but pre-Lexi, an event this cataclysmic would be clanging through my head like a church bell tower.

I chomp into a bread patty. "This feels bad enough, Ro. You don't have to make it harder."

"Explain why I should make it easier. Your problem is—wait, nope, I'm not doing the advice thing now." Ro flicks her hand and then retreats to her coffee. Changing her mind, she sets it down again. "This festival could mean the difference between selling off our family legacy and saving it, so maybe you could've rescheduled dumping Ben to Monday. He's done so much for us, it's bad karma hurting him before the festival, and we *need* all the good karma we can get."

My mouth filled with bread, I launch a counterattack. "I *said* I was sorry. I thought we sold all our reservations for the next few months."

"Short-term thinking, Grant!" Ro claps her hands together in a begging gesture. "If the buzz is good, we can keep booking through the winter. Almost all our summer revenue went into renovating the place and putting on the festival! We could be struggling again by Thanksgiving. And where will Ben be? I don't know. Where will you be? Jolly old England. Where will I be? The toilet."

Chomp-chomp-chomp. That's all I can do. It's just you and me now, bread patties. And Lexi, of course. Blessedly, Uncle

Paul saunters into the kitchen in a very Old Italian look: white dress shirt, dark slacks, and suspenders. "All right, Ro, that's enough," he says.

Ro tosses her balled-up napkin to the table. "Paul, I have to say my side—"

"All right, and you've said it. You're badgering the kid. His heart's broken."

"Paul . . ." Ro protests, but sadness is finally overtaking her anger.

Paul kisses the top of her head. "It's just a little rain. Today's gonna be beautiful. Grant did so much work for us. That fountain. Those dresses made of real flowers? People are gonna lose their minds, rain or no rain."

Ro's shoulders buckle, and both of us smile wearily at my uncle, who knew exactly what to say. My heart pinches remembering what Grandpa Angelo told Ben: that the outside people who come into this family are always patient nurturers.

Because our bloodline is as hot as a teakettle.

"I'm sorry, honey," Ro says, wrapping a desperate hug around me. Her touch is everything I need. The gentleness, the love, is so powerful I have to shut my eyes.

"Ro," I whimper into her shoulder, "I thought I was doing the right thing. I want him to be part of this family. I just want to be realistic."

Ro laughs heartily and retakes her seat. "When has a Rossi or a Bianchi ever been realistic?"

I have to laugh, too. "You're right. Why start now?" I toss the last bread patty over and over on my plate. "I have plans and . . . dreams. I can't ask him to drop everything and come with me. That's too soon."

Ro purses her lips. "You've been part of his life for a decade. If anything, you're too late."

My heart racing to my throat, I turn to her. "You think it's too late?"

Aunt Ro doesn't answer. She just looks tired.

"Is Ben still coming to the festival?" Uncle Paul asks, his body half-hidden behind the fridge door as he hunts.

I glance at my phone. No new messages.

"He said he would," I say, smoothing tension from my cheeks. "Said he'd be coming as a guest, so I think he'll be here when the foot traffic from the other festival houses finally reaches us." My eyes glumly stuck to the floor, I shrug. "At least he's not ignoring my texts."

Ro shrugs along with me. "Ben always comes back. He's my little alley cat." She smiles and rubs my knee. "You know, after Mom died . . . After you and Ben had that big blow-out fight, and you went back home . . . Ben still came around."

"Really?" I ask, my chest lightening with such a sweet thought.

"He did, every weekend. Your grandpa started getting worse, and no one else was around anymore. The house got so dark. Like someone switched off a light in me. Everything looked the same, but felt wrong. But Ben kept coming around to say hi. He'd stay for lunch. He'd talk with Dad. He'd even fiddle with the vegetable garden when Dad couldn't make it down the hill by himself anymore. Having him here was like a life preserver. I don't know why a teenage boy would want to hang around some sad old lady, but he did. Saved my life."

I squeeze Ro's hand under the table. "I don't think he ever liked going home."

Her eyes flare. "Definitely not. The way that family fought." She shivers and stares into her mug, like she's lost. "We never had kids. Ben's my kid." Ro smiles, pain in her eyes, and reaches for my chin. "Whatever you end up doing, he will always be part of this family."

I feel run through with a spear.

I never thought about how deep Ben's roots grew with my family. How when I smashed apart our friendship, I overlooked how much he meant to so many other people. How could I have let things get so strained? Twice!

"What do you want, Grant?" Ro asks. "Really. If you could wish again?"

Wishing.

Haven't I done enough of that?

After a thoughtful sip of coffee, my answer finally arrives, frighteningly simple: "I want to design in London, and I want Ben to come with me." Now a storm breaks across my face. "But I don't want you to be alone. And I don't want to make decisions for him."

Chuckling, Ro lands a kiss on my forehead. "First of all,

don't ever plan your life around me—except today, everything should be planned around me today! Second of all, it sounds like you just need to *ask* Ben what he'd like to do."

There it is. The simple thing I just can't do.

The thing I've been avoiding.

My smile becomes a wince as I ask my most vulnerable question: "What if he hates me?"

All of this fell apart because I'd rather blow up a great thing than ask a risky question and hear a disappointing answer.

Standing, Ro straightens the rose-colored shawl over her Mama Bianchi dress. "From the bottom of my soul," she says, "if you don't take this chance *now*, you will become a handsome, successful designer who lies awake in bed wondering, all those years ago, what Ben's answer would have been."

Satisfied that she's torn my still-beating heart from my chest, Ro walks out.

CHAPTER 28

THE ROSE FESTIVAL

Alone in the grand entryway, I gaze at Mama Bianchi's portrait and hear faint music outside. It's jaunty and whimsical string music from our gardens. Everyone is almost finished setting up. Meanwhile, in Valle, hordes of Rose Festival guests travel from house to house, admiring the most breathtaking assortment of rose beds for thousands of miles. And they're all ending up here.

The biggest, most famous rose assortment of them all.

There will be dancing, wine, fashion, and maybe even a wish or two.

We booked local photographers to do widespread coverage of Vero Roseto, the living sculpture garden, and the Wishing Rose installation. It's a one-two punch—Ro gets brand-new pictures for her website (redesigned by me), and I get my portfolio for University of the Arts.

Today will be an about-face from last year's show at the Art Institute, where I craved as much spotlight as I could get, gaudily dressing like an eighteenth-century prince, stomping the red carpet arm in arm with my influencer boyfriend, and decorating the cover of magazines I would later deface. This year, I am dressed in clean, simple blacks, and I plan on letting my work speak for itself. The old, desperate-to-please Grant Rossi is being put to bed. The new Grant is quieter and will *try* taking some personal risks.

Here we go.

On a piece of blue stationery, I write my note to Ben. I tend to be chatty, so this time, I keep it simple:

> You brought me back to life. I never want to be any-
> where you aren't.
> At five o'clock, when the festival is over, I'll be where
> you put mud in my hair.
> I'm going to make another wish today. If you're open
> to it, I want us to both make one at the same time.
> If not, I didn't want to leave without giving you this
> to keep.

I remove the small orange Nerf dart from my pocket—the one we fired at the Avengers in the laundry chute, the first thing Ben found when he returned to Vero Roseto—and wrap it in my letter. I seal it in an envelope labeled BEN and then text him:

I left something important for you under Mama Bianchi's portrait. I would really like to see you, but

if you don't want to see me, please don't leave without checking under the portrait.

The second I place the envelope beside the entry hall vase, my phone buzzes. It's Ben:

I promise I'll check.

Roller coaster goes up—he'll see my envelope. Roller coaster goes down—he didn't say if he wants to see me or not.

"That'll have to do for now, Mama Bianchi," I tell her portrait. After a big, catlike stretch, I engage in a staring contest with my great-grandmother. Over long seconds, I search for my face in hers. In my dream, she told me to prove to her I could beat this curse, that I belonged in the family myth, that I was worthy of a love like the others the Wishing Rose has brought together.

Ben and I rebuilt her home—we belong in this family *and* this myth. We have already proven our worth to both the living and spiritual inhabitants of Vero Roseto.

The only one I hadn't convinced was me.

Sadly, I lose the staring contest. She is, after all, oil on canvas.

"It's time to keep your legacy going," I tell her. "I don't know how you built this entire house, vineyard, and garden, all for a man who wouldn't get serious for you. The faith that required from you. The delusion. That could have blown up in your face. Fully unwell behavior." I raise my finger. "*If* he said no. But he said yes, so you became a legend." A pleasant sigh escapes me. "I really am just like you—I'm going to do something wild today. I just need that Mama Bianchi faith."

With that, I leave Mama Bianchi to her staring. Hopefully, when she sees Ben later, she'll put in a good word for me.

The sky is green and pregnant with coming storms, but Uncle Paul is right: it can't dampen the gloriousness of Vero Roseto's gardens. I stand atop the deck, hugging a post to keep myself from fainting with happiness. Look at what we did. An emerald-green lawn that used to be pale and dying; a tented, checkerboard sculpture garden of living, glamazon floral queens; and a freshly reenergized rose garden, its high green walls and canary drapes concealing the Wishing Rose and its river of tears.

Tonight, I will meet my fate there—either with Ben or without him. Tears indeed.

Crossing the lawn toward the sculpture garden, I pass photographers scurrying around to capture candids of the event before the town of Valle descends, but I ignore them. No posing today, Grant. The work will speak, not me.

At the winery patio to my left, a string quartet fills the air with gorgeous Italian melodies. Beside them, tables draped in cream-colored silk offer platters of antipasti, shrimp cocktails, stuffed mushrooms, and grilled vegetables. *That's for you, Grandpa Angelo.* Another table offers small glasses of Invidioso and Grato wines, along with carafes of coffee and sambuca. *Also for you, Angelo.*

Under the canary-draped tent, garlands of rose-tinted lights float like pixies around the living sculpture models. Each model has their own raised pedestal, as if they were carved topiary shrubbery. At the foot of each pedestal is a placard listing the names of the models, the kinds of flowers used in each design, and how many bulbs it took to craft the look.

Twist: A LOT.

Six models, six flower types: roses (white and red), tulips, lilies, magnolias, and hydrangeas.

I debated bringing non-roses into the festival, but we were just aching for a little differentiation to make them pop.

Dedicated dressers assist each model as we prepare for the coming crowds, letting them sip water, adjusting bulbs on the wire dress frames, or just fanning away this humidity before their makeup starts to run. Uncle Paul sneaks under the carriage of the magnolia model and tampers with her irrigation hose with a wrench.

"It just keeps splurting," says the magnolia model.

"Yeah, like a sprinkler," Paul says. His shoulders flinch. "Oop! It got me."

Every model is a beloved face from my Art Institute show last year, and while I wave congenially, I have to pay special thanks to my red rose diva:

Nick Hutchinson. My first boyfriend. A tiny cutie with chipmunk teeth who has transformed overnight into the

Queen of Hearts. The red rose silhouette is a slim-fit, femme fatale–style cocktail gown, a vibrant red bloom taking up every square inch. Hutch wears a corsage of pure baby's breath on each wrist and a heavy iron neckpiece of thorns. In lieu of a wig, he wears a monstrous headpiece of rose blooms, turban-like in how it makes him look like a faded, doomed movie star from the Silent Era.

Any negative feelings I ever had for Hutch vanish under his beauty.

Even though the show hasn't begun, he's already in place. This is game day for him.

"Queen," I say proudly.

"Do I look all right?" Hutch asks, his first glimpse of fear breaking the powerful visage.

I lean close to whisper, "The others are gonna have to fight to keep people's attention off you."

"Thank you," Hutch says on a hard exhale. "I'm really glad we got to, you know, be cool before I left."

"Me too." I squeeze his forearm to avoid mussing the baby's breath at his wrist.

Hutch giggles. "Weird, this is my first time at Vero Roseto. You kept me so far away, your dirty townie secret, and now I'm in drag in your grandmother's garden."

My laugh becomes a groan. "Yeah, the universe loves its little surprises."

"It's me, the universe's little surprise." Hutch does a slight magical flourish with his wrists, but it's *just* jerky enough for his rose headpiece to falter and slip down his forehead. He reaches for it, his balance overcorrecting, and I prepare myself to watch Hutch fall and ruin the most important look in the entire event.

But Uncle Paul's arms reach Hutch first. My uncle lunges, grabs him by his bare, exposed shoulders, and at last . . . Hutch steadies himself. Everyone breathes.

"Sorryyy," Hutch says.

"It's all right, just careful not to move your neck too much," I say, racing around the dress in circles to make sure everything is still intact. Luckily, only one errant rose didn't make it, but it's at the base in the back.

Hutch stretches his skinny chicken-wing shoulder blades to crack them. "It's hard. This headpiece is heavy."

"It's fashion! You look perfect. I believe in you."

Spinning around, I trot out of the tent with the spare rose in hand, grinning to myself that while Hutch and I have put the past behind us—and he does look like a million dollars in that gown—he must pay a small Bitch Tax and stand rigidly all day wearing a cumbersome headpiece.

I still have a drop of evil in me.

"Knock, knock," says a voice outside the tent, and five people rush in unceremoniously. My parents, my sister Kimmy, her little son Angelo . . . and Ben. My mom—a small, round woman with cheerful dark (dyed) curls—could be Ro's twin, even though Mom's older by six years. My dad is where

I get my height: a silver-bearded mountain man (literally how A. C. is gonna look in twenty-five years), he hangs to the back of the crowd as if he doesn't want to steal any focus.

Having been divorced for over a decade, my parents have long since learned how to behave at co-functions (unlike Ben's parents, who are now-and-forever oil and water).

Kimmy is keeping it plain in a T-shirt, jeans, and ballcap with her ponytail sticking out the back. Angelo runs in overexcited circles at the sight of all these gorgeous people in flower gowns. He has an enormous blue rose painted on his cheek.

And Ben—Ben, as threatened, is wearing Grandpa Angelo's hideous brown velvet wedding tuxedo. This boy is in the frilliest, most puffed-up seventies outfit imaginable, he looks grotesque—yet he is also the most fascinating person in the entire room.

I love him.

I almost say it out loud, but it wouldn't be right. It's not time yet.

"You're all here!" I gasp with joy, unable to look away from Ben. "You're here."

Ben smiles uncomfortably. "Yeah, Angelo was so excited to see the sculpture dresses, so we ran a little ahead of the crowd to get here first. But you should know, *everyone* is coming."

"For real?" I ask, a brick hitting my stomach. Ben nods. I have so much I want to ask him and tell him, but people are coming, and my family is already here. I need to not force things. There is no control. My only course of action is to stay present in the moment and appreciate that everyone I love is here.

"Did you see lots of flowers, Angel Baby?" I ask, scooping a screaming, giggling Angelo off his feet. He nods frantically. "What was your favorite house?"

Kimmy holds up her hand. "He *loved* the Blue Rose Cottage."

"I got this right here!" my nephew shrieks, jabbing at his painted cheek.

My heart lifts. The most eccentric, lovely elderly couple runs the Blue Rose Cottage. It's not very big or showy, but they exclusively grow white roses, which they align perfectly in a row, and then the hour before the festival begins, they douse their flower beds with a light blue paint. It only lasts for the afternoon before it runs and ruins the flowers, but in that window of time, it's pure wizardry.

When I set Angelo down, he gazes, open-mouthed, at the models, but it's Hutch in the red roses who seems to capture his imagination.

Ben walks him and Kimmy over to meet Hutch. All four of them are laughing, and my insides grow warmer. Whatever lies ahead for my nephew, he has a stronger, more loving family now at Vero Roseto, and he'll never feel like he has to make some desperate, bad wish in the dead of night.

Without warning, my mom wraps a tight hug around me. "Ro told me everything you've been doing," she says, voice trembling. "I grew up in this house. I thought we were gonna lose it."

Mom breaks the hug by patting my curls, and I wriggle away. "Not the hair, Ma."

"Oh!" She smacks me, suddenly dry-eyed, and then . . . it's my dad's turn.

Dad has improved so much in the last few years, but especially after a summer at Vero Roseto, marinating in not-the-best memories of everyone (including me), I can't help flinching as he approaches with that flat, sour look on his face he's always got.

"Ro says you're looking at London," he says.

"Uh, yeah," I say, businesslike with him as usual.

A smile splits his mighty beard in half. It's unnerving. What's happening?

Oh. A hug is happening.

One quick—but nice—clamp around my shoulders, and then it's over. "You're so talented," Dad says, and I fight the urge to check behind me to see if there's someone else he's talking to. But no, Mom's smile says it's me. "You're a really special guy. You're gonna get in. There's nothing you can't do."

"Dad . . ." I groan, wiping a quick tear before he sees.

With one last clap on my cheek, Dad points over my shoulder at Ben. Coyly, he says, "Take your little British guy with you. Seems like a sign to me."

Only my father would call a red-headed, brogue-spitting

Scotsman this family's known for a decade "British." But a sweet word about gay shit from my dad is like rain in a desert to me, so I let him walk away thinking he got the last word. Beaming, my mom flashes her eyebrows at me and follows him to view the other gowns.

As they leave, Ben returns, looking frighteningly good the longer I see him in my grandfather's vintage monstrosity. "Did you make Hutch's headpiece extra heavy on purpose?" he asks. I wink. "Shady."

"This fell." I present Ben with the stray rose bloom from Hutch's gown. He studies me as I thread the stem through his jacket buttonhole as a boutonniere. "Now you're a fashion baby."

"Thanks." His energy turns cold. Not cold, just . . . neutral.

Did he get my envelope yet? Probably not if they rushed over from the other houses.

It's okay. He'll get it in time. It's still early.

"So, look, um . . ." He pulls out the Nerf dart. My insides explode into goo. He scratches the back of his neck awkwardly, and it's so cute.

I'm in Hell.

"Grant, uh," he says, "I'm gonna think about it. Okay? I don't know if I'm up for that today. And I don't know if you are either. There's a lot of people here. Traci and A. C. are coming behind us. That British travel guy, actually, he came back." Ben lowers his voice. "With a boyfriend!"

"Mr. Cartwright?" I ask. This shocking information is the only thing that could've derailed my spiral from Ben's onslaught of a bummer reply.

"They look *really* happy."

I laugh, throwing my arms up. "Well, at least we know the Wishing Rose isn't homophobic. It just doesn't like me!" Ben's smile drops. "Oh. That was a joke. I'm not serious."

Ben frowns, overflowing with pity. "See . . . it's just gonna be a tough day, Grant, and you're not gonna be thinking clearly enough to do another rose wish. That'll be like a trauma buffet."

Oddly enough, Ben's *disbelief* in my wellness clears my anxiety. I appraise my would-be soulmate with the utmost sobriety. "Ben. My invitation still stands. At five, I will be where I said I'm going to be. I would love for you to join me, but it's up to you."

"Okay." He nods tentatively.

I need to get out of this tent and make sure our onslaught of guests is greeted properly. First impressions are everything. As I turn, Ben reaches for me. "Grant?"

"Yeah?"

"Just . . . when you go out there, have a good time? Don't worry about me or us, just focus on how brilliant you are and what you created."

I smile. "What *we* created. Angelo's garden is back because of you. It's *your* garden now. And this beautiful lawn is all you.

And the deck. And the entire rose garden! I designed the Rose Festival, but you . . . you rebuilt Vero Roseto."

Sheepishly, Ben has no choice but to smile. "Don't embarrass me. Get out of here!"

Outside the tent, Aunt Ro and Uncle Paul are already waving to a massive horde of humanity. At the end of the lawn, along the East Wing of Vero Roseto, hundreds of people—young and old, children and parents, packs of friends—flow toward us, like a medieval army if they were smiling and clutching bags of assorted flowers.

Here they come.

Aunt Ro, already performing Mama Bianchi, welcomes everyone, and I hurry to join her side. In the crowd, there's tons of unfamiliar faces, but it makes the familiar ones pop even brighter: Eshana, my Art Institute bestie, a small Indian girl with dark golden skin and black, chopped bangs. She beams as she wears a crown of white roses in her hair. My brother, A. C. (wearing a sash of bright flowers like a lei); my older sister Traci (her blond hair braided with daisies); Mr. Cartwright, the stately British travel writer (wearing a flowing blouse and slacks with a bright, rose-red ascot). He's linked at the arm with a man I assume is his boyfriend—like Mr. Cartwright, he's Black, but not as old, with a shaved bald head and dressed in a comfy cable-knit sweater.

That's everyone Ben warned me about.

However, there are some guests he did not.

In fact, these guests are probably why he was nervous to meet me later. Why he asked me to forget about us and to try to have a good time. The so-called trauma buffet.

Ben didn't tell me—and I forgot to confirm if they were coming—that my ex is here with his boyfriend.

CHAPTER 29

GOODBYE, PUMPKIN

I don't run from my ex, so I'm already impressed with my restraint.

To my knowledge, he never responded to my Instagram message, but here he is: Micah, a small, white twink with wavy dark hair and a child's simplistic sense of style. I loved him something awful, but then he realized he was in love with his best friend, Elliot—now his boyfriend, standing protectively by his side.

Elliot is kind, patient, and impossibly cute, like a woodland critter. He's the ultimate bunny, and I'm the ultimate beast. Micah really had no choice. Elliot is white, pretty, and chubby, with sandy-blond hair and a sparkling smile. He's also grown a faint blond beard, which I'm usually not fond of, but—*groan*—works on him. Micah and Elliot clasp hands, each of them carrying their own rose (which they likely bought for each other—*double groan*).

The boys stare, vaguely terrified, as if I'm going to start screaming and chuck them bodily off the premises.

Except . . . I already chucked them a year ago.

They wanted to stay friends, but I was hurt, so I abandoned them.

I did it with them, I did it with Ben, and I'll do it again with God knows who else if I can't break this curse *today*. Today is the day I settle my debts.

"You came!" I whisper, waving excitedly. Micah and Elliot return my wave with a relief that hurts my heart. Micah probably thought I'd never be nice to him again.

Behind me, Aunt Ro beckons the festival crowd deeper down the lawn toward the first stop on the tour: the living sculpture garden. I don't want to lose valuable time with these two, and what I need to say to Micah deserves privacy, so I run defense among the other friendly, familiar faces in the crowd. "One sec!" I mouth to Micah, and he nods enthusiastically.

Quickly, I dash through the crowd to hug Eshana and tell her, "These models are perfect. You saved my ass again, queen!"

"You can start paying me back right now," she says, clutching a bouquet of sapphire-blue roses. Her eyes dart around the premises. "Anyone single and straight here?"

I wince. "Unlikely. Ooh, one of our irrigation mechanics is bi."

"Okay!" Eshana brightens, her head swiveling left and right on the hunt.

"He's forty-two," I chuckle.

Her smile falls. "It's good to see you again, worm." On another laugh, she grabs my hand and looks deeply at me. "Your ex is here. You know that?"

On a deep breath, I announce, "I invited him."

Eshana is speechless. Slowly, a proud smile rises on her face. "You know," she says, slightly choked up, "for a while there, I was really worried about you."

"I know. I'm sorry I made you worry."

She throws one more Beloved Friend Hug around my chest and whispers, "Whatever you're doing, keep it up."

After I leave Eshana, I hurry over to two of my siblings, Traci and A. C. My brother rustles my hair, which I'm *trying* to be cool about—especially since Micah is here and I need to look perfect! I double back to grab Mr. Cartwright and his boyfriend before they reach the sculpture garden.

"Mr. Cartwright! Ben told me you were back!" I throw a hug around the man, who chuckles with delighted surprise.

"Grant, it has been a *divine* festival," he says, gesturing at the grounds. "Look at what you've done with the place."

I wave him off. "Ah, that's all Ben. I'm sorry about the weather, though."

"Don't be! The rain is for the flowers."

Mr. Cartwright is smiling harder than I'd seen him earlier in the summer. He's practically levitating off his toes. And I can guess why: he's dying to introduce me to his brand-new man!

I throw out my hand to the newcomer. "I'm Grant. Very cool to meet you."

Mr. Cartwright's boyfriend—Mr. Looks Comfortable in a Cable-Knit Sweater in August—shakes my hand with a moisture-soft grip. "Stephen Wilder," he says, American, unlike Mr. Cartwright's clipped British. "Got a gorgeous place here."

"Oh, it's, uh . . . it's home." With a swift glance at Vero Roseto's grand walls, I see it through Stephen's fresh eyes. It's a palace. I wish I didn't have to leave soon.

Returning to Mr. Cartwright, I say, "Don't want to keep you from the big show, but I'd really like to catch up as soon as you're done."

"I'd like that." He pets Stephen's shoulder, looking lost for words—a first. "We were going to the winery after this. Join us?"

My pre–rose garden plans now set, I wish Mr. Cartwright and Stephen a happy show and jog backward across the lawn toward the deck of Vero Roseto. The mass of townspeople suddenly breaks into three groups. One group heads straight for the rose garden to make a wish, Aunt Ro leads another toward the Blue Apple Orchard, and the rest slowly merge single-file into the living sculpture garden. A. C., Traci, Stephen, and Mr. Cartwright go with them.

Milling around just outside the sculpture tent, Micah glances anxiously back at me. My "one second" ask was quite a few seconds ago, and now I've backtracked to the patio. But I'm not being a coward—I have a plan. Waving at him, I gesture broadly to the phone in my hand. As fast as I can, I jump to my DMs with Micah and send:

> **I have something for you! Gotta get it upstairs.**
> **Meet me here on the deck in a minute?**
> **Bring Elliot too.**

Okay! his reply comes instantly.

Without thinking or planning, I dash inside the parlor, run up the East Wing stairs to my room, and find my vegan leather jacket, the one I sewed from scratch that's embroidered across the back with a pumpkin and vines. Vines so similar to the ones Mama Bianchi carved onto Vero Roseto. The jacket that got me into design school. The jacket I wore the day I met Micah. When I look at this jacket, I see him, not me. I used to hate that fact, but now I know why.

When I reemerge onto the deck, Micah and Elliot are waiting by the pool. I hold the jacket in a tight ball under my arm. Gotta keep it a surprise for just another minute.

"Come here, hug me!" I tell them both, and smiles break out over their faces as they envelop me in love. Micah's scent is exactly the same. I don't know if it's a deodorant, cologne, or just him, but it's The Micah Smell. It's extremely pleasant and very rich, and teleports me to Simpler Times.

All I can do is bite my lip to hold back a monsoon of emotions. With a flourish, I unfurl the pumpkin jacket. Instantly, Micah covers his face to hide his tears. Even Elliot brushes back a tear. "Oh my God . . ." Micah reaches for the sleeves, moved beyond words at the memento. It's priceless to him. Suddenly, he looks up, almost scared. "You're giving this to me?"

Sniffling back my own emotions, I nod. "It belongs with you."

Slowly, as if he might ruin it, Micah hugs the jacket close. When my hand leaves the material, I can almost feel my connection to the past break.

It's a gift, a sacrifice, and medicine to heal an old wound. By letting this jacket go, I'm free to accept the next gift the universe plans to send.

A gift that I hope is Ben's trust.

I hug Micah and Elliot one last time and tell them we should catch up as soon as I'm in the city again. With any luck, it'll be a double date. As they hurry up the lawn to see my living sculpture garden, the dark green clouds hanging over us finally make good on their threats, and the storm begins.

CHAPTER 30

THE ENVY CLUB

Since the rain finally started, the winery has become the newest hot spot for festival-goers caught without an umbrella. Although that's not stopping plenty of them from dancing across Vero Roseto's lawn in the downpour. As it's the last stop on the festival tour, people are shaking loose after what appears to have been a joyous day. Micah and Elliot twirl each other—my ex wrapped in the pumpkin jacket—while Eshana, Kimmy, and her son perform what I soon recognize to be flawless choreo from the "Rain On Me" video.

Oh, nephew. This really is gonna be a when, not if, situation.

From the winery's canopied deck, I can spy just inside the corner of the sculpture garden where volunteers help the models carefully escape my wire frame designs. Moments later, Hutch—back in street clothes and free of my murderous headpiece—runs outside, howling with laughter as he embraces the cleansing rain.

The one person I don't see is Ben.

It's twenty minutes to five. My chest fills with cement with each tick closer to the time I agreed to put myself out there, ask the big, scary question, and await my response. *God*, I hate Ben for putting me in this position of giving a shit about him. It would've been so easy to just spend a few weeks here, get Vero Roseto on its feet, and then fuck off to my new life. Nothing with Ben can just be simple!

With twenty minutes to kill, I have one last account to settle before Ben.

I've taken care of Micah.

I've taken care of Hutch.

I opened myself to the possibility that my sister will truly advocate for her son.

I took a back seat to my own work and let it speak for itself.

But before I settle things with Ben, I need to talk to Mr. Cartwright. I need my Envy Club—Team Invidioso— someone who's lived an older queer life, who knows that partnering with someone can be trickier than a fairy tale, much more complicated than straights or lucky gays would have us believe. Partnering requires trust, and some of us are challenged in that department.

How do I learn to do that after so much failure? Especially all the failure with Ben?

I run this question over in my head as I weave through the wine shop's tightening crowd. Every available seat is occupied by a roaring, wine-toasting local with bushels of roses. I squeeze by Traci, clutching a glass of chilled Invidioso, and

A. C., boisterously raising a hearty pour of red Grato. Judging from the pink flush on his pale white cheeks, I don't think it's his first.

"Little buddy!" my brother says, snatching me by the waist. Traci, not on her first glass either, happily paws at my soaked shirt like I'm a pretty kitty.

"Enjoying yourselves?" I ask.

"Grant, you saved the house," Traci says.

"Nah." I wave off her approaching hug. "It was Ben and Ro and Paul. Big group effort."

"You saved the house, little buddy," A. C. repeats, and he and Traci drag me into a sloppy hug like joyful zombies. I admit, it's been kind of powerful thinking of doing my art for a specific *purpose* and then watching it come to fruition. Personal art. Not art I think will say something about the world or ethics or capitalism, not art that's designed to people-please, but just . . . something that is a pure expression of me. Weird and grand and in love with my own drama as I am.

"We never thought this house would feel good again," A. C. says.

"Nope," Traci agrees, downing her glass.

"Our kids are gonna get to have what we experienced. Because of you."

I've been near tears too much today—and this whole summer—and year. "Ah, come on," I say, "you're killing me."

"We've been thinking," Traci says, pointing at A. C. "Grandma's looking down on you today. The rain."

"The rain!" A. C. says, gulping wine as a wave of grief comes over him. "Gram's tears."

"OKAY, OPERA," I say, dropping a quick hug on them—and ignoring the fact that I made a whole art installation of the Wishing Rose's tears, so I'm opera, too. But I'm going to blow my time window with Ben if I keep listening to more Italian nonsense. We mutter *I love you*s to each other, and I leave them to their next bottle.

At long last, I reach Mr. Cartwright and his boyfriend, Stephen, tucked away at a window bench, being very non-Italian in sharing their one sensible bottle of Grato in measured sips.

"Grant!" Mr. Cartwright says, patting a sliver of padded bench. I plop down, embracing the reality that I'm going to track water everywhere, and that's okay. From our window view, the warm summer rain continues to slap down. The sky is still dark, but golden sun punches through in spots like holes in notebook paper.

"You are drenched, young man," Stephen says.

"Yeah," I say, raking my fingers through my flattened mop. "My poor hair."

The two old men chuckle. "We would kill to have hair to mess up."

Mr. Cartwright gestures with his glass at the people dancing in the rain. "I see you didn't get up to any of that. It's like a production of *Hair* out there." Stephen and I laugh politely, but Mr. Cartwright is onto us. "Neither of you know what that is, do you?"

Now real laughter explodes as we both shake our heads.

Mr. Cartwright sighs longingly. Another hilarious reference wasted.

I check the time. Ten minutes left. There's no time for chitchat, so I jump in: "How long have you two been seeing each other?"

"Almost a year," Stephen says.

"A year?" I turn to Mr. Cartwright. "But you just came here for—"

"The Wishing Rose," he says, nodding. "I needed the courage to ask this one to be my husband." Stephen raises his hand to show off—yes, indeed—a diamond-encrusted ring. My mouth hangs open, and as usual, Mr. Cartwright understands. "I didn't say anything about being with anyone, and, Stephen, forgive me, but I needed the Wishing Rose to tell me if I was being a fool."

"A fool?" I ask.

"Grant, it's been hard," Stephen says, rapping his knuckles anxiously against the table. "We're long distance, Chicago to London."

I turn to Mr. Cartwright, startled, but with an odd kindling of hope. "I assumed you were in Chicago. You booked a trip here so fast after my rose garden video."

Mr. Cartwright nods while he sips. "I was in Chicago, seeing Stephen. I normally live in London, where I run my business. I'm pretty dug into the community." Inexplicably, Mr. Cartwright bites his lower lip as if he doesn't want to say what's next. "I didn't tell you last time—because you seemed sensitive about the subject—but before last year, I'd never been to Chicago. I write about travel, but Chicago hadn't been on my radar until I—like so many other gay people—followed along on Instagram what you were doing in the art world there."

I scoff. "It was my influencer ex. He brought in the numbers."

"But it was very striking art you were doing, Grant. We all witnessed it again today. The rose garden's installations, they're . . . astounding, but that's not even a strong enough word."

I shake my head aggressively. "There's no way my one art show that only performed once made it across the pond."

Mr. Cartwright doesn't blink. "Grant, now you're being rude. I am telling you . . ." He opens his palm to Stephen. "I have a fiancé now because I came to Chicago on a whim—so I could see your installation at the Art Institute. You have many more fans than you realize. And we've been waiting for you to come back."

The men watch me. My face hangs slack. None of this is computing.

I wrote off that whole era. It was so entangled with Micah, and later with how my attitude made everything fall apart, that I just . . . threw it all in the trash. But it brought these men together. It brought them here to Vero Roseto. Everything is blooming again.

It's five minutes to five.

"So, actually," I say, "I'm using the Rose Festival and my last installation as a portfolio to send to the University of the Arts in London."

Their faces brighten. Mr. Cartwright raises his glass. "I know a few alumni! They'd be lucky to have you."

It's too close to five o'clock to let myself smile. Swallowing hard, I say, "But . . . Ben . . ."

Clarity washes over Mr. Cartwright, and he winces. "You and Ben . . ."

I can't hide the fear from my face.

Stephen reaches across the table crowded with glasses and pats my wrist. "Long distance is nothing to be scared of. It's not the bogeyman, it's just . . . him." He and Mr. Cartwright share a soft, knowing glance. "If you have a real connection, that doesn't come around all the time. We know."

It's five. I stand abruptly, accidentally clattering a dish of charcuterie at the next table.

"I have to be somewhere," I say, my voice growing meeker by the second.

"Grant." Mr. Cartwright clutches my wrist. His intensity is serious. "You saved my life, now I'm going to save yours. Whatever you do, don't let him get away."

"Thank you."

Like a soaking wet bull, I charge through the winery, bumping chairs and tables as I exit as quickly as I can. When I meet the rain, I see the rose garden just ahead. My canary-yellow curtain keeps its magic separate from the rest of the world.

A place of magic and curses.

I sprint into the storm and run to meet my fate, whatever it is.

CHAPTER 31

WISH UN-GRANTED

The rain intensifies as I push through the curtain into the rose garden. Everyone is gone, either back home or chased inside the winery by the storm. Everything is so warm—that special summer lake weather that feels like they put the rain in the microwave for thirty seconds. Seven years ago, during a perfect Vero Roseto summer, this same rain caught me and Ben on Lake Valle in Grandpa Angelo's pontoon. A gleeful rain.

This kind of rain has never surrounded an unhappy memory in my life.

That's how I knew Ben would be here before I even saw him.

At the end of a corridor of luscious green walls we grew ourselves, Ben McKittrick stands beside the Wishing Rose bush, his back to me. The massive shrubbery shrinks him as he stands aside the flowing artificial rivers of tears we built. The storm has flooded our rivers, so now everything is tears, illuminated by the sapphire-colored footlights glowing in the dusk. However, the sky hasn't left us yet—I'm still able to recognize that Ben ditched Grandpa's frilly tuxedo, a memento too precious to ruin, for his gardener's tee and khaki slacks.

The rain plasters everything to Ben, leaving nothing about his body to the imagination. My own body, too. Every muscle I struggled to keep, every new curve I learned to love because of Ben, it's all on display as my shirt and dress pants stick to me like paste.

I am not the Grant Rossi I used to be. I'm somewhere between him and the new one.

And I'm ready to let go of this goddamn curse.

Ben doesn't hear me coming. His head is bowed to the bush, like a man praying. I approach him, one boot-step after another sloshing through inch-high puddles, gathering strength by the second. When I get close enough, his freckled bicep tenses, grasping one of the few remaining blooms not bought during the festival.

His eyes are shut. He's making a wish.

A low rumble of thunder cuts the sky. The powerful noise vibrates through my chest and pushes me toward courage. "Is that wish for me?" I ask.

Ben doesn't startle, or even move. "Haven't got round to making it yet. Been wondering how to say it."

My chest rises and falls on a painful throb. "Start with what you want."

"I want . . ." His jaw tenses. "A lot of things. Things that contradict each other."

I laugh heartily. I've been there. Asking an anxious homosexual what they want is like asking a child what their favorite dinosaur is: you're going to get thirty answers. We want so much. There's so much we can't have. And our tastes can be astronomically indulgent, not to mention fickle. The answers are many and constantly changing. So how could we be expected to make a single wish about something as thorny as who our hearts belong to?

The good news is, Ben doesn't have to make this wish alone.

Stepping behind him, wrapping my arms around his, I grasp the same crimson bloom. Our fingers interlock amid the petals.

"Open your eyes," I whisper.

Ben's muscular back expands and then deflates with a heavy sigh. "I want to go back in time, find you in the garden when you made your wish, and tell you . . . tell you nothing. I just would've kissed you. We deserved that. That's how our story deserved to end, not with all this shit. I want to go back and tell you 'Fuck you for leaving.' 'Fuck you for chucking me so easily.' I needed you. I know you haven't been happy either, but I needed you, and I'm sorry to tell you I've gotten real good at living without you."

Lexi be damned, my head is making the loudest noises it's ever made.

Through this chaos, my terrified lips somehow open. "Do you want me to go?"

Ben releases the rose and turns in my arms to face me. We're nose-to-nose, and his tight jaw has gone slack. Whatever hardness he's been carrying these last few years has finally been dropped. The boy reappears in his softened, rain-soaked features.

The silly boy, the boy I trusted, the boy I lost.

"I want you to take me," he whispers, almost begging. "Trust me. Don't second-guess me. Look at me and be *sure*, not be filled with . . . questions. I want you to see me like I see you."

This sweet guy. He doesn't get it.

"I trust you," I say, shrugging. "I don't trust me. I ruin things. I'm broken."

Ben's expression collapses. This isn't what he wanted to hear—and this isn't going well.

"Of course you're broken, you're gay," he says.

"Ummmmm . . ." Briefly, terror soars through my mind at the possibility that Ben has been a secretly self-hating homophobe this whole time.

Luckily, he takes my hand and, chuckling, explains himself. "Everybody queer I've ever met, just, we had to grow up too fast. We had to get harder and believe less, and it just made us . . ."

"Beasts."

"We deserve a second chance." He shrugs helplessly. "I love you, Grant. And I hate that. Because I don't know what to do with that information. I really don't."

I am sunk. Utterly sunk by his words. I don't even try to reach for glibness or cynicism. Instead, I reach for his shoulders. "I love you, too! I always have. I never stopped, even if it seemed like I did when I let you get away all those other times. Guys scare me *so* much that you're literally the only boyfriend I've ever fought for. Do you know what that means?!"

Ben blinks, a little afraid. "What?"

"It means I wasn't cursed to lose every boyfriend, and you weren't cursed to lose yours! Hutch, Brendan, Ruben, Dylan, Jon, Scott, Micah—I lost them because they weren't *you*. I was seeing Hutch when I made the wish to reveal who I really loved. And it did! Or at least, it was trying to, but I was being such a stubborn, emotional car crash, dumbass—"

Ben nods. "I agree, keep going."

I laugh like it's my first time. I couldn't drop my smile if I tried. "The rose was saving me until I found you again. It needed us to save this house, and . . ." I swallow hard. "And if we're really going separate places after this, then at least the rose made sure I didn't give up on us without a fight."

Ben clasps my face in his rough, chapped hands and kisses me. Wet with rain and coarse with his prickly stubble, the kiss—while far from my first with him or any boy—feels like my first adult kiss.

We separate but keep our heads pressed together. We breathe on each other.

Ben smirks. "I hate that goddamn rose, and I hate your GUTS."

Giggles overtake me. "I know! I made this *so* much more complicated than it should've been!"

"If all this magic hoo-ha talk is what it takes to get you to be my boyfriend already, I salute you and the damn rose."

My smile falls.

Boyfriend. That is what I want.

But like Ben said, the things I want contradict each other. I want Vero Roseto to thrive. I want to go to school to be the best designer I can be. I want Ben to admit he's homesick for Scotland. I want us to be together. I want too many things.

We hold each other in silence, my hand cupping the small of his back as the summer rain continues pooling up to our ankles.

"Will you two make your wish before the rose bush is underwater?!" a voice shouts behind us. At the curtained archway, Aunt Ro and Uncle Paul wait under a double-wide umbrella. They're still in their festival clothes, except both have thrown on knee-high Wellington boots.

Ben and I quickly separate to a close, but less intimate, proximity. Scowling, I say, "Ro, that's the *second* time you've snooped on my wish!"

She waves me off, her many bracelets jangling. "Grow up, Grant! I snoop on everyone's wishes—gay, straight, family members, guests. I'm Mama Bianchi, and you're on my turf, so get used to it!"

Ben and I chuckle, while Uncle Paul raises a testy finger. "There's been a lot of drama in this house caused by you two boys. At the very least you owe me and Ro a front-row seat to what we hope will be the *conclusion* of this opera."

I frown at Ben. "You and me? Without all the roller coaster stuff?"

Grinning slyly, Ben plops his head on my shoulder. "I wouldn't be interested."

Oh God, it's true. We might actually be in love with the fury of it all.

"Let's make that wish," I say, shaking a river's worth of rain from my curls. Ben and I approach the rose bush as the thickening clouds darken the summer evening. The shaft of light surrounding the gargantuan bush is angelic, the rain briefly illuminated in it like tiny scratches. We reach for the same bloom—a brilliant, red creature. An opulent bloom at the end of a path of a thousand thorns.

Just like us.

Gently holding the rose, I look at Ben, and his gold-flecked hazel eyes look back with the same mixture of fear and hope. "What do we wish for?" he asks.

I haven't been able to stop thinking about it. It feels risky to wish to be bonded to Ben forever when we both have so much growing to do. We both know such rigidity is not how you properly tend a garden. It also feels weird to wish for an end to both our curses—him never sticking around, me never keeping anyone—because we now know that's bullshit.

So, what then?

I just wish I could trust it'll all work out somehow.

My heart lifts. I glance back at my aunt and uncle, who are

smiling expectantly, and then back to Ben, eagerly awaiting my guidance. I am the seasoned veteran of rose wishes, after all.

"I wish," I say, not looking away from Ben, "to trust that whatever path we take—even if it ends up being away from each other for a time—it always leads back to you."

Speechless, Ben bites back a little gasp. His eyes are brimming.

He knows our journey still won't be easy.

He needs the same trust I do.

"I wish for that, too," he says.

As two curses come to an end, soothing, happy rain crashes down on Vero Roseto, feeding the beautiful grounds after such a horrible rot almost claimed it, almost claimed us all.

EPILOGUE

GRATO

FOUR MONTHS LATER

Winter in London hasn't disappointed.

Next month, I start design courses at the University of the Arts, but I moved a few weeks early to get acclimated before the holidays. It turns out, not only was my Rose Festival portfolio impressive, I have international fans who remembered my Chicago exhibit from last summer. "What have I been telling you?" Mr. Cartwright scolded. "You were only a failure in your own mind!"

I scoffed at him. "So, you get a fiancé and suddenly, you're not in the salty Envy Club?"

"Grant, sometimes being negative is more deluded than being positive. You are *loved*."

I am loved.

With those three impossible words, I renewed my passport, hugged my family at Vero Roseto goodbye, and flew to England to face my next chapter. For the holidays, Mr. Cartwright took his new fiancé on a European vacation to his favorite winter destinations—skiing in Switzerland, Babbo Natale street festivals in Italy, and the Santa Lucia crowning in Norway. This left him with a cozy, vacant English home during the weeks I'm waiting for my dorm to open.

Sometimes, the universe curses you; sometimes, it pulls you up.

Mr. Cartwright lives in an attic apartment in Camden Town (I refuse to be one of those Americans who move to London and call it a "flat"). Most stunningly, his apartment is the floor above his own bookshop café: Books, Bindery & Brekkie.

I don't have to manage anything, thank God. He employs a trio of booksellers who keep the business running downstairs while I dress mannequins upstairs. Although, the smells from the bookshop's bakery have me frequently descending the spiral staircase connecting the apartment to the shop to snatch another treat. I'm less of an employee and more of a bodega cat.

The day before Christmas Eve, the booksellers hang a sign letting people know we'll reopen in the new year. And as the sun sets on Books, Bindery & Brekkie, I shut the store lights and ignite the downstairs fireplace. Outside, the market is emptying as other stores shutter, their lights dotting the indigo winter dusk. It's so beautiful, but the quiet solitude finally hits me.

I'm on my own, grown and far from home.

I need to stop confusing independence for loneliness.

Over the next hour, I bake the store's famous sugarplum cake by candlelight. The vibes are cozy, my cussing is noisy, but the cake is a masterpiece. In fact, I'm sliding a moist, warm slice into my mouth when Ben McKittrick walks through the door along with a tinkling of bells.

Fastest swallow of my life. (Of the *cake*!)

Ben lingers in the doorway—tall, handsome, and bundled snugly. The last time I saw him was at Mama Bianchi's Halloween Haunt. In just two months, his rust-colored hair has grown longer and curlier, a whirling lion's mane peeking beneath his knit cap. The cold air has stung his pale cheeks blood-red. I can't even smile, I'm so stunned with happiness.

"Hey, shopgirl," Ben says, his Scottish accent pronounced from his time back home. He raises a frost-white rose, and both it and his fingerless mittens make me too weak to stand. "Got you a new rose. It's not the magical kind, but just to be safe, maybe don't make any wishes near it."

Blushing, I laugh. "It's beautiful. But we'll keep it away from me." Behind the counter, I raise my plated cake, exquisitely sugar-dusted. "I made you cake." Following a devilish impulse, I lick stray powder from my thumb. "Want some?"

"Depends. Is it just us?"

I nod. "For the rest of the holiday."

"Then it's cake time." Ben returns my wicked energy with a grin and latches the door. With that, Books, Bindery & Brekkie becomes a holiday hideaway where Ben and I can be alone in warmth, luxury, and . . . other things. Clutching his rose, he pulls me close with fearsome power. His two-day scruff claws at my lips as he refuses to do this tenderly. I'm just as starved. I pull him toward the stairs—but on our way, Ben backs me into a shelf of self-help titles, sending a few books toppling off the delicate display. Ben always did have a more aggressive approach to self-improvement.

I snatch his knit cap and cast it to the floor. Ben's ruddy mane unfurls like a camping tent taken out of the bag. My greedy fingers plunge into his hair, and as I pull on his tangles, his lip curls like an angry dog. We kiss, his lower lip swallowing mine as a familiar scent greets me. Not his body spray. Not lawn work. Not even sweat. It's . . . sour. Vaguely repellent. A touch of odious biology.

It's the smell of Ben's desire.

I'm so nasty, I missed this smell more than anything. Romance isn't just sugarplum cakes.

As Ben pins me against the shelves, we breathe heavily on each other, just breathing, until I say, "Take me upstairs."

The night fades into a blur of soothing warmth and stimulating pain. It's just us and the growing blizzard outside. I'm free of my depressing history, free of my anxious future, engulfed—for the first time in my life—in a beautiful present.

When I got accepted to UAL, Ben encouraged me to say yes. My decision helped him make his own: he wanted to return to Scotland. Our long-distance relationship could be doable!

I was terrified—still am.

But we're jumping into our futures together. Miles away, but together.

The next morning, the blizzard outside hits so hard, the air itself has body. Through the whiteout, I can barely see Ben's frost-colored rose sitting in a vase by the window.

Waking up next to Ben is shocking. Not that I thought he'd leave in the night, I'm just not used to this alien feeling of security. As Ben's bare shoulders stare at me from under our silver, pelt-like quilts, I fight the urge to beg him to stay forever. The moment Ben is back in my arms, I mentally count the days until he goes away again. Which would come first—the rose's death or Ben's departure?

Acid rises in my throat. Tears could easily begin, but I look at the rose, then back to Ben's curls and long, delicate neck. For now, both he and the rose are here, beautiful and powerful. I don't cling. He isn't mine to keep, and I'm not his. Ben McKittrick—the boy I thought my curse had stolen—is back. He could've stayed in Scotland. He could've met someone new. It's an exhausting journey traveling south to London, but he did it for me. I focus on that instead of fear.

In the end, the Wishing Rose did as we asked.

We didn't wish to be kept together forever. We wished for the one thing Ben and I needed most—the missing notches in our puzzle-piece hearts that kept us from clicking into place.

We wished for trust.

It didn't grow overnight. Trust, like Vero Roseto, needed to be planted, tilled, and nurtured daily, ritualistically, even when I didn't want to—even when the job was hardest.

But our trust bloomed, and my trust is as good security as I'll ever get.

"I'm hungry," Ben whispers beneath the pelts.

Kissing his neck, my sneaky hand travels south. "Me too."

He smacks my wrist. "Food first, beast." Ben's torso, contoured precisely to mine, squirms until he faces me. My lion. We dress in Mr. Cartwright's silk robes. After descending the spiral staircase, we weave through the bookstore's sections: rare first editions, the children's department, the mess we made of self-help. My sugarplum dream sits under a glass cake-saver dome. Beyond it is a giant kettle. Ben turns it on and readies two mugs as I carve two healthy slices of cake.

As my boyfriend hunts through various flavors of tea, I spin the frost-white rose around in my hand. It's so precious, I just want to keep staring at it. I must be staring too long, because Ben eyes me anxiously. "What are you doing over there, wish-maker?" he asks.

As I gaze at the still-dewy petals, my mind flips through five years of trauma like pages in a book. Hutch, Micah, my first go-round with Ben—all the boys the last rose cost me. Yet this rose feels like a sign that the loop of my curse is finally closed for good. In a way, the rose took away my boyfriends. In *another* way, the rose is why I'm here with Ben, my love of loves, spending an unforgettable week in a blizzardy bookshop in a magical city where I'm about to begin my future.

Shockingly, my heart rate is normal. My breath hasn't stopped.

It doesn't hurt anymore.

In fact, I didn't realize until just now that I haven't thought about any of my exes in months. They are finally where they belong—in someone else's story.

"I'm not wishing," I say. "There's nothing else to wish for."

Holding Ben's white rose, I don't look up. I don't want him to notice my tears. Grateful tears. I have everything I want, and at last, I realize I have it while I still have it. In my mind, Aunt Ro—dressed as Mama Bianchi—approaches, ready to hand me a glass of Grato.

THE END

ACKNOWLEDGMENTS

When you're creating a book for a traditional publisher, your creativity is always going dancing with the business side. Sometimes, that goes smoothly; other times not. Sometimes, you have all the time in the world to write a book—and sometimes, you have to sew your own parachute as you're falling. Which can be exciting in its own way. *Cursed Boys and Broken Hearts* was created like that. I was touring one book and revising another. And somewhere in the chaos of all that, Grant's second-chance story needed to get written.

Typical Grant, last in line.

But then something wonderful happened: *Cursed Boys* flew out of me and became my best, most personal book I'd ever written. It wasn't just going to be about Grant's second chance—it was going to be about my own. Vero Roseto is an amalgamation of my husband's Italian family and the home my mother grew up in—where I spent so many magical summers with my cousins until my grandmother's death when I was a teenager. The outside of Vero Roseto is fantasy—no vineyard or fabulous wishing roses—but the inside of the home is nearly identical to *my* Vero Roseto: the patio pool; the parlor just inside; the laundry flap leading into the basement, where my uncle kept fireworks and my grandfather kept pickled vegetables he grew in his personal garden; the other, lighter side of the basement that housed books, games, costumes, the billiard table, and most importantly of all, the ancient slot machine, which everyone in the family remembers fondly. Grant and his loved ones save Vero Roseto.

Unfortunately, I couldn't save mine. It gives me a great sadness to think about it, and like Grant, sometimes, I dream I'm there. I consider writing a book to be like creating a dream that you then invite readers inside to experience with you. This book, more than anything, is meant to be a recording of my memories of that home we lost, of those beautiful summers we can't get back, and to invite my nieces and cousins' children (and hopefully, someday, children of my own) inside the dream of Vero Roseto, so they can know what a marvelous thing a family can be—and how easily it can all fall apart if people stop trying.

With that, some heartfelt thanks are in order. To my mother, thank you for keeping your family all together as long as you could—even to this day. There's a lot of you in Aunt Ro. To my mother-in-law, you've kept your own family going through some terrible storms, something your own mother did that you took on after she was gone. I'm sorry I never got to meet her. There's a lot of you in Aunt Ro, as well.

When a book gets this personal, editing can get treacherous. My editor, Kelsey Murphy, and I navigated some rough terrain as we kept stumbling on creative issues in scenes that were emotional landmines for me. Once again, creativity goes dancing with business, and it isn't always smooth. Thank you, Kelsey, and Kate and the Dovetail team, for your patience while we figured out creative solutions to emotional sore spots. Additional thanks to designer Kaitlin Yang and illustrator Anne Pomel for another divine, golden cover, as well as the tireless folks at Penguin Teen's publicity, marketing, social, sales, and school and library teams. Without you, my stories would just be me talking to a brick wall. You actually get them into people's hands!

To Eric Smith, thank you for making sure I took that call about doing a rom-com—I would've never found Grant if I hadn't. To Chelsea Eberly, thank you for finding Grant (and Micah) their proper home. And thanks to Michael Bourret, jumping into the middle of a project already in motion is never easy, but you did it for *three* projects!

When you don't have a ton of time to draft a book, that means you don't have a ton of time to revise, so the first draft needed to hit the runway *hard*. I couldn't have done that without my personal creative team. To Terry, our talks about big memory places was my first indication that—oh my God—I might actually have something powerful here, so thanks for reading outside your genre just for me! To Stags, your love of all things *Micah* kept me motivated when my own confidence faltered, and I'm so happy I've learned to just shut up and listen to you. To David, thank you for all the worldbuilding work you did on *99 Boyfriends*, with Elliot, Micah, and Grant, so that by the time my fingers touched the keyboard to write Grant's story, I already knew him inside and out. And to Simeon, thank you for always reminding me that I'd already written my sweet rom-com—now I needed to get real: this was a love story between two Chicago gays, so they needed to be beasts!

To all the booksellers who've been such lighthouses for me in the dark, churning seas of publishing, thank you: most notably, Simeon and Stags again, Miracle, and James. And to Marco Locatelli, my friend and fellow writer, thank you for helping me with the Italian translations—language, meaning, and its effects are the lifeblood of writing, so without your guidance, I'd be wearing clown makeup.

Finally, to my husband, Michael, and our dogs, Marty and Malibu—thank you for being my home. *Cursed Boys* is the final chapter of a four-book-long "first act" about lost, lonely young queers finding their way home, and I could never have written these books confidently without you all. I wished for you, and I go on wishing for you.

Ti desiderio.

The 99 BOYFRIENDS *of* MICAH SUMMERS

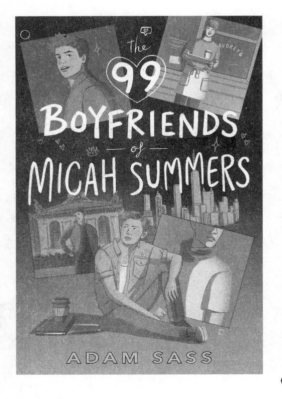

MICAH SUMMERS runs a popular Instagram full of drawings of his numerous imaginary boyfriends (ninety-nine so far)—though he's never had a real boyfriend before. But when a meet-cute with Boy 100 goes wrong, Micah embarks on a Prince Charming–like quest throughout Chicago to find true love—for real this time.